How Much

of

These Hills

Is

Gold

How Much

of

These Hills

Is

Gold

C Pam Zhang

RANDOM HOUSE
LARGE PRINT

Copyright © 2020 by C Pam Zhang
Penguin supports copyright. Copyright fuels creativity, encourages diverse voices, promotes free speech, and creates a vibrant culture. Thank you for buying an authorized edition of this book and for complying with copyright laws by not reproducing, scanning, or distributing any part of it in any form without permission. You are supporting writers and allowing Penguin to continue to publish books for every reader.

All rights reserved.
Published in the United States of America by Random House Large Print in association with Riverhead, an imprint of Penguin Random House LLC.

Cover design by Grace Han
Cover illustration by Maggie Chiang

The Library of Congress has established a Cataloging-in-Publication record for this title.

ISBN: 978-0-593-17184-4

www.penguinrandomhouse.com
/large-print-format-books

FIRST LARGE PRINT EDITION

Printed in the United States of America

10 9 8 7 6 5 4 3 2 1

This Large Print edition published in accord with the standards of the N.A.V.H.

To my father,
Zhang Hongjian,
loved but slenderly known.

This land is not your land.

Contents

Part One

Gold	3
Plum	27
Salt	45
Skull	55
Wind	63
Mud	69
Meat	75
Water	89
Blood	95

Part Two

Skull	101
Mud	105
Meat	117
Plum	135
Salt	151
Gold	163
Water	179
Mud	181
Wind	195
Blood	201
Water	209

Part Three

Wind Wind Wind Wind Wind   217

Part Four

Mud	261
Water	269
Meat	279
Skull	293
Plum	301
Wind	307
Blood	313
Gold	323
Salt	331
Gold	343
Gold	355

Acknowledgments   367

PART ONE

———◇———

XX62

Gold

Ba dies in the night, prompting them to seek two silver dollars.

Sam's tapping an angry beat come morning, but Lucy, before they go, feels a need to speak. Silence weighs harder on her, pushes till she gives way.

"Sorry," she says to Ba in his bed. The sheet that tucks him is the only clean stretch in this dim and dusty shack, every surface black with coal. Ba didn't heed the mess while living and in death his mean squint goes right past it. Past Lucy. Straight to Sam. Sam the favorite, round bundle of impatience circling the doorway in too-big boots. Sam clung to Ba's every word while living and now won't meet the man's gaze. That's when it hits Lucy: Ba really is gone.

She digs a bare toe into dirt floor, rooting for words to make Sam listen. To spread benediction over years of hurt. Dust hangs ghostly in the light from the lone window. No wind to stir it.

Something prods Lucy's spine.

"Pow," Sam says. Eleven to Lucy's twelve, wood to her water as Ma liked to say, Sam is nonetheless shorter by a full foot. Looks young, deceptively soft. "Too slow. You're dead." Sam cocks fingers back on pudgy fists and blows on the muzzle of an imagined gun. The way Ba used to. Proper way to do things, Ba said, and when Lucy said Teacher Leigh said these new guns didn't clog and didn't need blowing, Ba judged the proper way was to slap her. Stars burst behind her eyes, a flint of pain sharp in her nose.

Lucy's nose never did grow back straight. She thumbs it, thinking. Proper way, Ba said, was to let it heal itself. When he looked at Lucy's face after the bloom of bruise faded, he nodded right quick. Like he'd planned it all along. **Proper that you should have something to rememory you for sassing.**

There's dirt on Sam's brown face, sure, and gunpowder rubbed on to look (Sam thinks) like Indian war paint, but beneath it all, Sam's face is unblemished.

Just this once, because Ba's fists are helpless under the blanket—and maybe she **is** good, **is** smart, thinks in some small part that riling Ba might make him rise to swing at her—Lucy does what she never does. She cocks **her** hands, points **her** fingers. Prods Sam's chin where paint gives way to baby fat. The jaw another might call delicate, if not for Sam's way of jutting it.

"Pow yourself," Lucy says. She pushes Sam like an outlaw to the door.

Sun sucks them dry. Middle of the dry season, rain by now a distant memory. Their valley is bare dirt, halved by a wriggle of creek. On this side are the miners' flimsy shacks, on the other the moneyed buildings with proper walls, glass windows. And all around, circumscribing, the endless hills seared gold; and hidden within their tall, parched grasses, ragtag camps of prospectors and Indians, knots of vaqueros and travelers and outlaws, and the mine, and more mines, and beyond, and beyond.

Sam squares small shoulders and sets out across the creek, red shirt a shout in the barrenness.

When they first arrived there was still long yellow grass in this valley, and scrub oaks on the ridge, and poppies after rain. The flood three and a half years back rooted up those oaks, drowned or chased away half the people. Yet their family stayed, set alone at the valley's far edge. Ba like one of those lightning-split trees: dead down the center, roots still gripping on.

And now that Ba's gone?

Lucy fits her bare feet to Sam's prints and keeps quiet, saving spit. The water's long gone, the world after the flood left somehow thirstier.

And long gone, Ma.

Across the creek the main street stretches wide, shimmering and dusty as snakeskin. False fronts loom: saloon and blacksmith, trading post and bank and hotel. People lounge in the shadows like lizards.

Jim sits in the general store, scritching in his ledger. It's wide as him and half as heavy. They say he keeps accounts of what's owed from every man in the territory.

"Excuse us," Lucy murmurs, weaving through the kids who loiter near the candy, eyes hungering for a solution to their boredom. "Sorry. Pardon me." She shrinks herself small. The kids part lazily, arms knocking her shoulders. At least today they don't reach out to pinch.

Jim's still fixed on his ledger.

Louder now: "Excuse me, sir?"

A dozen eyes prick Lucy, but still Jim ignores her. Knowing already that the idea's a bad one, Lucy edges her hand onto the counter to flag his attention.

Jim's eyes snap up. Red eyes, flesh raw at the rims. "Off," he says. His voice flicks, steel wire. His hands go on writing. "Washed that counter this morning."

Jagged laughter from behind. That doesn't bother Lucy, who after years lived in towns like this has no more tender parts to tear. What scoops her stomach hollow, the way it was when Ma died, is the look in Sam's eyes. Sam squints mean as Ba.

Ha! Lucy says because Sam won't. **Ha! Ha!** Her laughter shields them, makes them part of the pack.

"Only whole chickens today," Jim says. "No feet for you. Come back tomorrow."

"We don't need provisions," Lucy lies, already tasting the melt of chicken skin on her tongue. She forces herself taller, clenches hands at her sides. And she speaks her need.

I'll tell you the only magic words that matter, Ba said when he threw Ma's books in the storm-born lake. He slapped Lucy to stop her crying, but his hand was slow. Almost gentle. He squatted to watch Lucy wipe snot across her face. **Ting wo, Lucy girl: On credit.**

Ba's words work some sort of magic, sure enough. Jim pauses his pen.

"Say that again, girl?"

"Two silver dollars. On credit." Ba's voice booming at her back, in her ear. Lucy can smell his whiskey breath. Daren't turn. Should his shovel hands clap her shoulders, she doesn't know if she'll scream or laugh, run or hug him round the neck so hard she won't come loose no matter how he cusses. Ba's words tumble out the tunnel of her throat like a ghost clambering from the dark: "Payday's Monday. All we need's a little stretch. Honest."

She spits on her hand and extends it.

Jim's no doubt heard this refrain from miners, from their dry wives and hollow children. Poor like Lucy. Dirty like Lucy. Jim's been known to grunt, push the needed item over, and charge double interest come payday. Didn't he once give out bandages on credit after a mine accident? To people desperate like Lucy.

But none of them quite like Lucy. Jim's gaze measures her. Bare feet. Sweat-stained dress in ill-fitting navy, made from scraps of Ba's shirt fabric. Gangly arms, hair rough as chicken wire. And her face.

"Grain I'll give your pa on credit," Jim says. "And whatever animal parts you find fit to eat." His lip curls up, flashes a strip of wet gum. On someone else it might be called a smile. "For money, get him to the bank."

The spit dries tight on Lucy's untouched palm. "Sir—"

Louder than Lucy's fading voice, Sam's boot heel hits the floor. Sam marches, straight-shouldered, out of the store.

Small, Sam is. But capable of a man's strides in those calfskin boots. Sam's shadow licks back at Lucy's toes; in Sam's mind the shadow is the true height, the body a temporary inconvenience. **When I'm a cowboy,** Sam says. **When I'm an adventurer.** More recently: **When I'm a famous outlaw. When I'm grown.** Young enough to think desire alone shapes the world.

"Bank won't help the likes of us," Lucy says.

She might as well have said nothing. Dust tickles her nose and she stops to cough. Her throat ripples. She retches last night's dinner into the street.

Straightaway come the strays, licking at her leavings. For a moment Lucy hesitates, though Sam's boots beat an impatient tattoo. She imagines abandoning her lone relation to crouch among the dogs, fight them for every drop that's hers. Theirs is a life of belly and legs, run and feed. Simple life.

She makes herself straighten and walk two-legged.

"Ready, pardner?" Sam says. This one's a real question, not a chewed-out spit-up line. For the first time today Sam's dark eyes aren't squinted. Under protection of Lucy's shadow, they've opened wide, something there half-melting. Lucy moves to touch that short black hair where the red bandana's come askew. Remembering the smell of Sam's baby scalp: yeasty, honest with oil and sun.

But by moving she lets sun hit. Sam's eyes squeeze shut. Sam steps away. Lucy can tell from the bulge of Sam's pockets that those hands are cocked again.

"I'm ready," Lucy says.

The floor of the bank is gleaming board. Blond as the hair on the lady teller's head. So smooth no splinters catch Lucy's feet. The tap of Sam's boots acquires a raw edge, like gunshot. Sam's neck reddens under the war paint.

Ta-tap, they go across the bank. The teller staring.

Ta-TAP. The teller leans back. A man appears from behind her. A chain swings from his vest.

TA-TAP TA-TAP TA-TAP. Sam stretches up to the counter on tiptoe, creasing boot leather. Sam's always stepped so careful before.

"Two silver dollars," Sam says.

The teller's mouth twitches. "Do you have an—"

"They don't have an account." It's the man who speaks, looking at Sam as one might a rat.

Sam gone quiet.

"On credit," Lucy says. "Please."

"I've seen you two around. Did your father send you to beg?"

In a way, he did.

"Payday's Monday. We only need a little stretch." Lucy doesn't say, **Honest**. Doesn't think this man would hear it.

"This isn't a charity. Run on home, you little—" The man's lips keep moving for a moment after his voice has stopped, like the woman Lucy once saw speaking in tongues, a force other than her own pushing between her lips. "—beggars. Run on before I call the sheriff."

Terror walks cold fingers down Lucy's spine. Not fear of the banker. Fear of Sam. She recognizes the look in Sam's eyes. Thinks of Ba stiff in the bed, eyes slitted open. She was the first to wake this morning. She found the body and sat vigil those hours before Sam woke, and she closed the eyes as best she could. She figured Ba died angry. Now she knows different: his was the measuring squint of a hunter tracking prey. Already she sees the signs of possession. Ba's squint in Sam's eyes. Ba's anger in Sam's body. And that's besides the other holds Ba has on Sam: the boots, the place on Sam's shoulder where Ba rested his hand. Lucy sees how it'll go. Ba will rot day by day in that bed, his spirit spilling from his body and moving into Sam till Lucy wakes to see Ba looking out from behind Sam's eyes. Sam lost forever.

They need to bury Ba once and for all, lock his eyes with the weight of silver. Lucy must make this banker understand. She readies herself to beg.

Sam says,

"Pow."

Lucy is about to tell Sam to quit fooling. She reaches for those chubby brown fingers, but they've gone curiously shiny. Black. Sam is holding Ba's pistol.

The teller falls in a faint.

"Two silver dollars," Sam says, voice pitched lower. A shadow of Ba's voice.

"I'm so sorry, sir," Lucy says. Her lips go up. **Ha!**

Ha! "You know how kids are with their games, please excuse my little—"

"Run on before I have you lynched," the man says. Looking straight at Sam. "Run on, you filthy. Little. Chink."

Sam squeezes the trigger.

A roar. A bang. A rush. The sense of something enormous passing Lucy's ear. Stroking her with rough palms. When she opens her eyes the air is gray with smoke and Sam has staggered back, hand clapped to a cheek bruised by the pistol's recoil. The man lies on the ground. For once in her life Lucy resists the tears on Sam's face, puts Sam second. She crawls away from Sam. Ears ringing. Her fingers find the man's ankle. His thigh. His chest. His whole, unblemished, beating chest. There's a welt on his temple from where he leapt back and banged his head on a shelf. Apart from that the man is unharmed. The gun misfired.

From the cloud of smoke and powder, Lucy hears Ba laughing.

"Sam." She resists the urge to cry too. Needing to be stronger than herself, now. "Sam, you idiot, bao bei, you little shit." Mixing the sweet and the sour, the caress and the cuss. Like Ba. "We gotta go."

What could almost make a girl laugh is how Ba came to these hills to be a prospector. Like thousands of others he thought the yellow grass of this land, its coin-bright gleam in the sun, promised even brighter rewards. But none of those who came to dig the West reckoned on the land's parched thirst, on how it drank their sweat and strength. None of them reckoned on its stinginess. Most came too late. The riches had been dug up, dried out. The streams bore no gold. The soil bore no crops. Instead they found a far duller prize locked within the hills: coal. A man couldn't grow rich on coal, or use it to feed his eyes and imagination. Though it could feed his family, in a way, weeviled meal and scraps of meat, until his wife, wearied out by dreaming, died delivering a son. Then the cost of her feed could be diverted into a man's drink. Months of hope and savings amounting to this: a bottle of whiskey, two graves dug where they wouldn't be found. What could almost make a girl laugh—**ha! ha!**—is that Ba brought them here to strike it rich and now they'd kill for two silver dollars.

So they steal. Take what they need to flee town. Sam resists at first, stubborn as ever.

"We didn't hurt nobody," Sam insists.

Didn't you mean to, though? Lucy thinks. She says, "They'll make anything a crime for the likes of us. Make it law if they have to. Don't you remember?"

Sam's chin lifts, but Lucy sees hesitation. On this cloudless day they both feel the lash of rain. Remembering when storm howled inside and even Ba could do nothing.

"We can't wait around," Lucy says. "Not even to bury."

Finally, Sam nods.

They crawl to the schoolhouse, bellies in the dirt. Too easy by half to become what others call them: animals, low-down thieves. Lucy sneaks around the building to a spot she knows is blocked from view by the chalkboard. Voices rise inside. Recitation has a rhythm near to holiness, the boom of Teacher Leigh calling and the chorus of students in answer. Almost, almost, Lucy lifts her voice to join.

But it's been years since she was allowed inside. The desk she occupied holds two new students. Lucy bites her cheek till blood comes and unties Teacher Leigh's gray mare, Nellie. At the last moment she takes Nellie's saddlebags too, heavy with horse oats.

Back at their place, Lucy instructs Sam to pack what's needed from inside. She herself keeps outside, probing the shed and garden. Within: thumps, clangs, the sounds of grief and fury. Lucy doesn't enter; Sam doesn't ask for help. An invisible wall came up between them in the bank, when Lucy crawled past Sam to touch the banker with gentle fingers.

Lucy leaves a note on the door for Teacher Leigh.

She strains for the grand phrases he taught her years back, as if they could be a proof stronger than the proof of her thievery. She doesn't manage it. Her handwriting scrawls end to end with **Sorry**s.

Sam emerges with bedrolls, scant provisions, a pot and pan, and Ma's old trunk. It drags in the dirt, near as long as a man is tall, those leather latches straining. Lucy can't guess what mementos Sam packed inside, and they shouldn't tax the horse—but what's between them makes her hair prickle. She says nothing. Only hands Sam a wizened carrot, their last bit of sweetness for a while. A peace offering. Sam puts half in Nellie's mouth, half in a pocket. That kindness heartens Lucy, even if its recipient is a horse.

"Did you say goodbye?" Lucy asks as Sam throws rope over Nellie's back, ties some slipknots. Sam only grunts, putting a shoulder under the trunk to heave it up. That brown face goes red, then purple from effort. Lucy lends her shoulder too. The trunk slips into a loop of rope, and Lucy fancies she hears from within a banging.

Beside her, Sam's face whips round. Dark face, and in it, white-bared teeth. Fear shivers through Lucy. She steps back. She lets Sam tighten the rope alone.

Lucy doesn't go in to bid farewell to the body. She had her hours beside it this morning. And truth be told, Ba died when Ma did. That body is three and a half years empty of the man it once held. At long last, they'll be going far enough to outrun his haint.

Lucy girl, Ba says, limping into her dream, **ben dan**.

He's in rare good humor. Employing his fondest cuss, the one she was weaned on. She tries to turn and see him, but her neck won't move.

What'd I teach you?

She starts on multiplication tables. Her mouth won't move, either.

Don't remember, d'you? Always making a mess. Luan qi ba zao. There's the splat of Ba spitting in disgust. The uneven thump of his bad leg, then his good. **Can't get nothing right.** As she grew older, Ba shrank. Eating rarely. What he consumed seemed only to feed his temper, which stuck to his side like a faithful old cur. **Dui. Thasright.** More splats, moving farther from her. He's starting to slur with drink. **Yaliddletraitor.** Given up on math, he filled their shack with language. A rich vocabulary that Ma wouldn't have approved. **You lazy sackash—gou shi.**

Lucy wakes up to gold all around her. The dry yellow grass of the hills sways jackrabbit-high a few miles outside town. Wind imparts a shimmer like sun off soft metal. Her neck throbs from a night on the ground.

The water. That's what Ba taught her. She forgot to boil the water.

She tilts the flask: empty. Maybe she dreamed of filling it. But no—Sam whimpered from thirst in the night, and Lucy went down to the stream.

Soft and stupid, Ba whispers. **Where d'you keep those brains you prize so much?** The sun's unforgiving; he fades with a parting shot. **Why, they melt clean away when you're scared.**

Lucy finds the first splatter of vomit flickering like dark mirage. The mass of flies shifts lazily. More splatters lead her to the stream, which in daylight reveals itself as muddy. Brown. Like every other stream in mining country, it's filthy with runoff. She forgot to boil the water. Farther down she finds Sam collapsed. Sam's eyes closed, Sam's fingers un-fisted. Clothes a foul, buzzing mess.

This time Lucy boils the water, builds a fire so fierce it makes her head swim. When the water is as cool as it'll get she washes Sam's fevered body.

Sam's eyes waver open. "No."

"Shh. You're sick. Let me help."

"No." Sam's bathed alone for years, but surely this is different.

Sam's legs kick without strength. Lucy peels back crusted fabric, holding her breath against the stench. Sam's eyes burn so shiny with fever it looks like hate. Ba's hand-me-down pants, bunched with rope, come away easy. At the join of Sam's legs, tucked into a fold of the underdrawers, Lucy bumps something. A hard, gnarled protrusion.

Lucy draws half a carrot from the indent between her little sister's legs: a poor replacement for the parts Ba wanted Sam to have.

Lucy finishes the job she started, hand shaking so that the washcloth scrapes harder than she means it to. Sam doesn't whimper. Doesn't look. Eyes turned toward the horizon. Pretending, as Sam always does when the truth can't be avoided, that she has nothing to do with this body of hers, a child's body, androgynous still, prized by a father who wanted a son.

Lucy knows she should speak. But how to explain this pact between Sam and Ba that never made sense to her? A mountain's risen in Lucy's throat, one she can't cross. Sam's eyes follow the ruined carrot as Lucy flings it away.

For a day Sam retches up dirty water, and for three more lies in fever. Eyes closed when Lucy brings oats cooked to porridge, twigs to feed the fire. In these slow hours Lucy studies a sister she almost forgot: the budded lips, the dark fern lashes. Illness sharpens Sam's round face, making it more like Lucy's: horsier, gaunter, the skin sallower, more yellow than brown. A face that shows its weakness.

Lucy fans Sam's hair out. Chopped short three and a half years back, it now reaches just under Sam's ears. Silk-fine and sun-hot.

The ways Sam hid herself seemed innocent. Childish. Hair and dirt and war paint. Ba's old clothes and Ba's borrowed swagger. But even when Sam resisted Ma's manners, insisted on working and riding out of town with Ba, Lucy figured those for the old games of dress-up. Never this far. Never this carrot, this trying to push and change something deep inside.

It's a clever job. Loose fabric in the underdrawers, sewn to form a hidden pocket. Well-done for a girl who refused girl's chores.

The stench of sickness clings to camp, though Sam's shits have stopped and she's strong enough to bathe alone. Clouds of flies persist and Nellie's tail won't quit its switching. Sam's suffered enough blows to her pride, so Lucy doesn't mention the stink.

One night Lucy comes back dangling a squirrel, Sam's favorite. It was trying to scramble up a tree with a broken paw. Sam's nowhere to be found. Nor Nellie. Lucy spins, hands bloody, heart ticking and ticking. To match its rhythm she sings a song about two tigers playing hide-and-seek. It's been years since any stream in this territory ran deep enough to support a creature bigger than a jackal; the song comes from a lusher time. This is a song that Sam, if Sam is scared and hiding, won't mistake. Twice Lucy thinks she sees a stripe in the brush. **Little tiger, little tiger,** she sings. Footfalls behind her. **Lai.**

A shadow swallows Lucy's feet. A pressure between her shoulders.

This time Sam does not say, **Pow.**

In the silence Lucy's thoughts circle and come down slow, almost peaceful, the way vultures drift without hurry—nothing to hurry once the deed's been done. Where did Sam stash the gun after they fled the bank? How many of its chambers are still loaded?

She speaks Sam's name.

"Shaddup." This is Sam's first word since **No.** "We shoot traitors in these parts."

She reminds Sam of what they are. **Pardners.**

The pressure slides down to rest on the small of Lucy's back. The natural height of Sam's arm, as if Sam grows weary.

"Don't move." The pressure lifts. "I've got my sights on you." Lucy should turn. She should. But. **Know what you are?** Ba snarled at Lucy the day Sam came back from school, left eye a plum. Lucy's clothes damningly clean. **A coward. A lily-livered girl.** The truth is Lucy didn't know that day, watching Sam face the kids who taunted, if it was bravery that made Sam yell. Was it braver to move loud or to stand quiet as Lucy did, letting spittle run down her lowered face? She didn't know and doesn't know now. She hears reins slap, hears

Nellie's whicker. Hooves hit the ground, each step trembling through her bare feet.

She says, "I'm looking for my little sister."

High noon at a settlement that's little more than two streets and crossroads. Every soul naps through the heat save two brothers who kick a can till the cheap metal ruptures. For a while now they've been eyeing a dog, a stray, trying to lure it with their rucksack of groceries. The dog hungry but wary, remembering old blows.

And then they look up at her, an apparition blown in to end their boredom.

"You seen her?"

Spooked at first, the boys peer closer. A tall girl with a long face, crooked nose, strange eyes over high, broad cheeks. A face made stranger by an altogether awkward body. Patched dress, old bruises slipping shadows under the skin. The boys see a child even less loved than they.

The plumper boy starts to say no. The skinny one jabs him.

"Maybe we did and maybe we didn't. What's she look like, huh? She got hair like yours?" A hand jerks out and grips a black braid. The other hand twists the bumpy nose. "An ugly nose like yours?" Now both pairs of hands are grabbing wrist and ankle, pulling narrower her narrow eyes, pinching hard at the skin stretched tight over her cheeks. "Funny eyes like yours, huh?"

The dog watches from a distance, with relief.

Her quiet perplexes them. The fat one grabs her throat, as if to milk her of words. She's seen his kind. Not those bullies who ran toward the task but the others, slow or lazy-eyed or stuttering, who trailed, reluctant. Those with gratitude mixed into their hate—because her strangeness let them into the pack.

For now the fat one holds her gaze, wondering, holds her throat, longer perhaps than he means to. She starts to choke. Who knows how long he would have held if a round brown body didn't come barreling into his back. The fat boy falls, gasping from the impact.

"Get off her," says the newcomer who hit him. Furious eyes, cut narrow.

"You and what army?" says the skinnier boy, sneering.

And Lucy, breath reentering in one shuddering whoosh, looks up at Sam.

Sam whistles, summoning Nellie from behind an oak. Sam reaches for a bundle on the horse's back. What Sam means to grab, none of the others will know. Lucy fancies she sees a gleam, hard and black as purest coal. But first, a fat white something plops from the trunk and lands in the dust.

Lucy, head spinning, thinks: **Rice.**

They are white grains, like rice, but they wriggle, and crawl, and split outward as if lost and seeking. Sam's face is impassive. A breeze insinuates itself among them, bringing the churning smell of rot.

The skinny brother skitters, shrieks: Maggots!

Nellie, good-natured well-bred mare, but shuddering, wild-eyed, barely contained, carrying fear on her back for five full days now, takes this voice as a message and finally decides to bolt.

She doesn't go far with Sam holding the reins. Nellie jerks, the load of pots clanging alarm. A knot loosens, the trunk slides, the lid bangs open. Spilling an arm. Part of what was once a face.

Ba is half jerky and half swamp. His skinny limbs dried to brown rope. While his softer parts—groin, stomach, eyes—swim with greenish-white pools of maggots. The boys don't see it, not truly. They run at the first suggestion of the face. Only Lucy and Sam look full on. He's theirs, after all. And Lucy thinks—why, this is no worse than his face in a dozen other permutations, monstrous with drink or rage. She steps closer, Sam's gaze a weight on her back. Gently, she lowers the trunk from the ropes that hold it. Pushes the body back inside.

But she'll remember.

More than drink and more than rage, Ba's face reminds her of that once she saw him crying and didn't dare go up, his features so melted by grief she feared her well-meant touch would dissolve his flesh. Expose the skull beneath. Now there it is, that peek of bone, and it is not so fearful. She shuts the lid and reties the latches. Turns.

"Sam," she says, and in that moment, with eyes full of Ba, she sees that same melting on Sam's face.

"What," Sam says.

Lucy remembers, then, tenderness, a thing she thought dead along with Ma.

"You were right. I should have listened to you. We've got to bury."

She saw more than she thought she could, bore it while those boys cowered. They ran, and their imaginings will follow all their lives at their heels. For her, who didn't turn away, the haunting may begin to be done. She feels a swell of gratitude for Sam.

"I aimed to miss," Sam says. "That banker. I only meant to scare him."

Lucy looks down, always down, into Sam's sweat-shiny face. A face brown as mud and just as malleable, a face on which Lucy has seen emotions take shape with an ease she envies. Many emotions but never fear. Yet there is fear now. For the first time she sees herself reflected in her sister. And this, Lucy realizes, this more than the school-yard taunts or the press of the gun's cold snout, is her moment of courage. She closes her eyes. She sits, face in her arms. She judges the proper way is quiet.

A shadow cools her. She feels rather than sees Sam bending, hovering, sitting too.

"We still need two silver dollars," Sam says.

Nellie chews a tangle of grass, calmed now that the burden's off her back. Soon the weight will return, but for now. For now. Lucy reaches for Sam's hand. She brushes something rough in the dirt. It's the boys' rucksack, abandoned. Slowly, Lucy swings it. Remembers the clank of it hitting her. She reaches in.

"Sam."

A hunk of salt pork, the greasy leak of cheese or lard. Hard candy. And waaay beneath, knotted in the fabric, hidden if her fingers didn't know where to look, if she weren't a prospector's daughter, one whose ba said, **Why, Lucy girl, you feel where it's buried. You just feel it,** she touches on coins. Copper pennies. Nickels etched with beasts. And silver dollars to lay over two white-swimming eyes, close them the proper way, sending the soul to its final good sleep.

Plum

It was Ma who laid down rules for burying the dead.

Lucy's first dead thing was a snake. Five and full of destruction, she stomped puddles just to see the world flood. She leapt, landed. When the waves quit their crashing she stood in a ditch emptied of water. Coiled at its bottom, a drowned black snake.

The ground steamed pungent wet. The buds on the trees were splitting, showing their paler insides. Lucy ran home with scales between her palms, aware that the world unfurled its hidden side.

Ma smiled to see her. Kept smiling as Lucy opened her hands.

Later, too late, Lucy would think on how another mother might have screamed, scolded, lied. How

Ba, if Ba were there, might have said the snake was sleeping, and spun a tale to chase the hush of death right out the window.

Ma only hefted her pan of pork and tied her apron tighter. Said, **Lucy girl, burial zhi shi another recipe.**

Lucy prepared the snake alongside the meat.

First rule, silver. To weigh down the spirit, Ma said as she peeled a caul of fat from the pork. She sent Lucy to her trunk. Beneath the heavy lid and its peculiar smell, between layers of fabric and dried herbs, Lucy found a silver thimble just large enough to fit over the snake's head.

Second, running water. To purify the spirit, Ma said as she washed the meat in a bucket. Her long fingers picked maggots free. Beside her, Lucy submerged the snake's body.

Third, a home. The most important rule of all, Ma said as her knife hacked through gristle. Silver and water could seal a spirit for a time, keep it from tarnish. But it was home that kept the spirit safe-settled. Home that kept it from wandering back, restless, returning time and again like some migrant bird. **Lucy?** Ma asked, knife paused. **You know where?**

Lucy's face warmed, as if Ma quizzed her on sums she hadn't studied. **Home**, Ma said again, and Lucy said it back, chewing her lip. Finally Ma cupped Lucy's face with a hand warm and slick and redolent of flesh.

Fang xin, Ma said. Told Lucy to loosen her heart. **It's not hard. A snake belongs in its burrow. You see?** Ma told Lucy to leave the burying. Told her to run off and play.

They're running, like Ma told them, but this time it doesn't feel like play.

All those years and still Lucy can't grasp the thing called home. For all that Ma praised her smarts, she's a dunce in what matters. Lacking answers, she can only spell. **H**, as the yellow grasses rustle. **O**, as she grinds stems underfoot. **M**, as she cuts her toe and watches a line of blood rise like rebuke. **E**, as she hurries up the next hill to catch Sam and Nellie disappearing down its slope.

What's home mean when Ba made them live a life so restless? He aimed to find his fortune in one fell swoop, and all his life pushed the family like a storm wind at their backs. Always toward the newer. The wilder. The promise of sudden wealth and shine. For years it was gold he pursued, rumors of unclaimed land and untapped veins. Always they arrived to find the same ruined hills, dug up, the same streams choked with rubble. Prospecting as much a game of luck as the gambling dens Ba haunted from time to time—and luck was never with him. Even when Ma put her foot down and insisted they make an honest living through coal, little changed. From coal mine to coal mine their wagon crossed the hills like a finger scraping the barrel's last taste of sugar. Each new mine drew men with the promise of high wages, but those wages fell as more men arrived. So the family chased the next mine, and the next. Their savings swelled and shrank in seasons as reliable as dry and wet, hot and cold. What's home mean when they moved so often into shacks and tents that stank of other people's sweat? How can Lucy find a home to bury a man she couldn't solve.

It's Sam, youngest but best-loved, who leads the way. Inland Sam treks, East through the hills. They start out on the wagon trail that once brought the four of them to town, its dirt tamped flat by miners and prospectors and Indians come before them— and, to hear Ba tell it, the long-dead buffalo before that. But soon Sam veers off, pointing those cowboy boots through untrammeled grass and coyote brush, through thistle and stinging cane.

A new, fainter track takes shape underfoot. Narrow and rough, hidden from pursuers. Ba claimed knowledge of such trails from the Indians he traded with outside town; Lucy figured those for empty boasts. Ba didn't show the trails the way he showed the scar on his bad leg that he swore came from a tiger.

At least, he didn't show the trails to Lucy.

They walk near to an empty arroyo. Lucy keeps her head down, hoping to see it fill before their canteens run dry. In this way she almost misses the first buffalo bones.

The skeleton rises from the earth like a great white island. Around it the hush deepens—maybe it's that the pinned-down grass has gone silent. Sam's breath hitches, close to a sob.

They've seen buffalo bone in pieces along the wagon trail, but never whole. Years of travelers have brandished mallets and knives, boredom and need, taking what was easy to find for cook fires or tent poles or idle carving. This skeleton is untouched. The eye sockets glimmer—a trick of shadow. Sam could walk through the intact rib cage without ducking.

Lucy pictures the bones clothed in fur and flesh, the animal standing. Ba claimed these giants once ran thick through the hills, and the mountains, and the plains beyond. Three times the height of any man yet gentle beyond reckoning. **A regular river of buffalo**, Ba said. Lucy lets that ancient image flood her.

They grow accustomed to bones, but see few living creatures apart from the trunk's attendant flies. Once, in the distance, what looks to be an Indian woman, her arm beckoning. Sam stands at quivering attention, the woman's hand lifts—and then two children run to her side. The small tribe moves away, complete as it is. The arroyo remains dry. Lucy and Sam sip sparingly from canteens, rest for a beat at the shady lee side of each hill. Always there's a next hill, and a next. Always, the sun. Their stolen provisions run out. Then it's horse oats for breakfast and dinner. They suck pebbles for moisture, chew dry stems till they soften.

And Lucy ignores most of all the hunger for answers.

Sam struck out saying only that Ba liked space. Wild spaces. But how wild? And how far? Lucy doesn't dare ask. The gun hangs heavy at Sam's hip, lending Sam's gait a swagger not unlike Ba's. Ever since Ma died, Sam's quit bonnets and long hair, quit dresses. Bareheaded, Sam dried out in the sun till Sam seemed a piece of cured wood: in danger of catching at the merest spark. Out here, there's nothing to quell Sam's burning.

Ba alone could change that. **Where's my girl?** Ba said, looking round the shack at the end of the day. Sam hid quiet as Ba searched, playing a game that was theirs alone. Finally Ba roared, **Where's my boy?** Sam leapt up. **Here I am.** Ba tickled Sam till tears sprang to Sam's eyes. Apart from that, Sam quit crying.

Five days on, the arroyo trickles. Water. Silver. Lucy looks round: nothing but the press of hills. Surely this is wild enough to bury Ba.

"Here?" Lucy asks.

"Ain't right," Sam says.

"Here?" Lucy asks again some miles later.

"Here?"

"Here?"

"Here?"

The grass shushes her. The hills roll up and around. On the Eastern horizon the inland mountains are a smudge of blue. **H**, she thinks as they walk. **O. M. E.** Her head aches with heat and hunger, the lesson no clearer. They spend a week drifting like the spirits Ma warned against, and then the finger drops.

It appears in the grass, looking like an overgrown brown locust. Sam's wandered off for a piss—any excuse to leave the flies and stench. Lucy bends to examine the insect. It doesn't move.

A dry crook, jointed twice. Ba's middle finger.

Lucy starts to yell for Sam. Then a thought strikes her like a blow across the cheek: if the finger's lost, why, the hand's in no position to be dispensing slaps. She takes a breath and throws the trunk open.

Nellie steps nervous as Ba's arm springs out, accusing. Lucy gags, holds steady. The hand has not one but two missing fingers, two exposed knucklebones staring out like blind eyes.

Lucy walks farther and farther out, searching the grass, till Nellie and the trunk are out of sight. Then she looks up.

Ba taught this trick when Lucy was three or four. Playing, she'd lost sight of the wagon. The enormous lid of sky pinned her down. The grass's ceaseless billow. She wasn't like Sam, bold from birth, always wandering. She cried. When Ba found her hours later, he shook her. Then he told her to look up.

Stand long enough under open sky in these parts, and a curious thing happens. At first the clouds meander, aimless. Then they start to turn, swirling toward you at their center. Stand long enough and it isn't the hills that shrink—it's you that grows. Like you could step over and reach the distant blue mountains, if you so chose. Like you were a giant and all this your land.

You get lost again, you remember you belong to this place as much as anybody, Ba said. **Don't be afeared of it. Ting wo?**

Lucy chooses to quit searching. The finger might've dropped miles back, indistinguishable by now from the bones of hare and tiger and jackal. The thought emboldens her. When she returns to the trunk, she grabs Ba's hand.

In life Ba's hand was huge and ornery and she'd no more touch it than she would a rattler. In death his hand is shriveled, wet. Hardly resists. It sticks, soft, as she pushes it back inside. A series of pops like dry twigs burning. When Lucy pulls away, Ba's hand and its missing fingers are hidden.

She washes in the stream and considers the finger still in her pocket. Look at it this way, and it again resembles an insect. A talon. A twig. Just to see, she drops it into the mud. A curl of dog shit.

The grass sways to announce Sam's return, and Lucy sweeps her bare foot over the finger.

Sam crosses the stream humming, one hand fastening the drawstring pants. A bit of gray rock peeps out the top. The rest of the rock is a long shape under fabric.

Sam stops.

"I was just . . ." Lucy says. "I was just thirsty. Nellie's back there. I was just . . ."

Lucy stares at Sam's pants, Sam at Lucy's stuck-out foot. Their secrets so poorly hidden. For a moment it seems one of them will ask, and behind the question a dozen answers might tumble.

Then Sam hurries on past. Great rips occupy the air: Sam yanking grass to clear space for the fire. Lucy swivels to help, the finger sinking underfoot. A dry land, this one, hungry for richness. She bears down harder, kicks dirt over. She gives the mound one firm slap with her foot. Ma warned of haunting, but what can one finger do? It's got no hand, and no arm to launch it, no shoulder to swing it, no body to put force behind the blow. **The proper way**, Ba said as Lucy watched across the room, Ba teaching Sam how to swing.

———

That night Lucy stirs oats one-handed, the hand that touched Ba at her side. The sticky feeling clings. And like one half-heard tune that recalls another, she remembers Ma's fingers. How they clutched her the night Ma died.

Sam is talking.

Night, only night, draws words from Sam. When lengthening shadows have drenched the grass blue, then black, Sam tells tales. Tonight it's about a man spotted on the horizon, mounted on buffaloback. The first night Sam mentioned pursuers, Lucy didn't sleep a wink. But no tigers ever came leaping, no jackals on leashes, no posse of sheriff's men. These stories are only a comfort to Sam, like another child's favorite blanket. Most nights Lucy is grateful to hear Sam's voice, even if it adopts Ba's bluster. Tonight the comparison doesn't soothe.

"That's ridiculous," Lucy interrupts. "There's no historical evidence." **Teacher talk**, Ba called this, sneering. Lucy likes how the long words distract from her dirty hand. "The books say buffalo are extinct in these parts."

"Ba said what a man knows to be true is different from what he reads."

Most nights Lucy would retreat. Tonight she says, "Well, you're not a man."

Sam in silhouette cracks the knuckles of one hand. Lucy bites her lip.

"I mean you're not grown yet. We're kids, aren't we? We need a house and food. And first we need to bury. It's already been two weeks since he—"

Sam jumps up to stomp a spark that leapt from the fire. It's caught a clump of grass. They should have made their firebreak bigger, should have worked longer. Should have, should have. Each small act teeters close to disaster these days—the wink of a star like a search party's lantern, the clop of Nellie's hoof like a gun being cocked—and increasingly Lucy lacks the energy to care. She's scooped so hollow the wind is liable to carry her away. **Let the hills burn**, she thinks as Sam stomps far longer and harder than the spark called for. Sam always finds some distraction when Lucy comes close to speaking the word.

Died, Lucy says to herself. **Dead, death, died.** She lays the words down, as she imagines Ma's trunk laid down in the earth. Soil falling over the latches and the wood. Handfuls, then shovelfuls, pounded neat. They've got silver. They've got water. Why does Sam keep looking?

"What makes a home a home?" Lucy asks, and for the first time in days, Sam looks her full in the face, on account of the three-legged dog.

Lucy first saw the dog across the lake born of the storm-swollen creek. This was the day after Ma died, and across steely water the dog flashed white. Lucy mistook it for a ghost till it ran—no ghost had that hobble. The stump of the dog's back leg poked out, red and chewed-looking. It limped like Ba. Lucy didn't give chase. She was looking for signs of where Ba had buried Ma.

The dog was there again the next day, and again Lucy found no grave. It was there the next day, its maimed body cutting a perfect arc through the air. The dog was there, and the dog was there, and the dog was there as Lucy searched in vain for the grave Ba refused to speak of. The dog learned to walk, run, chase blown leaves, while at home Ba got clumsier. He stubbed his toe, misjudged steps, fell against the bench where Lucy sat. Girl, bench, man, clattered together. Lucy close enough, for the first time since Ma died, to feel Ba's whiskey breath. They stumbled trying to stand. Ba yanked her straight, and kept yanking till she was pressed against the wall, his fist at her stomach.

Day by day Lucy spent more time studying the dog. Its grace among the broken things. On the day she quit searching, the day the lake dried up and the valley lay exposed with no sign of the grave, the dog approached. Close-up its eyes were brown and sorrowful. Close-up it was a she.

Lucy fed the dog in secret behind the house. Scraps of what Ba didn't eat, he who mostly drank. She didn't fear discovery; Ba's world had narrowed to the inside of a bottle, and Sam's world to the space around him.

Then came the day that drink ran dry. Ba went to work in the morning and surprised Lucy on his return, flour and pork in one arm, whiskey in the other. Sam tagged behind; Sam's hands, like Ba's, black with coal dust. Lucy's clean fingers held only scraps of dinner, and the dog's snout.

Proper reward, Ba said as he hefted the bottle, **for a hard day's work**. He swung between the dog's eyes.

As the dog toppled, Lucy held still. She'd learned true hurt from fakery. Sure enough the dog leapt up when Ba looked away, a piece of pork in its mouth.

Lucy couldn't help smiling, despite Sam's warning shake. Ba saw. Something was planted that day, in the remnants of Ma's garden—an ache, a sour crop.

That was the start of a new balance. For days at a stretch Ba stayed sober enough to work the coal mines. A few swigs at breakfast held his hands steady on a pick. On paydays he brought home his reward, and a jangly rhythm swung his fists round and round. Lucy learned the steps of her part: quiet, nimble, spinning away. If she was quick enough, Ba's fists hardly clipped her. Sam learned the steps that cut between Ba and Lucy when the dance grew too violent.

Lucy asked, once, with Ba fallen from a missed

swing, if she should help in the mines too. He laughed in her face. A gap showed in his teeth, and that sight startled her worse than any blow. When had he lost it? When had a hole opened up in the man she knew, without her seeing it happen? **Mining is a man's work**, he spat out. Sam helped him rise, Sam who dressed like a boy and worked like one and was paid like one too. Sam whose hands grew calloused and nicked, strong enough to support Ba's body.

Their family, too, learned to move on three legs. And then the dog returned.

One night Ba called them out behind the house. There Lucy and Sam found him petting the dog's hindquarters, which stuck out from a barrel of lard. Good leg, stump leg, and flag of tail between. Ba stroked that tail, then reared back and slammed his boot into the good leg.

"What makes a dog a dog?" Ba asked. This time when the dog tried to run, two bad legs dragged behind two good. It could only crawl. Ba crouched and laid a finger on Lucy's knee. "It's a test. You're fond of tests, smart girl like you."

He twisted Lucy's skin. Sam moved closer so that Ba couldn't pull his arm back all the way. The bark, Lucy answered. The bite. The loyalty. Pinches grew down her calf as she spoke.

"I'll tell you," Ba finally said. Not because Lucy trembled, but because his own bad leg did. "A dog's a cowardly creature. What makes a dog a dog is **it can run**. That's no dog. Ting wo."

"I'm not a dog. I promise, Ba, I wouldn't run."

"You know why your ma's gone?"

Lucy jolted. Even Sam cried out. But Ba would take that answer to his death. He shook his head. Spoke over Lucy's shoulder, as if the sight of her disgusted him.

"Family comes first. You bring a thief among us, Lucy girl, and you betray us. You're as good as a thief yourself."

Funny thing was, Ba's lesson did bring a part of their family closer. **What makes a dog a dog?** Sam and Lucy came to swap the words as a joke, a riddle. By incantation stripping it of its origins: the cold night, the broken creature. When Ba staggered home and fell asleep in the water trough, when he searched for a boot he'd flung out the window, they whispered, **What makes a bed a bed? What makes a boot a boot?** These words stretched between them as other distances grew: between their heights, between the shack where Lucy sat reading and the wide world of open hills and hunting sites that Sam explored at Ba's side.

Tonight, Sam looks at Lucy across the campfire. Those feet quiet at last from their stomping.

For a moment, Lucy hopes.

But the old spell of the words is broken. Sam walks alone into the grass.

Fool that she was, Lucy thought Ba's death would return Sam to her. Thought that the jokes Sam shared with Ba, the games and confidences, would fill the emptiness inside Lucy. Lucy thought they might even speak of Ma.

Sam doesn't return that night, though Lucy waits up for hours. When at last she smothers the fire, she piles the soil higher than needed. Both hands are caked and filthy by the end. She should have known. A dog can't stand on two legs, and neither can a family.

Piece by piece, step by step, they part with bits of themselves. Hunger reshapes them. Two weeks on and Sam's cheekbones emerge like rocky outcrops. Three weeks and Sam shoots up taller, thinner. Four weeks and Sam begins to range the hills alone after they make camp, returning with a shot rabbit or squirrel. Pistol swinging at that growing hip.

Lucy does her own hunting while Sam is gone. Hers more like panning. She shakes the trunk and collects a toe, a piece of scalp, a tooth, another finger, each part buried with a slap on the mound. That slap ought to feel enough like home to Ba. And if it doesn't? What makes a haint a haint? She pictures a spirit toe floating behind, trailing its cloud of flies. Each small burial drops a fistful of soil into her hollow, filling her for a little while.

Then comes a string of days when nothing drops. Silent days, hardly a word spoken. Lucy shakes the trunk hard enough to rattle. She's sweating by the time a piece falls loose. It's as long as a finger but thicker. Softer, with wrinkled skin. No bone that she can see. It gives under her toes, like a dried plum.

She understands.

Dirt-speckled and shrunken, it bears little resemblance to what she saw by accident the night Ba buried Ma. He came up from the lake dripping, shedding wet clothes. Soon he stood in underpants. As he reached for his bottle, Lucy caught a swing of flesh through the thin cloth. Darkly purple, a strange and heavy fruit.

What makes a man a man? The parts that Ba and Sam hold so dear didn't look like much even then. This time, Lucy slaps the burial mound twice.

Salt

Then comes the night of Nellie's near escape.

She'll never know exactly how, but Lucy likes to think it began as most escapes do: in the dead of the night. What's still called the hour of the wolf. Decades back, before the buffalo were slaughtered and the tigers that fed on them died too, a lone horse in these hills would have quaked in fear of carnivores come slavering. Though there are no tigers, Nellie trembles like her ancestors. She's smarter than most people, her master claimed. She knows there are things more fearsome than any living threat. The thing strapped to her back, for instance, that dead thing she can't shake. Nellie waits till the stars stare through their peepholes of sky and the two sleepers lie quiet. Then she commences to dig.

Nellie digs through the hours of the wolf, the snake, the owl, the bat, the mole, the sparrow. At the hour of earthworms stirring in their burrows, Lucy and Sam wake to the knock of hooves against the stake.

Sam is quicker. Four strides and Sam's caught the reins in one hand. With the other, Sam slaps Nellie. Hard.

The mare only snorts, but the sound echoes in Lucy along with the sound of other slaps by other hands on other parts. She leaps between girl and horse. Sam's hand halts in midair. Only then, her neck loosening, does Lucy admit she didn't know if Sam would stop.

"She tried to run," Sam says with arm still raised.

"You scared her."

"She's a traitor. She'd've made off with Ba."

"She's got feelings too. She's—"

"Smarter than most people," Sam mocks, lowering her voice to ape Teacher Leigh. It's half-convincing. A fit to Sam's new, leaner face. They both of them go quiet. When Sam speaks again it's still in a borrowed voice, not quite a man's but not quite Sam's own. "If Nellie's so smart then she understands loyalty. If she's so smart she can take her punishment."

"She's worn out by the weight. I'm tired too. Aren't you?"

"Ba wouldn't quit on account of being tired."

And maybe that was Ba's problem. Maybe he should've made peace with what they had before he died dirty in his bed, not a clean shirt to his name. Lucy presses a hand to her hot scalp. Her head buzzes. Strange thoughts have been taking residence in her empty spaces. Sometimes it seems the wind itself whispers notions at night.

"Let's let her rest a while," Lucy says. "Anyhow, we can't have much farther to go." She looks around at the hills. Not a soul to speak to since they left the two boys at that crossroads a month back. She's got to ask, for Nellie's sake if not her own. "Right?"

Sam shrugs.

"Sam?"

Another shrug. This time Lucy perceives the softening in Sam's shoulders as doubt.

"If we keep on," Sam says, "we might find a better place."

The next place might be better, Ba said each time they packed up for a new mine. Better never came.

"You don't know where you're going," Lucy says. And then, unbidden, she is laughing. She hasn't laughed since Ba died. These aren't her forced **ha-ha**s but something raw and hurting as it pulls free. If Sam means to chase Ba's dream of wildness, they'll never quit wandering. And maybe that's what Sam wants: Ba forever on their backs.

"Don't be stupid," Lucy says when she catches her breath. "We can't last."

"We could if you were stronger." Those words are Ba's words. As the sneer is Ba's, and the swing of Sam's hand aiming once more for Nellie.

Lucy grabs Sam. Touch is a shock—Sam's wrist-bones so small and fine despite that brashness. Sam tugs away, pulling Lucy off-balance. Lucy flings an arm out—and her nails graze Sam's cheek.

Sam flinches. Sam who's never quailed before, not from the kids and their stones, not from Ba at his drunkest. But why would Sam? Ba didn't ever aim to hit Sam, as Lucy just did. The morning light is stark now, Sam's accusing eyes as wide as twin suns.

Coward that she is, Lucy flees. The blows resume behind her.

She climbs. Up the biggest hill she can find, thirsting plants reaching up the hem of her dress, which is too short now, and faded from travel. The grass so parched it draws blood, hatching her legs with delicate pattern. At the summit, she folds her knees to her chest. Puts her head between and squeezes her ears shut. **Ting le?** Ma asked, holding her hands over Lucy's ears. Silence for that first moment. Then the throb and whoosh of Lucy's own blood. **It's inside you. Where you come from. The sound of the ocean.**

Salt water, poison to its drinkers. In Teacher Leigh's history book, land stops at the ocean that borders this Western territory. Beyond: blank blue, sea monsters drawn among the waves. **The savage unknown**, the teacher said, and it troubled Lucy that Ma spoke so yearningly.

For the first time, Lucy understands the desire to travel so far from the life she's known. She meant for them to leave Sam's violence when they fled town. But violence lives in Lucy too.

"Sorry," Lucy says. This time to Ma. She hasn't taken care of Sam as Ma bid her. She doesn't know if she can. And then, because Sam isn't there to witness weakness, Lucy finally lets herself cry. She licks the tears as she goes. Salt's expensive, missing from their table for many years. She cries till her tongue shrivels. Then she chews a blade of grass to clear the taste.

The grass tastes of ocean too.

A second blade proves just as salty. Lucy stands, looking over the hilltop. There: a gleam of white.

She walks till she reaches the edge of a huge white disk that crunches underfoot, burning her scratches. Height of the dry season and all through the hills, the shallow pools and creeks are disappearing. Here a whole lake has gone, and left behind a salt flat.

Lucy stands long enough for the clouds to gather, the world to swirl around her. She thinks of the plums Ma pickled in salt, the way they took a form more potent than their origins. She thinks of Ba salting his game. Of salt to scour iron. Of salt in an open wound, a burn that purifies. Salt to clean and salt to save. Salt on a rich man's table every Sunday, a flavor to mark the passage of the week. Salt shrinking the flesh of fruit and meat both, changing it, buying time.

The sun's swung low when Lucy descends. Sam's face is mottled, but not on account of shadows. Sam rages—yet there is fear behind it. What here in this emptiness could scare Sam?

"You left," Sam spits out between a string of cusses, and Lucy understands. She broke the unspoken contract of their lives. Always it's been Sam who ranges wide while Lucy sat, waiting. Sam's never been left behind.

Lucy speaks, gently, as she would to a spooked horse. Of salt and pork, venison and squirrel, while Sam refuses. Yells louder.

"It'll mean we can keep looking," Lucy says. "Nellie's not as strong as you." She pauses. "Nor am I."

This soothes Sam, but what convinces is the wind that insinuates itself between them, carrying the flies and the odor of Ba. Both siblings pale. So when Lucy says certain Indian tribes honored their warriors this way, Sam relents at last.

Does it matter that agreement was bought with a lie?

For the first time they untie the ropes from Nellie's back. Freed, the mare rolls in the grass, leaving a black mash of flies.

What makes a man a man? They tip the trunk. Is it a face to show the world? Hands and feet to shape it? Two legs to walk it? A heart to beat, teeth and tongue to sing? Ba has few of these left. He lacks even a man's shape. He's shaped by the trunk as a stew is shaped by its pot. Lucy has salted meat gone green at the edges, and meat frozen for days. Nothing like this.

Sam approaches the salt flat at a run. By evening it's as if one great white moon has sunk to the ground, leaving a lesser in the sky that rises, unconvincing. Sam leaps high and slams down those boots. A crack splits the surface, twice as long as Sam is tall. The boom like close thunder. Lucy peers up at the now-dark sky. Sure enough the clouds are circling.

She shoulders the shovel. Where Sam leaps, Lucy follows, prying hunks of white. Goose bumps swim on Lucy's skin despite the heat. This here's a familiar rhythm. The digging. The heat. Even the boom like laughter from a man full-grown. Lucy looks up to find Sam looking back.

"It's near as pretty as gold," Sam agrees. Then, "Wish he coulda seen it."

———

Sprinkled over Ba's body, the salt looks like ash. Flies flee the onslaught, but the maggots can't escape. In their death throes they look for all the world like small white tongues, curled in screams.

It takes four blistering days for Ba to transform to something other. Time to rest Nellie and let her eat her fill of grass. Sam turns the parts, using the shovel to give them an even coat of salt. From time to time Sam chops apart a joint, a knot of flesh. At a distance Sam looks to hold an enormous spoon.

Burial is just another recipe, Ma said.

Ba dries up smaller than Lucy, smaller than Sam. They pour him into the empty rucksack: the startling brown flower of his ribs, the butterfly of his pelvis, the grin stuck to his skull. And lengths and lumps they can't identify, hardened mysteries that may hold the answer to questions Lucy never could ask. Why'd he drink? Why'd he sometimes look like he was crying? Where'd he bury Ma?

They leave the stained trunk behind. Once, Ma carried it across the ocean. Now it's a gift to the flies. Lucy feels an unexpected pang of pity for those flies, which followed faithfully for weeks, buzzing and mating and birthing young. Countless lives lived on the bounty of Ba's corpse, a generosity of the kind the living Ba never showed. They're doomed to die by the hundreds. Each morning will dawn on more black bodies cold in the grass. If Lucy had a handful of silver, she'd scatter it in their midst.

Skull

Teacher Leigh claimed Nellie for the fastest horse in a hundred miles, come from a line of breeding older than the Western territory. He never raced her. Said it wouldn't be fair sport to the cowboy ponies.

Now they test the truth of it. Sam mounts first, Lucy behind. The two of them, and the rucksack of Ba, are still lighter than the trunk was. Nellie paws the ground, eager to run despite her skimpy diet of grass. Lucy expects an answering impatience from Sam.

Instead, Sam leans forward and whispers. The mare's gray ears twitch back, subtle as speech.

And then Sam whoops.

Nellie stretches long, long—legs flicker over grass

and they are flying, the wind shrieking, the sound from Sam's throat raw and thrilling, at once Ba's pride and Ma's husky rasp and something all Sam's own, wild as a beast—and Lucy realizes the sound isn't from one throat. It's hers too.

If this is a haunting, then it's a good one.

Were a traveler to go by wagon, it takes a month to cross the Western territory. The main trail that they left starts at the ocean in the West, bumps against the inland mountains to the East. There the trail turns North, hugging the range till it flattens. East the trail loops, into the gentle plains of the next territory. A clear path, well-traveled. Easy enough to find again if they wished. But Sam, drawing in the dirt that night, has other plans.

"Most people do this," Sam says, tracing the first part of the wagon trail with a stick. Sam depicts mountains as Ma did: clusters of three peaks.

"And then," Lucy says, picking up her own stick, "most people keep going." She draws the next piece of trail that crosses into the neighboring territory.

Sam scowls. Taps Lucy's stick away. "But no one goes here." Taking up a thinner stick, Sam draws a new line. This one splits from the wagon trail. "Or here." The line cuts clean through the middle of the range. "Or here." Now it leaps to the side as if shoved. "Or here." When Sam is finished, the map holds a wriggling snake of a trail, one that loops and circles, cuts through the mountains, wends South, jumps North, leans into the far Western coast.

Lucy squints. Sam's new line seems to end where it begins, so many times does it curl. "No one would go that way. It's senseless."

"Exactly. **No one would.** This here's all the wild places." Sam studies Lucy. "Ba said that's where to find buffalo."

"Those are stories, Sam. The buffalo are dead."

"You read that. You don't know it."

"Nobody's seen buffalo in these parts in years."

"You said we could keep looking."

"Not forever." Sam's line represents months of travel through the most rugged, unbroken places. Maybe years.

"You promised." Sam turns away. The red fabric across Sam's back is faded, stretched tighter than when they set out. A line of stomach peeps from the shirt's bottom edge—Sam has grown. A dark splotch forms, unaccountably, at the corner of the dirt map though Sam's stick doesn't move. The splotch spreads, Sam's shoulders shake. The darkness is wet. Sam—is Sam crying?

"Promised," Sam says again, quieter, the words before and after unheard except for a sloshing, and this time Lucy hears, **He promised he wouldn't die.**

Lucy knew of Ba's dying for years. All she lacked was the day. Though he lived not even two decades, Ma's death aged him. Ba refused meals and took whiskey like water. His lips sank into his leathery face, his teeth loosened and spotted, and his eyes went red, then yellow, then a mix of both like fatty beef. Lucy wasn't truly surprised to find his body. It's been years since she mourned Ba's broken promises.

But it was different for Sam. Ba saved what little tenderness was left in him for Sam.

"Shh," Lucy says, though Sam is silent. "Hao de, hao de. We'll go. We'll look."

Lucy knows they won't find a thing. Not one buffalo. The truth of those wild places is written in books. But Sam trusts only two sources: Ba, and Sam's own eyes. One is lost. The other will see the empty mountains soon enough. It may take a few weeks more, but soon, Lucy hopes, Sam will lay Ba down.

From atop Nellie, the hills roll by with a speed that makes them liquid. The ocean Ma spoke of, remade in yellow grass. The distant mountains draw closer till one day Lucy sees: why, they're not blue. Green brush and gray rock, purple shadows held deep in ridges.

The land, too, regains color. The stream widens. Cattails, miner's lettuce, clusters of wild garlic and carrots. Hills grow craggier, valleys deeper. From time to time, the grass bursts full green in the shade of a grove.

Is this, then, the wildness Ba sought? This sense that they might disappear into the land—a claiming of their bodies like invisibility, or forgiveness? The hollow in Lucy shrinks as she shrinks, insignificant against the mountains, the gold light filtered green through unbent oaks. Even Sam is gentling in a wind that tastes of life as much as it tastes of dust.

One day Lucy wakes to birdsong, and it isn't a dream of the past that holds her. It's a new vision of the future, clinging like dew.

There was a kind of miner's wife who faced inland and sighed, **Civilization**. Such wives came from those fertile plains on the far side of the mountains, tugged West by letters from miner husbands. The letters made no mention of coal dust. The wives arrived in cheerful dresses that faded fast as their hopes in the strong Western sun.

Soft, Ba scoffed. **Kan kan, they'll die off quick**. He was right. When cough came, those wives crumpled like flowers tossed to fire. Their widowers remarried sturdy women who fixed eyes to their tasks and never looked inland.

But Lucy liked to hear about the next territory, and the next one, even farther East. Those flat plains where water is abundant and green stretches in every direction. Where towns have shade trees and paved roads, houses of wood and glass. Where instead of **wet** and **dry** there are seasons with names like song: **autumn**, **winter**, **summer**, **spring**. Where stores carry cloth in every color, candy in every shape. **Civilization** holds the word **civil** in its heart and so Lucy imagines kids who dress nice and speak nicer, storekeepers who smile, doors held open instead of slammed, and everything—handkerchiefs, floors, words—**clean**. A new place, where two girls might be wholly unremarkable.

In Lucy's fondest dream, the one she doesn't want to wake from, she braves no dragons and tigers. Finds no gold. She sees wonders from a distance, her face unnoticed in the crowd. When she walks down the long street that leads her home, no one pays her any mind at all.

They've nearly reached the foot of the mountains, one week later, when the rib in the sky thickens. Wolf moon, rarest kind. Bright enough that after sunset and star rise comes moonrise. Silver pries their eyes awake. The blades of grass, the bristles of Nellie's mane, the creases of their clothes—illuminated.

Across the grass, an even brighter glow.

Like two still sleeping they rise from their blankets and walk. Their hands brush. Did Sam reach across? Or is it a coincidence of strides grown similar thanks to Sam's new height?

The light comes from a tiger skull.

It's pristine. The snarl untouched. Chance didn't place this skull; the beast didn't die here. No other bones surround it. The empty sockets face East and North. Follow its gaze, and Lucy sees the very end of the mountains, where the wagon trail curves to the plains.

"It's—" Lucy says, heart quickening.

"A sign," Sam says.

Most times Lucy can't read Sam's dark eyes. Tonight the moonlight has pierced Sam through, made Sam's thoughts clear as the blades of grass. Together they stand as if at a threshold, remembering the tiger Ma drew in the doorway of each new house. Ma's tiger like no other tiger Lucy has seen, a set of eight lines suggesting the beast only if you squinted. A cipher. Ma drew her tiger as protection against what might come. Singing, **Lao hu, lao hu**.

Ma drew her tiger in each new home.

Song shivers through Lucy's head as she touches the skull's intact teeth. A threat, or else a grin. What was the last word of the song? A call to the tiger: **Lai.**

"What makes a home a home?" Lucy says.

Sam faces the mountains and **roars**.

Wind

Wind blows down the slopes, a change-smell in the air. By the moon's keen light, Sam readies the site for burial.

Around the tiger, Sam lays a circle of stones. **Home**, Sam calls this. To one side of the circle, their pot and pan and ladle and knife and spoons. **Kitchen**, Sam calls this. To the other, their blankets. **Bedroom**, Sam calls this. At the edge, branches stuck upright. **Walls**, Sam calls this. Over the branches, woven grass mats. **Roof**, Sam calls this.

The center Sam keeps empty till last.

It's close to dawn by the time Sam finishes. The grass ceiling is clumsy and gaping, the pan still clumped with oats. Sam is a poor housekeeper on account of having no practice. All the same, Sam shooed Lucy's help away. Now Sam walks to the tiger skull and holds the shovel aloft. Does Sam's hand quiver as the blade sinks into dirt?

Sam stops. The quivering continues. Maybe it's lack of sleep. Maybe something else. Sam's face is dry. Sam stares at the skull as if expecting an answer.

Lucy comes up and takes Sam's hand. Today she encounters no protest as she lays Sam down and tucks the blanket beneath that trembling chin. There's no hurry now. They'll bury come daybreak. Till then, Lucy offers to sit vigil.

And all the rest of that night the wind blows with particular fierceness. Blows Sam's house down, blows straight through Lucy's threadbare dress and blanket, down her throat and into her hollows so that she's cold from the inside. A slapping wind. Quick gusts against her cheeks. It means the rainy season is coming.

Though **coming**'s too strong a word, unless it's meant as Ba meant it, saying **I'll come home tonight** and meaning the next morning, the next night, the next Monday, red-eyed and fuming with whiskey. Rain's coming in the way Ba was and was not coming: a far-off, brooding cloud. While Sam sleeps, the wind blows loud enough to keep Lucy awake. A wind unlike the daytime wind, a wind like a voice, low and blustering through the grass. **Aaa**, the wind says. And sometimes, **Uoooo**. And sometimes **iiiiiiin**, sometimes **aaaaaaan, ben daaaaaan**. Can't sass wind or beg wind, so Lucy does what she's learned to do: keep quiet. She lets the wind batter her and sting her eyes. She lets the wind blow gifts from far-off places. Withered leaves it brings, long-fingered as hands. Fine dirt that yellows her hair. Gifts or warnings? Smells of wet and rot. Cicada husks, which on first reckoning she mistakes for fingers and toes, which on third, fourth, fifth reckoning she takes for the ghosts of fingers and toes. The haunting comes in the way the wind blows down her throat with vengeful force, fills her ears with words she won't dare remember by day. **Aaaa**, the wind screams, claiming her with coldness. **Eeeeeer**, the wind screams. **Nu eeeeeer.** Wind's blowing up and as Sam sleeps, Lucy sits and listens. Listens. Listens.

And then it is day.
  Sam has the shovel,
  Lucy the ladle.
  Burial zhi shi another recipe, Ma said.
  "Ready?" Sam says.
  Aaaaaard, the wind says.
  And Lucy says, to herself, **Remember? How**

he taught us to prospect. Remember? How his wrists were spotted with oil burns. Remember? His stories. Remember? His nails bitten to the quick. Remember? How he snored when he drank. Remember? His white hairs. Remember? His bluster. Remember? How he loved pork cooked with peppers. Remember? The smell of him.

They dig a hole. The size of a pistol. They dig. The size of a dead baby. They dig. The size of a dog. They dig. The size of a girl who wants only to lie down and rest. They dig though there's soon space enough for a rucksack, two rucksacks, four. They dig and the grave takes on a shape like the one inside Lucy, a hollow filled with the smell of loam and morning breath. They dig until sun crawls down the backs of the hills, drops shadow over the lip of the grave.

Cowaaaaaaard, the wind says sadly.

Lucy knows better than to talk back.

Sam opens the sack.

Ba falls in a jumble. No hope of straightening him. Already the soil, so dry and so thirsty, is drinking him up. He sinks. Where will he go? Down to mix in a common murk alongside Ma's bones, in the grave Lucy never saw?

Sam reaches into a pocket. For a moment the bulge of fist recalls the bulge of the gun Sam drew in the bank. They gave up so much for these two pieces of silver—she hopes this grave was worth their thieving.

Remember? How he taught you to ride. Remember? His boots that held the shape of his feet when empty. Remember? The smell of him, not after he quit washing, not after the drink, but the smell before.

And still Lucy doesn't speak. As Sam doesn't move. Sam holds those pieces of silver till Lucy realizes: Sam wants her gone.

As she did on many nights, Lucy leaves Sam and Ba alone together. She doesn't see what passes at last between father and daughter, father and false son.

Mud

They sleep. Not down in the grave but on the soft, loose mound born of it. The hole is filled in, tamped down, but they couldn't quite return the dirt they originally took. For the first night since they fled near on two months ago, Lucy sleeps heavy. Dreamless. Though she doesn't remember Sam coming to bed, there in the morning is Sam's body beside hers, dirty and stinking of life.

Wet has visited overnight, those distant clouds issuing damp breath. Sam's face is beaded. Dirt's thickened to mud on their skins. When Lucy tries to clean Sam's cheek, her finger leaves a streak of even darker brown.

She cocks her head, raises a second finger. Draws a second streak parallel to the first.

Two tiger stripes.

"Good morning," Lucy says to the skull that guards the grave. It ignores her, of course, as it ignores the Western hills behind. It faces the mountains' end. On this morning, the air boding a new season, it seems Lucy can see farther than before. Squint, and can't she see the peak of the last mountain? Squint, and don't the clouds resemble lace? Squint, and can't she see a new white dress, and broad streets, and a house of wood and glass?

Lucy presses her fingers to her wrist. Her thighs. Her cheeks and neck and chest, avoiding the new soreness there. On the surface she's no fatter and no thinner than she was the night before, but something inside has changed, laid to rest with Ba's body. Wet on her cracked lips. She smiles, small at first, wary of tearing dry flesh. Then bigger. She licks her lips.

Water is coming back to the world.

Quietly, so as not to wake Sam, Lucy moves through the camp unmaking the home Sam built for burial. She unweaves the grass mats and lays the blades over the grave to hide it. She drops the stones back in the stream. She plucks up the branches and smooths mud over their holes. She packs their gear. She saddles Nellie.

By the time Sam sits up, looking around in bewilderment, Lucy has made Ba's gravesite look wild once more, as he liked.

"Wake up, sleepyhead. It's time to go."

"Where?" Sam says thickly.

"Onward. To hot meals. White bread. Meat. A nice long bath." Lucy claps her hands. "Clean new clothes. A bandana and pants that fit for you. A new dress for me." She grins at Sam, who blinks in that sticky way. Lucy faces the tiger skull and points. Then she pulls her hand up. Squints down its line as if down a gun's barrel. She aims at the horizon. "Once we get past the mountains, we've plenty of time to find a new home."

And Sam says, "We **are** home."

Sam stands. Walks East as Lucy wants. But Sam stops too soon. Plants a foot on the tiger's skull.

"Here," Sam says, clearly now.

One foot raised, head thrown back, hands on hips: Sam doesn't realize the image this calls up. Lucy's history books were filled with conquering men who stood this way. Flags waved behind them in land emptied of buffalo and Indians.

Lucy drops to her knees, trying to nudge Sam's boot away. Sam stands firm. Gone the tapping impatience.

"Spurs!" Lucy says. "A proper town will have proper spurs."

"I don't need 'em for Nellie. Just like we don't need any old town."

"We can't survive out here. There's nothing. No people."

"What'd people ever do for us?" Sam runs the tip of a boot over the skull's teeth. An eerie music rises from the dead mouth. "There's tigers here. Buffalo. Freedom."

"Dead tigers. Dead buffalo."

"Once upon a time," Sam says, and what can Lucy do but listen?

———— ◇ ————

Once upon a time, these hills were barren. And they weren't hills yet. They were plains. No sun, only ice. Nothing grew till the buffalo came. Some say they crossed a bridge of land over the Western ocean, and that the bridge sank from the weight of their passage.

The buffalo's hooves plowed the earth, and their breath warmed it, and in their mouths they carried seeds, and in their hides they carried birds' nests. Their hooves made gullies to hold the streams, their wallows made valleys. They spread East, South, through mountains and plains and forest. Across the territories so that there was a time they walked near every inch of this country, bigger with every generation born, stretching up to fill the open sky.

And then, long after the Indians, came new men, from a different direction. These men sowed bullets in place of seeds. They were puny and yet they pushed the buffalo back, and back, till the last herd was rounded up in a valley not far from here. A pretty valley with a deep river running through. The men intended to rope the buffalo instead of killing them. They intended to tame them, and mix them into their cattle. Shrink them down to size.

But when the sun rose, the men saw that hills had risen overnight.

Those hills were the bodies of a thousand thousand dead buffalo that had walked into the river and drowned.

The hills stank so high the men were forced to leave. Even after birds picked the buffalo clean, the river never flowed again, and what grew back between the bones wasn't the same green grass. It was yellow, cursed, dry. No good for planting. No one can settle these hills the proper way till the buffalo decide to come back.

———◦———

A dozen times Lucy has heard this story. It was Ba's favorite. But Teacher Leigh laughed and showed, in a book, the truth of the last herd of buffalo, kept in a rich man's garden far to the East. The creatures in the drawing did not stretch skyward like these ancient bones. Captivity had diminished them to the size of docile cows. **Pure sentiment**, the teacher chided. **A pretty little folktale.**

After that, when Ba told any story, Lucy no longer saw buffalo parting the grass with broad shoulders, or tiger stripes slipping through shadow. She saw only the empty space in Ba's lying mouth, where once there was a tooth.

"Like you said," Lucy reminds Sam. "This is cursed land."

"What if **we're** not cursed? The buffalo came from across the ocean—just like us. And the tiger marked Ba special."

"You can't trust everything Ba said. Besides, things are different now. The territory's been civilized, improved. We can follow suit."

The tiger's snarl sits in Sam's mouth. This time it points at Lucy.

Meat

Sam quits speaking of hunger, of cold. Of the low gray clouds that stalk at the horizon. As if Sam means to out-stubborn the truth of the house that won't stand, the tiger skull that for all its snarl can't protect from starvation now that the oats have run out, and the bullets too. Lucy tries to speak of their future. Sam has words only for the long-dead past.

Despite the overcast days, Sam shines ever harder. Brighter. Each morning Sam admires her reflection in the stream, like any girl—but warped. Sam doesn't put up her hair or brush it. Sam hacks her short hair shorter till bare scalp shows through. Delights in lost pounds, and the sharpening of elbows and cheeks.

And yet, in these vanities, Lucy sees Ma's likeness.

Once Sam studied Ma as Sam now studies herself. Ma transformed each morning before heading to the mine with Ba. She hid her hair under a cap, her white arms in sleeves. Bending to tie her boots, Ma's face nearly touched the ashes. Like the story of a serving girl raised from cinders—only the wrong way round. It was a costume, Ma explained. Just till they saved enough. When Sam clamored for a costume too, Ma opened her trunk with its sweet and bitter perfume. She ripped a red dress for a bandana.

Sam shone so fierce with joy that day, Lucy had to look away.

Of all their faded and travel-worn clothes, that bandana alone holds its color. Sometimes Sam hums while tying it. A song to which they've both forgotten most of the words. The melody is Ma's.

Worn down, arguments nibbled by hunger, Lucy dozes day and night. She dreams of green trees with heavy fruit, of fountains spitting chicken broth. Pale fur creeps down her limbs. Her teeth pain her. She shivers and grinds her jaw, dreaming of an animal roasting, the flesh overcooked, oversalted, dried like jerky—

When she blinks awake this particular afternoon,

the smell of meat persists. A line of smoke splits the sky, rising from a copse at the foot of the mountains.

Saliva fills Lucy's mouth. Sweet at first, then bittered by fear. Cooked meat means killed meat, means men with guns and knives. She wakes Sam from her nap. **Run**, Lucy mouths, indicating the smoke, Nellie, the trail where they can still slip away. Sam yawns slow, rolls those shoulders in a shirt so frayed the movement seems like to split the cloth.

Sam reaches for the frying pan. As if this is another day of easy living, as if there's bacon or potatoes to fry, as if Sam is blind, still, to the impossible fantasy of living life alone in these hills.

"Swing with your whole arm," Sam says, passing the pan to Lucy. Sam takes a sharpened fish spear and strikes out toward the smoke. Calling behind, "This is ours to defend."

This is what they find in the middle of the copse at dusk:

A dying fire.

A staked horse.

A dead man half-buried in leaves.

No stench yet, though flies buzz at his beard. He's wrapped in a coat of many pelts like some creature from tale. This is the jackal's hour, when edges disappear and the line softens between the real and the not.

"Look at that," Sam breathes. Then Sam is sliding through the branches, aimed at the dead man's bags—and the plump bird laid atop them.

That leaves the man to Lucy. It's easier this second time she kneels by the dead. At least his eyes are shut instead of squinted, his furs clean though his beard and nails are filthy. Lucy can't help stroking the pelt, up and down and up and—

The dead man grips her wrist and says, "Don't cry, girl."

Lucy wrenches back as the man sits, molting leaves. A rifle lifts up with him. Jackal hour. The leaves that covered him go black in the shadows. But the hand around her wrist—that's real. His breath, the gleam of his weapon, the spit at the corner of his mouth—they're real. As are his eyes. Strange, round eyes with much more white than iris. They roll up and over Lucy.

"And you there, don't come any closer."

Sam stops with one of the man's skinning knives in hand. Plundered bags lie behind, all the proof needed of their intentions.

"You tricked us," Sam howls, stomping in place. "You wanted us to think you were dead, you hun dan piece of low-down lying—"

"Please, sir," Lucy whispers. "Don't hurt us. We meant no harm."

The man drags his eyes from Sam. Looks at Lucy. A lingering look that pauses at her mouth, continues to her chest, belly, legs. His eyes prickle her skin. She wets her lips, parts them to speak. Nothing comes out.

He winks at her.

"Don't do anything you'll regret," the man calls to Sam. They're the wrong words. "Listen careful." Sam bristles, newly shorn hair on end.

And then the man says, "Boy."

Sam's eyes flash, brighter in that dusk than the knife. Lucy thinks again of Ma in the ashes, and Sam's rapt gaze. That look of transformation.

Sam drops the knife.

"That too," the man says, nodding toward the pistol.

Sam releases Ba's empty gun. For a thing so heavy in Lucy's mind, it makes no thump in falling.

"I don't aim to hurt anyone, except maybe these durn flies," the man says. "You know that, right?" He addresses Lucy, who's spinning her trapped wrist. He lets go so sudden she falls. "Easy." His eyes go to her legs, new-exposed under the hem of her dress. "Easy."

"We weren't going to hurt you, either," Sam bluffs.

"'Course not. Aren't we all passing through? This spot belongs to none of us travelers."

Sam tenses. Lucy expects Sam to shoot back,

Our land. Instead Sam says, "That's right. It belongs to the buffalo."

"I'm glad they'll share it," the man says solemnly. "Speaking of sharing, I've got a brace of partridges, if you folks can do without salt."

"I don't need salt," Sam says, as Lucy says, "We've got plenty." They took a hunk from the salt flat for eating.

"There's what a man needs, and what he likes." The man pats his belly, as round as his eyes. "Company, for instance. It gets lonely out here. I'll take some of your salt and thank you for it. I could also use a girl."

His eyes spin toward Lucy like empty plates.

She offers to launder his clothes. Cook his dinner. His eyes widen, till at last he howls in laughter. He wipes spittle from the corners of his lips with two dirty fingers.

"I could use a girl, but you're a **girl**, aren't you?"

Lucy doesn't know what he means, but she nods.

"You're tall for your age. I mistook you. How old are you? Eleven? Ten?"

"Ten," Lucy lies. Sam doesn't correct her.

Later, Lucy will understand. The language of his looking that she's too young to speak. She's nervous through dinner though the partridges are so plump that Sam whistles. Lucy leans close to the sizzling meat and warms her hands.

"You come from mining folk," the man says, offering his own palms. Flecks of blue live under his skin, like a shoal of tiny fish. Lucy has only the one spot where coal dust got caught in a wound. "How'd you get away so clean and pretty?"

"I only worked the doors," Lucy says, looking away. Her hands shame her. Sam's hands are nicked blue all over, just like Ba's, and Ma's under her gloves. Lucy worked so little before she went to school, and Ma died, and Ba no longer wanted her help.

"We're not miners," Sam says.

One drunken night Ba put his palms to the stove, intending to burn the marks clear off. It took a week for his blisters to pop, another for the dead skin to slough. The color remained on the new skin. Coal hides deep. **We're prospectors**, Ba insisted. **This isn't but temporary, to get by. Ting wo.**

"We're adventurers," Sam continues in singsong. "We're not like anyone else." Sam leans forward and narrows those dark eyes. "Outlaws."

"Sure," the man says in his agreeable voice. "Outlaws are the most interesting kind of folk."

He proceeds to tell of those other interesting folk. Sam's face, on the hotter side of the fire, glows. On her side Lucy can feel the wind at her back. The man gives Sam a taste of partridge and nods gravely at Sam's judgment. Lets Sam carve the meat. Only when they're finished eating does the man ask, "So where do you come from? You some kind of mutts?"

Sam stiffens. Lucy shifts closer, ready to lay a steadying hand on Sam's shoulder. Though this man took longer than most to get here, his destination is the same. Lucy never knows how to answer. Ba and Ma gave no clear answers. They spoke around it in a jumble of myth. Half-truths not found in Teacher Leigh's histories, mixed with a longing that made Ma's words fly up and apart. **There's no one like us here**, Ma said sadly and Ba proudly. **We come from across the ocean**, she said. **We're the very first**, he said. **Special**, he said.

To Lucy's surprise, Sam gives the only correct response.

"I'm Sam." That chin, rising. "And that's Lucy."

It's broad cheek, yet the man seems pleased. "Hey," he says, raising his hands. "Dogs are my favorite people. I'm a mutt myself. I didn't mean it that way. I meant, I'm mighty curious about where you came from just now. You got the look of travel on you. And the look of running scared."

A glance passes between Lucy and Sam. Lucy shakes her head.

"We were born in these hills," Sam says.

"Never left them?"

"We've lived all sorts of places. We've gone miles and miles."

"Then of course you know what's in these

mountains," the man says, a smile playing on his face. "I don't have to tell you about the creatures that hid up there to escape the miners. And of course you must know everything past the mountains, out on the plains and beyond. Of course you know there are things bigger than buffalo. Like the iron dragon."

Sam, rapt.

"Bellies full of iron and smoke," the man whispers. He's as good a storyteller as Ba. Maybe better. "Trains."

Lucy doesn't show how the man's caught her attention too. Teacher Leigh spoke of trains. According to this mountain man, the trains have advanced even farther West in the last few years.

"There's a station in a town right past the mountains. I hear talk of laying track across the range, but that I'll believe when I see it. No man on this continent can do it. Mark my words."

The fire burns low. The two partridges are reduced to bone, yet a hunger remains in Sam. The man, obliging, drops tale after tale into Sam's open mouth. About trains and other iron contraptions, smokestacks belching like enormous beasts. About wild forests far to the East and ice to the North. He's talking about deserts when Lucy yawns. A big yawn that takes her over. When she reopens her watery eyes, the man is glaring.

"Do I bore you, girl?"

"I—"

"Here I thought you two might take amusement from an old man's tales. God knows there's little enough adventure out West. That place?" His voice hardens. "What would a body want with those hills? Them miners picked the territory clean. Can't walk a step without falling into a hole dug by everlasting fools."

Sam says nothing.

"There's plenty more marvels out East. And more space than in this blasted territory. The worst kinds of people crawled West to pan for gold."

"What kinds of people?" Sam says.

"Killers. Rapers. Disgraced men. Men too small or stupid to make a living back home."

"My ba said—" Sam's voice squeaks. "Ba said the Western territory was once the prettiest land anyone ever saw."

"You couldn't pay me to go any farther West." The man throws a partridge bone in that direction. "It's dead and they're all over there sticking their heads in shafts, telling each other the sun's a rumor too."

A ripple like laughter runs through his words. But he hasn't lived on that land or worked it, hasn't seen morning strike the hills and gild them—how else could he step so lightly over them?

"My ba—" Sam says.

"Maybe your ba was one of them fools too."

Some men grow drunk on whiskey. This mountain man seems drunk on his own talk. Loose and careless. He's left his skinning knife by the fire, smack between him and Sam.

Lucy sees Sam see it.

She thought she wished Ba's spirit gone. But in this moment, she desires that vengeful squint back in Sam's eyes.

The mountain man thumps Sam's back, chuckling, saying it was a joke, calling Sam **boy**, likening Sam to an Indian boy he kept for a winter and used to help set traps, asking if Sam would like to hear about that. Sam leaves the knife be. Yes, Sam says. Yes, yes.

Sam hates women's work. Takes perverse pride in loose stitches and half-burnt food. Yet there Sam stands in the morning, stirring the breakfast pot with the sun showing just so through the trees. As pretty a sight as if Lucy had dreamed it—except for the mountain man calling out advice.

The slop Sam dishes up looks like mud and tastes like meat. Pemmican, the man names it. Dried venison and berries pounded fine. Lucy eats so fast she chokes, wishing she was brave enough to spit out the food.

This morning Sam feeds the man right back. A feast of words tip into his round, dinner-plate eyes.

Sam explains the gun and the banker, the two boys and their groceries. The man laughs, ruffles Sam's hair, and follows them back to their campsite.

What right does Lucy have to suspect a man who checks Nellie's swollen knee, who gives them horse oats and a bag of pemmican too? Who draws a map on a piece of hide and circles a town just past the mountains?

"I wager you'll like it, boy. There's a trade fair soon, the biggest for hundreds of miles. That town's big enough that you'll run into fine ladies as well as Indians and vaqueros and outlaws—all sorts of characters a sight tougher than me."

To him, Sam doesn't say, **We're staying here**. Sam says, "Where are **you** going?"

"What's the town called?" Lucy breaks in.

The man says, "Sweetwater."

Oh.

Lucy's mouth floods. Even in the hard years, they had their tastes of sugar and salt. But no amount of coin in mining country could buy a drink of clear water. **Sweetwater** glows in Lucy's mind like the tiger's skull, and she hardly even cares when the man rests a hand on Nellie to hold them a minute longer.

"You remember that Indian boy I kept? I been thinking. Might be I could use another boy. These fingers of mine"—he spreads his hands—"they aren't as nimble as they used to be. Might be I could use smaller hands to help me, and pass on what I know."

The silence presses like the storm clouds. No longer so distant.

"That's kind of you," Lucy says, her stomach clenching. "But we've got plans. For our family."

The man looks her up and down one last time. "Best get off before the rain."

Water

Storm days. The sky opens after they leave the mountain man. Rain falls with such force that it explodes to white mist where it hits the earth, raising a boundary, a ragged caul. Twice Nellie steps into what seems mere puddle, and sinks to her chest before leaping back. A slower horse would have drowned them.

Buffalo bones provide the only firm ground. They stop for the night before a particularly large skeleton. Sam touches the skull first, as if asking permission. Then they crack the brittle ribs from the spine. Stacked together, the bones curve to sturdy cradles.

The rain pauses on the fourth day. They've

reached the mountains' end. Nellie clops up a low, rocky foothill—the last hill—and from there they look down at the plains.

Grass spreads low and flat and green, like good velvet rolled out for their aching feet. There's a band of river in the distance, and a blot that must be Sweetwater. Lucy breathes deep of this new world. Its scent so damp and so heavy on her tongue.

She moves forward—

Wind taps her shoulder. Not hard and blustering as it has been these days of storm, but plaintive. Soft. It's the sadness in the wind that makes Lucy look back.

From afar, the hills of her childhood look washed clean. She's lived her share of rainy seasons, but she lived them down in the muck. Where thin soil became soup, each day waterlogged by the suck-tide of living. From afar she can't see how dangerous the West is, how dirty. From afar the wet hills shine smooth and bright as ingots—riches upon riches stacked to the Western horizon. Her throat tightens. A tingle high up in her nose, behind her eyes.

It passes. She figures it for the rememory of old thirst.

Meeting the river—

All Lucy's life, water meant thin, choked rivulets flowing downstream of mines. This river is wide, a living thing. It beats its banks and it **rages**. Ma said Ba was water too, and Lucy never understood, before this day, how that could be true.

They camp that night on the bank. Come morning: Sweetwater. Lucy draws her blanket close, then recoils. It stinks of trail dirt and old sweat, months of baked suffering. The river's cleanness comes as rebuke.

"I'm leaving you behind," she says into the cloth.

Sam's head turns. "What?"

Lucy kicks the blanket away and stands. Already she feels cleaner. The night is cool and damp.

Water to purify, Ma said.

"Once we get there," Lucy says, with a nod to Sweetwater's lights, "there's not a soul who knows who we are, or what we did. And we don't have to tell. If someone asks where we're from—we can say anything. I've been thinking. We don't need any history at all."

Sam's face tips up.

"It's a chance to start over. Don't you see? We don't have to be miners." Or failed prospectors. Or outlaws, or thieves, or cast-off students, or animals, or prey.

Sam leans back on elbows and says, so easy, "If they don't want us, then we don't gotta stay. We don't want them, either."

Lucy looks down in astonishment. Absurdly, Sam grins.

Three months they've traveled in fear and in hiding, and Sam saw it as a game. Sam who's at home wherever Sam goes, shining through hardship. The map Sam drew, the path Sam meant to take—it didn't represent months or years, Lucy realizes. It was the start of a lifetime.

"I can't," Lucy says. "I've got to stop."

"You're leaving me?" Sam's face twists, as if it wasn't Sam talking of departure, Sam the one so restless. "You're leaving me."

There's no mistaking Sam's anger. This time Lucy doesn't give way. She hardens her spine. Sam's always claimed anger as a birthright. Who gave Sam that right?

"You're so selfish," Lucy says, her heart beating hard all the way up her throat. Her voice thrums with it. "All you do is want and want. Do you ever ask what I want? You can't expect that I'll follow your whims forever."

Sam stands too. Once Lucy looked down, always down, into her little sister's face. Now it's level with hers. The face of a stranger. A face to which she can't say:

That sure she wants clean water and nice rooms, dresses and baths—but those are only things. Beyond them, she doesn't know. The hollow inside her doesn't hold what it once held, as the grave they dug couldn't accommodate all its old dirt. Dig too deep, miners know, scoop away too much of what is good, and you tempt collapse. Ba's body, Ma's trunk, the shack and the streams and the hills—she left them willingly, expecting that at least Sam would remain to cross over to the future.

But Lucy can't ask. Can't speak. The stink of her own filth chokes her. She pulls her dress over her head, shutting out Sam's face. Then she shucks her shift, too, and jumps into the river.

Water knocks thought right out of her. A cold slap. A grateful muffling. She kicks down for a handful of sand and scrubs her neck and shoulders, her armpits, her wrist the trapper held, her fingers that touched Ba's fingers. She breaks the surface six layers lighter. Scrubs slower at her chest, where the skin is sore and puffy. She can't quite reach her back. She calls to Sam to lend a hand.

Sam turns away. Above the faded shirt, Sam's cheeks glow true red. Surely Sam can't be blushing. Lucy swims back to the bank, asks again for help. Again Sam refuses.

"Selfish," Lucy says through the thrashing waves. She grabs for Sam's boot.

Sam is dragged into the water fully clothed. Lucy yanks Sam's collar and rubs at caked grime, ignoring the bubbles that stream from Sam's mouth. All Sam's stubbornness is, down here, turned to foam. **Now your back**, Lucy says, handling Sam as Ma handled her in the tub. **A firm hand is what you need**, Lucy says, tugging down Sam's pants before she remembers who said that—Ba—and why.

Something tears. Lucy's hand brushes foreign hardness. She's left holding a piece of Sam's pants as Sam dives for the bottom. Water is Lucy's element. She passes Sam easily, scooping up the long gray rock that was kept hidden. Yet Sam swims on as if the rock doesn't matter.

That's when Lucy sees what else Sam dropped. It fell quick; after all, silver is heavier than common stone. Twin flashes at the river's bottom. Not buried, not muddied, not left with a body.

Ba's two silver dollars.

Lucy kicks back to the surface, passing Sam. There is a moment in which they're close enough to touch. One could reach out and arrest the other's motion, suspending both between the surface and the bottom. Neither one does. Sam keeps diving as Lucy heaves onto the far bank and lies panting in the green grass of a new land.

Family comes first, Ba said, and Ma too. For all his blows and temper, this belief of his Lucy respected to the end. This belief her sole inheritance.

But now?

Sam is emerging at last. Water slicks Sam's hair, sogs Sam's clothes so that the skinny bones beneath show through. In the dark, a creature unknown to Lucy stands with hands full of silver stolen from the dead.

Blood

In the morning Sam is sat by Lucy with shoulders straight and solemn. Sam commences to talk as if speech is a coin hoarded for these past three months.

"Wasn't doing nobody good buried," Sam says as Lucy folds her blanket.

"It's stupid superstition," Sam says as Lucy picks grass from her dress.

"It won't even matter," Sam says as Lucy combs her hair with her fingers and braids it as best she can. "You know what happened to that dead snake of yours? Ba took the thimble back. I **saw** him. And nothing happened, right? Right?"

A week ago Lucy would've lapped up these confidences. Now they turn her stomach.

"He told me that the living need silver more'n the dead," Sam says as Lucy prepares to head to town. "He told me a long time ago not to bury him proper." Sam says, quieter, "Said he didn't deserve it. I swear, I meant to leave the coins with him anyhow, but that night it was like he told me himself. Over the grave. Didn't you hear him?"

Lucy studies Sam from one side, from the other. Hard as she squints, she can't see where Sam's stories end, where Sam's lies begin. If there is, to Sam, any difference.

"Wait," Sam says, gripping Lucy's elbow. "And Ma. He said that Ma—"

Lucy pushes Sam away. "Don't. Don't talk to me about Ma."

Sam doesn't come forward again. Lucy steps back. They stare at each other. Lucy steps back, and steps back, and back, and a part of her rejoices, a part of her already in Sweetwater, already rehearsing her orphan's story—a small, clotted part of her relieved that Sam won't be there, that Sam with Sam's strangeness won't have to be explained.

Lucy turns.

One last time Sam calls. The fear unmistakable. "Lucy—**you're bleeding**."

Lucy puts a hand to the back of her dress. It comes away wet. She lifts her skirt to find her underdrawers bloody too. Yet somehow, beneath, the skin is unbroken. She feels no pain despite the slick between her thighs. Sniff her fingers and there, beneath the copper tang—a richer rot.

Ma said there'd be cake to celebrate this day, and salted plums, and a new dress for Lucy. Ma said this day would make Lucy a woman. The blood trickles free, leaving a hollow ache. Just another thing Lucy loses with little pain. Though there is no cake, no celebration, she feels with a certainty heavy in her body the truth of what Ma said: she's no longer a little girl.

Sam's face is stripped younger by horror, as if Lucy wields a new and frightful power. For the first time Lucy, looking at her little sister, feels pity course through her along with the blood. This is a different sort of leaving behind.

"I'll come back soon enough," Lucy says, relenting. "I'll bring something to eat. After I find work."

Sam drifts away as Lucy washes the stain. When the fabric is as clean as it'll get, and wrung only slightly damper than the damp day, when she's stuffed grass in her underdrawers and swallowed cold water to ease her stomach, she squints down the bank. Catches sight of the figure in the trees.

"I'm heading to town now," Lucy calls.

The figure lifts its head.

"You'll be here?" Lucy says.

She meant it as a command. But the distance between them, and the river's crashing, unmake her meaning. What she says comes out a question.

PART TWO

———◦———

XX59

Skull

Ma is their sun and she is their moon. Her pale face shifts over the threshold of the new house, inside to out, light to shade, as she readies space for the tiger.

Outside, the family waits.

This house is really a shack, set alone at the valley's edge, a long uphill walk from the creek. Gapped walls, tin ceiling. What Lucy can spy of the inside is twilit, on account of the single window. No glass—just stretched oilcloth, yellow and cloudy, admitting weak light and smudged shapes. Lucy's heart sank at the sight after two weeks of travel, but the mine boss who led them here didn't leave much choice. **It's this or you camp with the trash outside town,** he said, spitting. He would've said more, but Ma put a warning hand on Ba's chest and said, **It'll do**.

Ma's voice is husky and low, with the crackle of kept fire. Its roughness strange against her mannered movements, her smooth face. A stopping beauty in that mismatch. The mine boss reddened and went on his way. **Ying gai care what other people see in you**, Ma has said while straightening Lucy's posture, neatening Sam's braids, scolding Ba for his love of the gambling dens and Indian camps on the fringes of town. **What people see shapes how they treat you, dong bu dong?**

But once the boss left, Ma drooped. Inside the shack the shadows reached for her. Her beauty's been worn thin by travel, during which she acquired a sickness that made her retch up her food. Her beauty now hardly covers her bones. As Ma moves in the house, Lucy can see the shape of her skull.

"Girls," Ma calls when she's swept a portion of dirt floor smooth. Her breath jerks and pulses at her throat, seeming like to tear the skin. "Fetch me a stick."

Sam runs around one side of the shack, and Lucy the other.

Lucy's side lies half in shadow, thanks to a plateau that looms over the valley's edge. She kicks through heaped rubbish: dead grass, burnt wire, ashy sticks. At the bottom, a promising piece of wood. She tugs and a sign comes free.

HENCOOP, it spells once she's brushed off the soot.

Those aren't burnt twigs—they're feathers. And this isn't a house. Ma calls again as Lucy stomps the sign back into the rubbish.

"Hao de," Ma says when Lucy returns. "That's all of us together."

Despite sickness, Ma is smiling. She holds the stick that Sam found as if it's something precious. For all the worry that chased them here, there is a hum of hope in the air, as there always is at the start of this ritual. **A proper home**, Ba said before they set out. **A settling-down kind of place this time.**

Ma begins to draw her tiger.

Ma's tiger is like none other. Always eight lines: some curved, some straight, some hooked like tails. Always in the same unchangeable order. Only if Lucy squints, looks away, watches from a slant, does the tiger that Ma draws flicker, for a moment, like a real tiger.

By the last stroke Ma is hunched in pain, skull once more straining through her skin. The protection is complete.

Quick then, bad leg forgotten, Ba is at Ma's elbow, steadying. He calls for the rocking chair.

Sam hurries it over the threshold, the plates piled on the seat beginning to slide. Lucy lunges to catch one. As she does, her foot smudges the last line of the tiger.

She considers telling. But Ma would insist on doing the whole ritual over, and Ba would scowl and call Lucy **da zui**, and say there's a time and a place to use her big mouth. Lucy says nothing, as she says nothing about the pungent house, the imprint of old chicken shit unmistakable. Learning to keep her own secrets.

Mud

Six days a week Lucy wakes first. It's the hour of the mole, an absolute dark, as she slips past her sleeping family.

Sam in the loft bed beside her, Ma and Ba on a mattress at the foot of the ladder—she circumvents them by memory as much as by sight, as she circumvents the heaped clothes, the bags of flour, the sheets, broom handles, trunks. The house has the close, stale musk of an animal's burrow. Last week a tub of creek water overturned, not improving the odor.

Once, Ma might have made it inviting. A bunch of sweet grasses, a strategically spread cloth. Nowadays her sole occupation is sleep. Her cheeks look ever more gouged or bitten, as if something nibbles her in the night. She hasn't eaten a proper meal in weeks. Says she can stomach only meat, which they lack the coin to buy.

Ba promised meat when they got to this big new mine, and a garden, good clothes, proper horses, school. Too many men beat them here. Wages are lower than promised. With Ma sick, it's Lucy who puts off school to accompany Ba to the mine, Lucy who wakes first, fixes breakfast.

She sets a pan on the stove. Too loud—Ma stirs at the clang. If woken, Ma argues endlessly with Ba. **The girls are hungry. / I'd be earning more if we'd gotten here sooner. / But we didn't. / Not on my account. / Say what you mean. / All I mean is this taking sick was awful inconvenient. / You think I did this on purpose? / Sometimes, qin ai de, you can be right stubborn.**

Quiet, quiet, Lucy presses potatoes down into the pan. The oil leaps and scalds her hands, but at least the hiss is muted. Two potatoes in a cloth for her and Ba, one on the table for Sam. She leaves a hopeful fourth on the stove for Ma.

Two miles to the next valley. Ba splits from Lucy when they reach the mine, heading down the main shaft with the men. That leaves Lucy to face her tunnel alone.

She looks East. The sky is still a bruise's deep blue, yet she lingers as if she could afford to wait for sunrise. She crawls down. Colors disappear, then sounds. The black is entire by the time she reaches her door. Nothing else for a long while, until the first knock.

Miners emerge as Lucy drags the heavy door open and wedges her arm in the gap to hold it. Walls reappear at the slice of lanterns. She hardly feels the welt on her forearm. It's nothing compared to the pain of the miners leaving, sight snuffed out.

In the long idle periods she rubs her body against the shaft wall, or screams experimentally. Five enormous bites of potato at what she guesses for noon. The food tastes of earth, too.

"Not forever," Ba promises at the end of the day that might as well be the beginning. It's dark again. The usual sorrow passes over Lucy like the line of sunlight over the distant hills. Where other miners cluster in fours and fives—slapping backs, exchanging greetings and complaints—Ba and Lucy walk apart. He smooths her wiry hair. "Ting wo. I got a plan. You'll have that school soon enough if you want it, nu er."

She believes him. She does. But belief only makes the pain worse, just as, in the tunnel, the desired lanterns hurt her eyes.

———

The shack is another darkness till Ba touches match to lamp. Ma dozes, Sam runs wild somewhere in play. Lucy starts dinner while Ba changes behind a curtain. He'll gobble his food and head across the creek to a second job cutting firewood for widows. They need the extra coin. Night after night. Day after day. The slow trickle of savings, emptied so quick by the needs of their stomachs.

Tonight, something different.

The fourth potato is gone from the stove. Finger-marks split the pan's congealed grease. Joy floods Lucy, strong as missing sunlight: Ma must have eaten.

Yet Ma's cheeks look hollow as ever, Ma's fingers clean. The only whiff on her breath is old vomit.

"Did you see?" Lucy asks the moment Sam comes through the door. "Did she eat?"

Sam, skin bronzed, flits through the house like a piece of caught daylight. Over the course of the day Sam's lost ribbons, bonnet, a piece of fabric torn from her hem. Gained, instead, this smell of sun and grass.

"Potatoes again?" Sam asks, sniffing at the pot of dinner.

"Did you keep an eye on Ma, like I asked you?" Lucy swats Sam's hand away. "It needs another ten minutes. Did you watch her? We talked about this. You didn't have a single other thing to do today."

"Quit nagging!"

Sam dodges Lucy and grabs for the pot lid, which slips away, clattering. Sam's outstretched fingers are shiny and slick. Sam marked by sun, grass—and grease.

"That potato wasn't for you," Lucy hisses. "It was Ma's."

"I got hungry," Sam says, clear-eyed, not trying to deny it. "Ma wasn't eating it anyhow."

Sam's no liar, no thief. Simply lives by a code of honor all her own, refusing to bend to other rules. Scoldings erode to laughter because Sam makes even stubbornness charming. On the worst days, Lucy wonders if this is the real reason Sam hasn't been sent to the mines, a reason more enduring than young age: that Sam is too pretty to be harmed.

Lucy clutches the bruise on her arm. There are more on her shoulders and back if she consults the tin mirror. "I'm telling Ba on you." But Ba will just pinch the baby fat on Sam's cheeks. "I'll tell him," she adds with sudden inspiration, "and see if he thinks you're grown enough to work."

"No!"

Lucy crosses her arms.

Through gritted teeth, Sam says, "I guess I'm sorry."

Ma likens an apology from Sam to water from dry firewood. Lucy savors the triumph till her stomach grumbles. "I'm still telling."

"Don't! If you don't . . . I'll show you what Ma ate."

Lucy hesitates.

"Tonight," Sam adds, grinning. And then Sam is off, running crash into Ba as he emerges in clean clothes, axe and pistol hanging from his belt. Sam begs, as usual, to be taken along.

Some time later, Ma walks out the door with a dreamer's shambling gait.

Lucy figures it for a visit to the outhouse, but Sam beckons her to follow. She leaves her book without marking the page. Anyhow she's read each of the family's three storybooks so often the drawings are faded, the princess's face a blur atop which she can imagine her own.

Way down the slope of valley, the prick of distant lights. Ma turns away from them. She heads to a plot of land at the very back of the shack, where all evidence of others is obscured. There she roots in the earth, bare-handed, as if hoping for vegetables in the garden Ba hasn't yet planted. Deep, unladylike grunts—then she pulls something free.

Hidden, Lucy and Sam crouch too. The night is warm, Lucy's back sweating. She can see the white stripe of Ma's neck, the wings of shoulder blades through fabric. Nothing else. Then she hears the chewing. Ma half-turns, holding a long something—carrot? Yam? The caked soil makes it hard to discern.

"What is it?" Lucy whispers.

"Mud," Sam says.

It can't be. Ma reproaches Sam for picking food off the floor, wipes each plate twice—once for dryness, once for shine. Yet dark grains stand out against Ma's cheeks. Sam isn't quite right, though. Ma licks till a flat edge shows through the thing in her hand, then a round joint, gleaming. She holds a piece of bone.

"No," Lucy says, louder than she intends. Her cry is masked by crunching.

Sam watches the rest, seemingly at home in the night, in the dirt with skirt hiked and one braid dragging. Lucy averts her eyes, not wanting to witness what else Ma might eat: earthworms, pebbles, ancient twigs, buried eggs and leaf mold, the scritch-scratch of beetle legs. A feast of the land's dank secrets.

Used to be that Ma and Lucy kept one another's secrets. Each day on the wagon trail Ba and Sam disappeared at dusk to hunt or scout; and each day Lucy and Ma were left alone among hills emptied of noise. Into that wide, wide quiet Lucy spilled her fear of the mule, how she'd nicked Ba's knife, how she envied Sam. Ma drank Lucy's words in, as her skin drank in the gilded late afternoons. Ma knew how to hold a secret in silence, sometimes murmuring, sometimes tipping her head, sometimes brushing Lucy's hand. Ma **listened.**

In turn, Ma told Lucy how she rubbed lard on her hands to keep them soft, how she had tricks for bargaining with the butcher's boy, how she chose, very carefully, who she associated with. In these moments, Lucy knew that Ma loved her best. Sam might have Ma's hair and Ma's beauty, but Ma and Lucy were joined by words.

Yet tonight, Lucy intends betrayal. She stays up long after Sam snores. She can't sleep. Close her eyes and in seeps, like moonlight, the shine of Ma's teeth. When the door creaks open below, Lucy waves Ba up.

"Say that again," Ba says when Lucy has told. He stands on the rungs, face level with hers, conspiratorial. "Man man de. What was she eating?"

Oddly, he grins when Lucy asks if they should open Ma's trunk. It holds fabric and dried plums, and most of all fragrant, bitter medicines that Ma brews into healing soups.

"Go to sleep," Ba says, descending. "Your ma's not sick. I'd wager good money on it."

Lucy waits till he's out of view, then rolls off the mattress and puts her eye to a knothole in the floor.

Below she can see Ma huddled in the chair, Ba approaching to wake her. Ma's eyes fly open first. Then her mouth.

Ma cusses at him.

Lucy has never heard Ma cuss—but she's beginning to understand that night is a different territory. How many years and centuries were swallowed with those bones? Enough, this night, to make it seem as if something else clambers out of Ma's throat. Something enormous, ungentle. **History**, Lucy thinks suddenly, remembering a drunk who spat at their wagon two towns back. While Ba and Ma stared ahead, the drunk shouted about the land, and claims to it, and who belonged by law, and what should be buried. Lucy doesn't remember the man's precise words, but she recognizes in Ma's spitting, rising voice the same fearsome creature. It must be history.

Ma asks the hour. She calls Ba a liar. She asks how many widows there can be. She accuses him of gambling again.

When she pauses for breath, Ba says, "You've been eating mud."

Ma snatches her blanket higher, likely to hide the filth beneath her nails. Cloth across dry hands like the sound of snakeskin being shed. "You have my own children spying on me? Ni zhe ge—"

"Don't you see what it means?" Ba drops to his knees. Ma tilts back, surprised. "Qin ai de." Ba's hands take up Ma's clawed ones, stroke them gentle. "These cravings. This sickness. This strain between us. It must be a baby."

Ma shakes her head. Her cheeks catch pools of shadow. She looks scared. Though Ba's voice is too quiet for Lucy to catch the words, she hears the old singsong of promises. Ma smiles partway through, and then her face changes once more. Goes hard. This hardness Lucy will remember years later. Trying to decide if it was resolve on Ma's face, or courage, or coldness. Trying to call it to herself.

"I thought we couldn't—" Ma says, though the argument has slunk from her voice. "And I wasn't sick with the girls. I didn't get this hunger."

Ba laughs so loud that Sam wakes. Two bright slits in the dark—Sam's eyes sting Lucy. Both of them hear Ba say, "It's a boy. What else could be so greedy?"

In the morning, Ba takes to the hills with the tools of his old prospector's trade, shut up two years back. Lovingly, now, he sharpens his pick and hefts his shovel, fans his little brushes out.

The pick pries bones from the hillside rocks; the shovel digs them. Brushes shiver, biggest to smallest, along the dug-up lengths. Exposing the old white. Ba grinds the bones down and mixes them into water.

Lying back in bed, her too-thin hands shaking on the glass—Ma drinks. Her throat swells and falls. Hours of Ba's work, centuries of life, disappearing into the baby.

History, Lucy thinks, and shivers.

Meat

But bone is temporary; they await payday. When it arrives the next week, the tunnels are charged as if a storm brews belowground. In the evening the mine boss appears on the ridge like some odd, huffing star to set up his table. He shuffles papers, stirs the crate with its pouches of coin. Counts, recounts. Lingers.

A string of miners ravels out, too long to see to its end. Minutes pass, an hour, impatience twitching the line. Lucy sticks by Ba. She means to hold the proof of her work in her hands.

Stars are up by the time they reach the table. One glance at Ba and the mine boss tosses a pouch, already looking to the next man. Ba unfastens the drawstring right there and commences to count. The boss clears his throat again and again.

"It's short," Ba says, tossing the pouch back. Behind him men shift and crane, murmur angrily.

"Rent for that fine house." The boss flicks up a finger. "Coal." Another finger. "Your tools." Another. "Your company-issue lantern." Another. "And a girl earns one-eighth wages. Now git."

Ba's hands clench. The men behind shuffle closer, begin to yell. **Can't you count, boy? Can't see, more like. Not outta them eyes.**

Someone says, **Like trying to fit a cow through a chink in the wall.**

This last is met with a roar of approval. The word passes from mouth to mouth, till it spills from every direction in the dark. Ba spins to face the insult, and Lucy trembles. Ba in the fullness of anger is fearsome. Those rare times he spanks her, he grows tall despite his bad leg. He fills the room.

The men only laugh louder. **Chink!** they bay from half a hundred throats. The hills echo with the sound, till the land itself is laughing.

Ba in anger, eyes squinted, is to them only funny.

Ba sweeps the coins from the table and walks away. His gait is wild, his bad leg swinging far to the side. Yet Lucy can hardly keep up. It could even be said that Ba runs.

———

"Mei guan xi," Ba says when he hands the coins to Ma. "Next payday we'll have enough for steaks. Salt and candy. Seeds for the garden. And sturdy boots for the girls. Mark my words. I promise."

Far from the mine, far from the hooting miners, Ba's voice in the shack is overloud. Past promises layer his words as grit layers their walls.

Ma says, quietly, "The baby."

The baby's got six months of growing, yet this stops Ba cold. He stares down at the coins, and when he looks up there's an old glint in his eye. "I know I promised I wouldn't gamble, qin ai de, but I swear I feel the luck. Here more than ever. If I took just a few coins—"

Ma shakes her head. "The mule. The wagon."

Ba loves that old wagon, which he coddles like a living thing. At each stop he paints the wheels afresh. **This is freedom**, he likes to say. **With this, we can go anywhere.** Now his face reddens.

Ma touches her belly. "For the baby."

Wordless, Ba slams out the door. They hear the grind of wheels, the mule's clop, departing. At the last moment Sam rushes out too.

Selling the wagon buys meat—of a sort. Enough for the butcher's leavings, those scraps still ragged with gristle and bone. Ma stews them for hours, the house ever-thick with cooking.

What others don't want comes cheap. Pigs' feet cooked to jelly, vertebrae that Ma sucks clean and spits, clattering, to her plate. Ma resumes her place at the table and sits longer than the rest. For hours each night she peels meat from bone and fills the house with gnawing. A crack splits the air and Lucy looks up, half in terror and half in fascination. Expecting Ma's smile cracked too.

"Why are we eating this?" Lucy complains.

"The baby," Ma says, and Lucy imagines tiny teeth chattering beneath Ma's dress. "The more meat he eats, the more meat he'll grow. Yi ding make him strong."

"But why do **all** of us have to?" Lucy says, knowing she pushes her luck. As expected, Ba tells her to shut her big mouth.

Sam, usually stubborn, swallows down two plates without comment.

Ma's face smooths. Her hollows fill. She recommences her chores. The house becomes, if not clean, then no longer dirty. Now it's Ma who sweeps twice a day, Ma who goes to the store and haggles. Ma with her voice to make shopkeepers shave a few cents from a bill, or wrap up an extra trotter with a wink.

And Ma recommences to brush Sam's hair when she brushes her own. A hundred strokes each night, untangling what Sam tangled in those few weeks of wandering. Neatened once more, bound by braids and bonnet, Sam no longer runs free all day. Sam grows prettier at Ma's feet, and quieter too.

Not so the baby. Mouthless, the baby speaks with Ma's borrowed voice. The baby can silence Ba, stop Lucy's questions, make Sam go sullen. What the baby demands, he gets.

"Look at him eat," Ba says in admiration one night. Ma smiles a smile distended around a chicken neck. Yet Ba stares as if he's never seen lovelier. "He'll be as strong as three men."

"Dui," Ma says. "**If** we feed him right." She spits her mouthful of chewed-up bone. "This isn't enough. Ying gai red meat. Not just bone."

"I got a plan," Ba says, as usual. But he mumbles it, shamefaced, instead of shouting.

That night he leaves earlier than usual for his woodcutting job. Ma kisses him goodbye without rising from the table. She's fixed on the last film of stew in the pot, the scrape and whine of her spoon setting Lucy's teeth on edge. Ma doesn't offer a bite to Sam or Lucy, as she once would have. Lucy asks if the baby isn't selfish. After all, she and Sam didn't make Ma sick. Ma laughs and laughs at the question. Explains, very gently, that boys are expected to raise a fuss.

Ba's late nights stretch later. He yawns through mine shifts. Each morning, half-asleep, his feet rise and fall through the blue-soaked hills in a driving rhythm: **The baby. The baby.**

On the morning of the next payday, Ba still hasn't returned. A tense breakfast, the three of them staring out the propped-open door at the empty stretch of field, the other miners' shacks, the creek, the South side beyond. Ma's eyes tick steadily to the pistol Ba forgot to take last night, left heavy on its hook.

Ba returns from an unexpected direction, swinging from behind the house with a clink and a clatter. He throws a bulging pouch on the table.

"Where—" Ma says.

"Payday. I collected early." Ba's voice swells with pride like the pouch's seams. "Didn't I promise you, qin ai de?"

"It can't be," Ma says. "Zen me ke neng?" But the truth spills free. Coins lie hard and weighty in her counting hands. She smiles. Ba flicks up his fingers, as the mine boss did, and explains. The house, the tools, the lantern—all paid for last time.

"Nu er," Ma says to Lucy, some of that coin-shine in her face too. "No more mines. Tomorrow, you and Sam go to school."

There are new dresses laid out in the morning. Lucy reaches for the red one, but Ma nudges her to the green.

"This suits you," Ma says, pulling Lucy to the tin mirror. Lucy stares, unblinking, into her own long face, made longer by the warped metal. "Like school will suit you. That teacher will see your true value."

Lucy thinks of her one-eighth wages. "Even if I'm not a boy?"

Most times Ma's voice is banked fire, cozy. Now its crackle rises. "Nu er, I don't want to hear that self-pity. Rang wo tell you something. When I first came to this territory, I had nothing except . . ." Ma looks down at her hands. She's careful to wear gloves outside the house, but here her skin is exposed. Roughened by callus, flecked blue by coal. "Girls have power too. Beauty is a weapon. And you—"

Above them, Sam's feet hit the ladder. Ma lowers her voice, puts her forehead against Lucy's. "Not the kind of weapons your sister plays with. Help me out, Lucy girl. Sam's . . . different. Ni zhi dao. Family comes first. Keep an eye on her."

As if Lucy ever needed reminding. Truth is, her eye can't help but follow Sam, who strides out of the house in the red dress that calls gold to the surface of Sam's brown skin. All eyes follow Sam. Though they hold hands across the creek and down the main street, gazes skitter past Lucy, straight to Sam.

What is it about Sam? Lucy has long studied her sister, trying to see what strangers see. That bold gaze swinging round, limbs in perpetual motion.

Like a wild creature, Sam holds the promise of movement. People watch for the sheer pleasure of seeing what shape Sam will cut through the grass.

The schoolhouse appears as a cool white beacon. But first there's the expanse of yard to cross, no shelter apart from a dead oak. Little boys' eyes blink from its leafless branches, bigger boys peer from spots against the trunk. And in the grass, among the curves and wriggles of the tree's reaching shadows, sit rings of girls. Their eyes glint hardest.

Lucy steps smaller and smaller, slower and slower, as if she could disappear like a rabbit into tall grass. The others, miners' children all, wear faded calico and gingham. Ma's good dresses are a brand. Lucy lets go of Sam's hand, crossing her arms over the rich embroidery on her chest. **Stand tall**, Ma says. **Speak up**. How often has Lucy seen Ma pry silence open with her voice?

"Good morning," Lucy says.

But Lucy isn't Ma. A few eyes blink incuriously. A boy laughs in the tree.

One of the girls steps forward. Other girls match her pace as geese trail their leader in a flock. The lead girl has beady eyes and unruly red curls.

"This is nice," she says, tugging the sleeve of Lucy's dress, and then Sam's. Girls swarm at that signal, stroking the embroidery, the ribbon in Lucy's hair, speculating among themselves how much each yard of fabric cost. The questions aren't directed at Lucy, exactly, but they flow easy around her. She tries to answer—**It's brocade. Thank you. Thank you, thank you**, even to those comments she isn't sure are kindly meant. Her voice goes quieter. These girls don't wait for her to answer. They don't need her to speak. She sees a way forward and through them, maybe—a new, silent way.

Through the press of bodies, Lucy gives Sam an uncertain smile.

Sam is holding still for the moment, but impatience begins to twitch Sam's mouth. **Let them**, Lucy begs silently. **Please let them do this. It isn't so bad.** Now the girls are admiring Sam herself. **Her skin looks like brown sugar, don't you think? I dare you to lick it. Look at her nose! Like a doll. And that hair—**

The first girl, the redhead, grabs Sam's glossy, half-loosed hair. "Pretty," the redhead croons, her own hair a frizz around her head. She lifts Sam's braid to her nose to sniff.

Two quick smacks ring through the courtyard. The redhead is left empty-handed, mouth hung foolishly open. Once set in motion, Sam can't seem to stop. Sam slaps and shoos the whole flock away, birdlike shrieks rising. Soon Sam stands alone.

"You all talk too much," Sam says.

A shifting in the yard. Like water on the first cold day of the year, what flowed through to greet them now begins to freeze. There's a moment when Sam could apologize—when Lucy could. But Lucy's tongue is thick and clumsy. "You idiot," she says under her breath. "You idiot, Sam."

"It's just dumb **hair**," Sam says scornfully, and tosses it over her shoulder.

A girl steps forward and spits. Misses. Saliva runs off Sam's shiny skirt, leaving the red that much deeper. The next girls don't make that mistake. The next girls use fingers, and nails.

School seems little different from the mine. The mockery, the bruises on Lucy's skin, the weight of so many gazes like the press of the underground dark—and even that same taunt Lucy heard on payday, passed down by miners to their children.

No difference until the bell rings and they enter the schoolhouse.

The order makes Lucy's heart ache. Desks, chairs, planks, chalkboard, maps—all fall in perfect lines. A clean room, airy. No sign of the territory's persistent dust. Real glass windows line the front, so that the first few rows look washed in butter. Kids sit two to a desk, leaving the very first and the very last empty. Lucy and Sam stand at the back till the teacher enters.

He came, it's said, on the long, hard trail from the East. But his thin white shirt would soil in minutes of travel, and his gold buttons would be lost or stolen. His is a costume absurd for trail or mine, possible only in this spotless place that he walks, greeting students by name. The girls who spat and pulled now beam at him with hands folded. Changed by his regard. He stops for a full minute to speak to one boy, who flushes at the attention. At the end of that talk, the teacher sends the boy to the very first, unoccupied desk.

It's a victory march. Lucy watches, along with everyone else, the pride that lengthens the boy's gait.

When the teacher arrives at Lucy and Sam, he rocks back on boots as polished as the planks. "I've heard of you two. I hoped to see you here one day. Welcome to my schoolhouse, which draws the border of civilization a little farther West. You may call me Teacher Leigh. And where do you come from?"

Lucy falters, takes heart from the teacher's kind gaze. She describes the trail they took from the last mine, but the teacher shakes his head.

"Where are you **really** from, child? I've written at length about this territory, and never encountered your like."

"We were born here," Sam says, mulish.

Lucy says, guessing, "Our ma said we come from beyond the ocean."

The teacher smiles. He seats them at the backmost

desk and lays a book before them. It's so new he must push the pages flat, and Lucy can't help it—bends to the pages to breathe in the ink.

When she lifts up, the teacher says, very gently, "This isn't for smelling or eating. This is called **reading**." He points to the alphabet that marches in letters half the size of his hand.

Lucy colors. She reads those letters, and the ones in the next book, and the words in the next one, and the next, the books getting thicker and the print smaller. Finally the teacher borrows the book from the boy at the first desk. He claps after Lucy reads a full page, sounding out those words she doesn't recognize. A roomful of eyes look back.

"Who taught you?"

"Our ma."

"She must be a very special woman. You'll introduce me one day. Tell me, Lucy, what would you most like to learn?"

No one has ever asked that question. Lucy's mind stumbles with the enormity of it. Inside that neat, closed schoolhouse she thinks all of a sudden of the open hills, their endless wander. Ba's bidding comes to her: **Don't be afeared**. How many books can there be? She hadn't dared imagine till now. Then she remembers the word.

"History," she says.

The teacher smiles. "'He who writes the past writes the future too.' Do you know who said that?"

He bows. "I did. I'm a historian myself, and may require your assistance in my newest monograph. What about you, Samantha? Are you a reader too?"

Sam glares. Doesn't answer. Silence simmers off Sam's brown skin, stirred thicker by every question, till at last the teacher gives up. He leaves Sam in the back and offers his hand to Lucy. Down the aisle she steps, all eyes watching—Sam's eyes too. She crosses into the sunshine that falls square on the first desk, and the boy sitting there hunches his shoulders high, as if to block the sight of her. But here he can't help seeing her. None of them can. He slides over. Makes room for Lucy.

"He says we're gifted," Lucy announces that night, pushing steak around her plate. Ma cooked up a special dinner, but Lucy is too occupied with telling to chew. She doesn't mention that the teacher said that only to Lucy. She doesn't mention the school-yard, or Sam's silence in the back of the room. "He wants to meet you, Ma. He said you must be brilliant too." Ma pauses with her hand on the ladle. Goes faintly pink. "He wants to meet all of us. And he wants to give me special lessons. He said there's people back East who'll want to hear about me, and maybe I could go with him the next time he talks to—"

"I don't like this," Ba says. He, too, has left his steak untouched. He grimaces at the char. "What's this teacher doing fishing around?"

"He's writing a history," Lucy says, as Sam says, "Nosy."

"I don't see what's so bad about the girls asking where they come from," Ma says. "Gao su wo, what else did the teacher say?"

"**We** can teach the girls," Ba says. "Not some stranger with his lies. Fei hua. I've half a mind to stop this."

They weren't lies, though. They were histories, set in ink. Lucy's hands still harbor that scent. Even the chicken shit fades in comparison.

"They'll learn," Ma says, "how to be something other than coal miners."

Silence pools through the room. In the mine, silence is deadlier than quake or fire. It precedes a fatal gas, invisible and scentless, its only sign this hush.

"We're not miners," Ba says.

Ma laughs. Her throat crackles with danger.

"We're—" Ba stops himself. The word he reaches for can't be said. It was banished from their family two years back, when Ma insisted on a different way of living. Ba doesn't say it, but they four feel its weight. **You just feel it**, Ba explained many years ago when he first taught Lucy to dowse. When he could still call himself a prospector.

"Then what do you call what we do?" Ma says,

standing. "People who live zhe yang? In this kind of place?"

Ma draws her foot back and kicks the floor. No ring of boot on planks. Just a heavy sort of sigh. Dust blooms up, grit scattering over the steaks. Lucy starts to cough. Sam too. And still Ma kicks till the room is a haze, till Ba seizes her from behind.

"Fa feng le," he pants, lifting Ma so that her feet kick the air. "Mining's what we do for now. Not who we are." He lowers Ma cautiously, then reaches for her belly. "We're saving up. Remember? I promised."

"Time with this teacher is a kind of saving up too. Not like what you do, gambling at those dirty camps. Don't think I don't know where you sneak off to. Dui bu dui, Lucy girl?" Ma looks sharp at Lucy, as she does when she shares a secret.

Hesitantly, Lucy nods.

Ba clenches the fabric at Ma's belly. Then he lets go. She glides back to her seat, her body parting the dust. Drawing a clean line between Lucy and Ba.

"The teacher's stuck-up," Sam says.

Ma **tsk**s, but doesn't object when Ba snorts, when Sam sits in Ba's lap and whispers. That night Ma is blind to manners, pretending she doesn't see the grit speckled over the steak, or Sam's laughing in a spray of half-chewed food. Lucy catches, over and over in Sam and Ba's whispering, the word **plateau**.

———

Ma washes the leftover steak, and fries it, and tucks it between bread for the next day's lunch. Lucy learns to swallow what scratches: the dust, the schoolyard insults, the spit that runs down her face and into her mouth, Ba's black moods at any mention of Teacher Leigh. Her big mouth learns another function.

The pay Ba collects seems only to increase. Two months pass, the family fortified by meat. Ma's belly domes and she coaxes the garden into sprouting. Ba takes extra shifts at the mine and stays out late every night. Lucy, happily, and Sam, reluctantly, go to school.

Later, Lucy will blame the meat for what happens in the schoolyard. The meat makes Sam's skin and hair brighter, a shine that won't be dulled by dust. Lucy will blame the meat, and even later she'll blame the cost of that meat, and the long desperate days worked to pay that cost, and the men who set that price, and the men who built mines that paid so little, and the men who emptied the earth and choked the streams and made the days so dry, and the claiming of the land by some that leaves others clutching only dusty air—but think too long and Lucy grows dizzy, as if sun-stunned on the open hills. Where does it end, that hard golden land that haunts her?

In any case, thinking comes later. The end of Sam's schooling dawns on a sunny, treacherous day. Heat makes the schoolhouse an oven, hottest where Sam sits at the back. Sam undoes her braids, lets down that shining hair.

Maybe, if they'd shared a desk, Lucy would have kept an eye on Sam as she was bid. Maybe she would have rebraided Sam's hair. But Lucy is last to leave at the day's end, when kids kick and shove to be free. All day tempers have itched at their clothes.

By the time Lucy gets outside there's already a circle.

It looks like a game of Cowboy and Buffalo. The kids playing Cowboy are gathered around. In the middle, playing Buffalo, is Sam.

The Cowboy who steps up to lasso is the redheaded girl. Instead of a grass rope, she holds scissors. Instead of throwing, she seizes Sam's hair. The redhead turns to the crowd to make a joke or declaration. In that moment, Sam gives a yell she fancies for Indian war cry. Sam grabs the scissors.

The circle tightens. Lucy can't get past the bodies. Can't see what's happening inside. The way the game usually ends is with the Buffalo lying dead on the ground.

But when the circle reopens, Sam still stands. A thick black rope lies in the dirt. No—a snake. No—a piece of Sam's hair. Sam still holds the scissors, Sam who cut a hunk from her own head.

"You can have it," Sam is saying. "It's just dumb hair."

Ma would scream, but Lucy laughs. She can't help it. An ordinary game, and yet Sam's cut and shaped it for her own. Look at Sam's shine. Look at the girls who gasp and clutch their own braids. Only Lucy understands that this is Sam's victory.

Then Teacher Leigh is striding across the yard. The redhead sees him and drops to the ground. She holds her stomach, writhes in the dirt, points at Sam. The scissors sharp in that chubby hand.

For the first time, Sam looks uncertain. Sam steps back, but again the circle tightens, entrapping. Boys scramble up the dead oak. Their arms laden. They throw. A meaty flower opens on Sam's cheek. Not fruit: the tree bears rocks.

Plum

A plum, Ba says tenderly as he studies Sam's face. Though the bruise on Sam's cheek, swelling from the cut that just missed Sam's eye, bears little resemblance to the fruit Sam loves.

Lucy, sickened, turns away. Ba grabs her chin. Forces her to look.

"Didn't I say?" Ba asks. "**Stick by your family**. I didn't raise you this way. Not as a coward. Not as a girl who—"

Ma puts herself between them. Her belly, against Ba's stomach, saying: **The baby**. Today Ba won't be silenced.

"I told you," he says, glaring now at Ma. "School's no place for Sam."

"Bu hui happen twice," Ma says. "Sam will be a

good girl now, won't you? I'll speak to the teacher. There's value to be had from schooling. Kan kan Lucy. How well she's doing."

Ba pays Lucy no mind. He's looking at Ma. A deadly hush falls once more in the room. It seems to seep from a place older and deeper than Lucy and Sam. From out of that place, Ba says in a peculiar, cold voice, "Didn't you learn your lesson?" As if Ma isn't Ma but a little girl like Lucy. "I figured the two hundred would rememory you against thinking you know best."

The words mean nothing to Lucy, or to Sam, who returns her confused gaze. Two hundred is a nonsense number. Yet Ma clutches the table. For all her regained weight, she looks sick once more.

"Wo ji de," Ma says, pressing her hands to her face. Hard, as if she means to push through to bone. "Dang ran."

Though Ba's won this argument, he looks even worse than Ma. The juice has left him. His bad leg wobbles. Sam rushes to him, and Lucy to Ma, and once more the house is split.

That marks the end of Sam's schooling.

Sam's wish comes true. The red dress is laid away, a shirt and pants cut down to size. **Boys get paid more**, Ba says, and Ma doesn't argue, though she draws the line at cutting Sam's hair. It's braided to hide the missing portion, tucked under a cap.

Ma's been awful quiet since the fight. A distance in her eyes. She startles when Lucy speaks, as if surfacing from a shaft.

"I want to stay home today," Lucy repeats.

"School?" Ma says, blinking. She turns away at last from the oilcloth window, where she's been staring at the smudge of horizon.

"Teacher Leigh said not to worry." He came wading among the Cowboys, crying, **Desist, you little beasts!** He took Sam's scissors and helped the redhead up. **Go home,** he said to Lucy. **And don't worry about returning tomorrow.**

Lucy's grateful for the pardon. Thing is, the teacher forgot to mention when she should return. A week passes with no word. Sam's plum grows backward: black to purple to blue to unripe green. Ba still won't look at Lucy. Ma won't look at Ba. The shack more stifling than usual. Come Sunday, Lucy can bear it no longer. With Ba and Sam at the mine working a spare shift, she decides to visit the teacher. Weeks ago he mentioned extra lessons, and told her where to find his house.

To her surprise, Ma's eyes uncloud. Ma insists on going along.

———

A ways down the main street on the South side of town, a sign reading LEIGH points them up a narrow path. The teacher lives on a road that is his alone, which starts out dirt and becomes gravel. Soon neat rows of coyote brush rise on either side, their tops trimmed and even. The dusty leaves hide the rough backsides of the stores, the view of the miners' half of the valley. And they hide the people that look at Ma even sharper than they look at Sam.

When they arrive at the teacher's house with its two stories and stone chimney, its porch and eight glass windows, its accompanying stable with a gray horse that must be the teacher's Nellie—a house so orderly it makes Lucy's heart beat fast—Lucy finds that she wishes Ma far, far away.

Easy enough to tell tales of Ma to the teacher. In the flesh there's no hiding Ma's bare feet, slick, one toenail cracked. And for all that Ma disguises her belly under a skirt, her rough hands under gloves, nothing can disguise her voice. Next to history, Teacher Leigh's favorite subject is elocution. There's wrongness in Ma's speech. Her lilt. Her way of swallowing some sounds and lingering too long on others.

"I want to talk to him alone," Lucy says. And then, to stop Ma from protesting, "I can do it myself. I don't need you."

Ma doesn't smile so much as bare her teeth. "Kan kan. You've grown up." She takes a step back, then swoops close to Lucy's ear and says, "Nu er, you remind me of myself at your age."

A part of Lucy has waited her whole life to hear this. There's a warm whoosh in her ears, her heart riding high in her chest. If they were alone on the trail she might well whoop into the dusk, and never care who heard it. Here she's mindful of the glass windows, the dignified hush of the coyote-brush lane. She keeps still. She waits for Ma to step back against the wall, hidden from sight. Only then does Lucy knock.

"Sir," Lucy says when the door opens. "I'm here, please, for the extra lessons."

The teacher frowns, as if at a slow student. "Lucy. You must know it's poor manners to come visiting uninvited."

"I'm very sorry. That's the thing, sir, there's so much I don't know. I'd be honored to learn from you."

"I enjoyed teaching you. You're a smart girl, and so unusual. It's a shame—what a sensation you would have made back East had I included your development in my monograph!" Lucy starts to smile. Teacher Leigh puts his hand on the doorframe. "But that little tableau of violence was unacceptable. Savagery runs in your blood, and I can't have my other students disturbed. I must think of the greater good."

Lucy holds her smile, though it's leaden now. "I wasn't fighting, sir."

"Lies don't flatter your intellect, Lucy. I saw you in that circle. And I heard from the other students how Samantha instigated the affair. No—results don't matter. I saw your intentions."

The teacher lets go of the door as Lucy says, "I'm not like Sam. I'm not."

Lucy could shove her arm through the gap, could grab for what she wants so desperately. That would only prove what the teacher suspects.

And then Ma grasps the knob. Teacher Leigh looks at her gloved hand, indignant. Up her arm, her shoulder. Into her face.

"Thank you for teaching Lucy," Ma says.

That husky voice, unexpected against Ma's smoothness. Ma who skins rabbits still twitching, who hauled the mule from a sinkhole. As if in answer, Ma speaks slower. A knife dragged through honey.

"We've walked a fair piece. May we come in for a glass of water?"

Ma gives Lucy the piercing look that says, **This is our secret**. Then she's smiling at the teacher, the smile sweetened like the voice is sweetened. Nothing changes. Everything changes. The teacher steps back, holding the door wide open. Some power leaves him and moves to Ma. She steps through.

———

Ma sinks into the teacher's horsehair couch as if she's sat there every day of her life. Her skin glows against the open window. She belongs here, of a piece with the lace curtains, the honeyed wood, the thin white teacups with their gold rims.

Lucy looks away, looks back. A thrill runs through her each time. Ma set in the center of that parlor like a picture in a frame. To judge by his face, the teacher feels that same thrill.

He pours tea and sets out cookies with dark, oozing centers. "The jam is made from cultivated hothouse plums. Not like these sour, wild trees in the West. My folks back East send the jam by train and then wagon, but once you taste you'll see it's well worth the extra cost."

Ma refuses, giving Lucy another look. **Don't be beholden**, Ma likes to say. Her gloved hands stay tidy in her lap. Miserably, Lucy leaves the cookies alone too.

"Tell me about yourself," the teacher says.

Light shifts down the couch, down Ma's body as the hours pass. Illuminating one piece at a time: the soft cheek, the long neck, the crease of an elbow, the ankle peeping just above the skirt. The shadows of Sam's wildness are vanquished from this room—Ma proof that decency lives in Lucy. Teacher Leigh and Ma discuss where she came from, the latest news from back East, the cultivation of plants and gardens, Lucy's reading, and how Ma taught her.

"And yourself?" Teacher Leigh says. "Where did you learn to read?"

Lucy's heard the story half a hundred times. **Your ma was a poor student**, Ba starts. And Ma jumps in: **Poor teacher, more like. Your ba couldn't sit still**. Together they recount how Ba taught Ma to read, interrupting and joking, silly as children.

Ma smiles. Looks down at her teacup, so that her lashes scatter shadows on the porcelain. "I picked it up here and there."

"And where was that?"

Ma gives a tinkling laugh that fits this room. No kin to her other laugh that crackles. Roars. "I think Lucy should be the one to answer your questions. She's a smart girl. I know she'd love to be in a classroom again."

Who could refuse Ma?

As they leave, Ma dips her head to Lucy and asks if she is happy.

Sunset leaves a glaze on the coyote brush. The world looks good enough to eat. Teacher Leigh's hair is corn silk as he waves from the porch, Ma's lips marrow-dark.

"I'm happy. But, Ma? Why didn't you tell him about learning to read?"

The house disappears from view. Rather than answer, Ma shucks her glove. Her fingers root in her pocket and emerge dirt-speckled. "Try this," she says, reaching for Lucy's mouth.

Lucy catches a hint of sweetness. Cautiously, she licks.

"From all the way back East," Ma says, pulling a handful of plum cookies from her pocket. "Fang xin, Lucy girl. Did you see how many he ate? He won't notice. He's a good man under his ruffles. Ying gai accept those extra lessons."

Lucy abstains as Ma eats. The sweet fades to sour on her tongue. "But why did you **lie**, Ma?"

"Don't whine." Ma wipes her fingers. "Ni zhang da le. Old enough to know what's a lie, and what's better left unsaid. Remember I taught you about burying? Well, sometimes truth needs burying too."

The cookies, and all traces of Ma's gluttony, are gone. Her face has a cat's satisfaction. So neat and clean that Lucy asks, meanly, "Like the two hundred?"

Later, Lucy will wonder what might've been different had she been kinder. Less selfish. Or as smart as Ma believed her to be, capable of reading what was written on Ma's trembling lip. Ma says, so softly, "I'll tell you when you're older. Xian zai help me out, Lucy girl. Don't tell your ba about this visit, or your lessons. Hao bu hao?"

Lucy wants to ask, **Why not now? What's older mean?** But Ma smiles again, a smile Teacher Leigh didn't see, because this smile has no place in that light-filled parlor. And Lucy is reminded that what makes Ma most beautiful is the contradiction of her. Rough voice over smooth skin. Smile stretched over sadness—this queer ache that makes Ma's eyes look miles and miles away. Brimming with an ocean's worth of wet.

"I won't tell," Lucy promises the woman who keeps her secrets.

Ma takes her hand and they walk in silence back-down to the main street, coyote brush receding as they leave the teacher's land. The town reappears.

And they see the clouds.

Strange clouds, too low and too early—the wet season is months away. Men spill from the stores, the saloon. They stare at the swift-moving clouds rushing from the direction of the mine, risen up from the ground to darken the sky. Ma squeezes so hard that Lucy yelps.

They last saw clouds like this a year ago on the trail. Mistook them for locusts till a boom lit the horizon orange. For three days fires raged, a distant mine burning. And Ma—Ma who braved storm and drought, who once set her own broken finger—Ma sank her head to her knees and shiv-ered. Didn't look up till they were long past. **She doesn't like fire**, Ba said brusquely when Lucy asked. **Shut that big mouth.**

Now Ma hitches up her skirt and runs, drag-ging Lucy along. Other women are running too, barefoot women, a flood of miners' wives heading home. Flashes of calf and thigh; the ragged pant of breath. Nothing ladylike about this dash. Ma, eyes wild, doesn't appear to notice.

Ma stumbles crossing the creek. In the space opened up by her falling body, Lucy sees that the clouds have overtaken the sun.

Ma twists. Her shoulder hits the ground in place of her stomach. Darkness stains her dress—but it's only plum jam.

"Ni zhi dao, Lucy girl, what happens to bodies in a fire?" Ma says as Lucy drags her up. Now they pass the other miners' shacks. Lanterns glow within; the open doors punch yellow into the false night. "I know." Women and girls stand outside, looking toward the clouds. "Fire leaves nothing to bury." Lucy hums, as if soothing a panicked mule. "The haints yi bei zi follow. They never let you go." Ash begins to fall. The bigger pieces like moths, which Ma always hated. She claimed that moths are the dead come visiting.

But there are no ghosts in their shack. Just Ba and Sam, the table set, a waft of good cooking.

"You're filthy!" Sam says with glee.

Ba stands, holding two plates. "Lai," he says. "Wash up after you eat."

At the table, legs swinging, Sam hums Ma's tiger song.

Ma steps back. "Where were you?"

"The mine." Ba steps forward with a plate. Ma steps back again. "Right, Sam? Tell your ma."

"We worked hard," Sam says with a full mouth.

"When?" Ma says.

"We got back not long ago. Must've just missed you." Ba frowns at the stain on Ma's dress. Reaches. Ma twists away as if dancing, though there's no humming now, no music in the silent room. Sam's head turns like a wary creature to track Ma. "What happened to you?"

Ma slaps Ba's hand aside. The plate falls, doesn't break. Spins round and round, whining.

"Leave it," Ma hisses as Ba stoops. His out-stretched hand is as clean as his face, the nailbeds pink. How long since they were black with coal? Lucy can't recall. "Where were you?"

"The mine."

"Fei hua."

"Might be we stopped along the way to explore. Can't quite remember—"

"Liar." Ma rips the dirty oilcloth from the window, and the eerie horizon shows.

"I can explain," Ba says, staring out. "We left early. Ting wo—"

"I thought you were dead."

"We're safe, qin ai de." Ba moves to hug her.

Again Ma says, "I thought you were dead." She steps back. Her shoulder meets the door. And Lucy sees for the first time how Ma's eyes could be what the kids say: small, unlovely, mean. Ma studies

Ba as she studies food gone rancid. Judging what good is left, and what to toss out. "I thought you were dead." Three times she's said it now, flat and strange, like a spell. "What's real, then? Na ge outside is real. Ni ne? What does that make you? Some kind of haint?"

"Let me explain. We didn't mean to scare you. We were working to—to make you happy."

"Me?" The words come rasping out of Ma. "You aim to blame **me**? Cuo shi wo de? Mine?" The unbroken plate left the promise of a crash in the air. "What's real, then? Which of your promises? Ni bu shi dong xi, ni zhe ge—"

Ma made of their hard life something orderly. Amid grass and dirt, from wagon beds and hard-used houses, Ma wrangled for them a life of soft voices and clean speech. A life of braided hair and swept floors, cut nails and pressed collars. **What people see shapes how they treat you**, Ma said again and again. Now something's come loose in Ma, her hair unwinding around her dirty face, her words unwinding into cusses.

Ba steps forward. No place for Ma to flee, unless it's out the door. Her fingers grip the knob as Ba pushes his fist against her mouth.

Ma stops talking.

When Ba pulls back, he leaves something yellow between Ma's lips. Something all the light in the room rushes toward.

"Bite down," he says.

Ma's fingers are still on the knob. One push and she could be gone.

She bites.

She spits a pebble into her hand. The print of her teeth in its soft yellow surface.

"This is real," Ba says. "I had to make sure. I only meant to keep it secret till I ascertained it would be enough."

"You've been prospecting," Ma says. The forbidden word billows round the room. A hot, singed smell. "You promised you'd quit. The widows? The woodcutting?" Ba shakes his head. "Kan kan, this is what I think of prospecting."

Ma tips the pebble to her mouth and swallows. Like bone and like mud, another piece of the land slips into her. Sam wails. Ba looks shaken. But then he grins.

"Mei wen ti," Ba says. "Plenty where that came from."

"I ate it," Ma says, slumping. Poor posture pushes her belly out, rounded now as the hills are rounded.

"**He** ate it," Ba says, and this time Ma lets him touch her. "Why, he'll be rich. Come here, Sam. Show your ma."

Sam comes forward with a dirty old pouch. Lucy recognizes it for the same one she used in the mine to hold a rag and a candle stub. In Sam's hands that same pouch releases a gleaming shower. Lucy thinks of the fairy tale: the good sister and the bad. One passed through the door and soot stuck to her.

Marked her all her life. The other passed through and came out dazzled.

Someone says, "Gold."

For the first seven years of Lucy's life, Ba was a prospector. Seven years of life lived as if windblown, drifting from site to site on the rumor of gold.

Ma set her foot down two years back. One night she left Lucy and Sam in the wagon, and for hours she and Ba talked in the open hills. Snatches drifted back, Ma's voice holding forth on hunger and foolishness, pride and luck. Ba was silent. Come morning, the prospecting tools were packed away. Ba nursed sullenness for a month, gambled and drank. It was Ma who first mentioned coal mines.

Since then, Ba's put away most of the gambling, and most of the drinking too. He blusters of fortunes made in coal, as he once blustered of fortunes made from other materials. The forbidden word went unsaid—till now.

Tonight, as ash from a burning mine falls through their window, Ba tells them about the gold.

How he heard rumors about these hills, plied from old prospectors and Indian trackers. Here, where a dried-up lake sits on a plateau, and where lone, mad wolves can still be found. How Ba figured that a quake a year back, and the digging of a big mine, might have unearthed something unseen for a decade. He prospected in secret, under guise of woodcutting in the dark.

"I struck gold early on," Ba says as he kneels, washing grime from Ma's feet. "That second payday—that was the gold. I walked ten miles south to trade it for coin at some little outpost—that's why I was gone all night. Didn't I promise you a fortune? We can buy whatever you want, qin ai de. Whatever **he** deserves. We're special." Ba turns to Sam and Lucy, grinning. "Girls, you know the only thing in this territory more powerful than a gun?"

"Tigers," Sam says.

"History?" Lucy says.

"Family," Ma says, hugging her stomach.

Ba shakes his head. Closes his eyes. "I mean to buy a big parcel of land out in these hills. So big we won't need to see another soul. We'll have all the space in the world to hunt and breathe. That's the kind of place I aim for him to grow up in. Imagine that, girls. That's proper power."

They all of them go quiet, imagining. Till Ma breaks the spell. Doesn't say yes, and doesn't say no. She says, "This is the last time you lie to me."

Salt

A new kind of morning, now.
The oilcloth Ma ripped from the window is never replaced, the shack brighter with nothing between them and the sun. They eat breakfast as a family again, four together chewing, teasing, offering, squabbling, planning, dreaming. Illuminated—every gesture lit by the promise of morning. At last Ba and Sam tug on their boots and heft their prospecting tools, which are hidden in a fiddle case. They head to the gold field at a leisurely pace, the deception of the miner's hour done. Isn't it easier, Ba says, with no more secrets?

Each Sunday right after Ba and Sam set out, Lucy leaves the house on a journey of her own. Unknown to all but Ma, she goes to Teacher Leigh's for extra lessons.

Lessons in politeness. How to drink tea and pretend fullness. How to refuse food—cookies, cakes, crustless sandwiches. How not to stare at the salt that arrives in its silver box. All that heaped white gleaming. How not to want its clean burn on her tongue.

Lessons in answering questions.

What does your family eat?

Can you describe the medicines in your mother's trunk?

How long has your family traveled?

What are your hygiene practices? How often do you bathe?

At what age did you grow your first adult tooth?

Lucy doesn't like answering half so much as she likes watching the teacher write her answers down. The fresh ink so crisp and fine. On an empty stomach, the fumes make Lucy dizzy.

What does your father drink? How much?

Can you describe his attitude toward violence?

Would you call it savage?

What is your mother's breeding?

Does she perhaps come from royal stock?

The teacher improves Lucy's answers. Brow furrowed he scratches out, rewrites, pauses to ask Lucy to repeat herself. On that blank page he orders her family's story with words neatened as the school-house is neatened, the parlor, the rows of coyote brush that shut out what's unpleasant to see. Lucy's story set down as part of the teacher's monograph on the Western territory. One day she'll hold that book, heavier even than Jim's ledger. She'll lay it before Ma. She'll smooth its pages and hear its living spine crack.

Lessons in imagining herself better.

Nights, Ma counts. Each fleck and pebble passes into her hands. She weighs them on a scale, scribbles down their value in coin. Then she squirrels the gold in pouches—big and small, fat and thin—hidden around the house.

And she grows stingy, despite the bounty. Ma declares an end to steaks and salt and sugar. A return to bony cuts. Only one new dress for Lucy. Practical boots for Ba and Sam. Sam throws a tantrum at this news, keening for the promised cowboy boots and horse.

"We're saving," Ma says, the crackle so strong in her words that Sam stops midyell.

Pouches in the stovepipe, behind the tin mirror. Down the coal bin and in the heel of an old shoe. The shack that was once a hen coop acquires a new gleam. Lucy's dreams glint with half-seen light.

Ma, too, seems to peer at something just beyond view. She's often idle, sat by the window with chin propped. The line of her neck dreamy.

Ba kisses the spot where Ma's shoulder curves to neck. "A nugget for your thoughts."

"The baby," Ma says, eyes half-shut in pleasure. Three months since they arrived, and Ma's stomach pushes against her loosest dress. "I'm imagining how he'll grow up."

Some Sundays, when the teacher's hand is too cramped to write, he tells the story of his own raising, so far from here as to be fairy tale.

Back in the East. An older, more civilized territory. Seven brothers, a doting mother, a father who ruled from a distance, his kingdom a fragrant heap of cedar wood shipped near and far. Teacher Leigh the special one. The smart one. Among his frivolous brothers, he alone thought bigger. **Some men are drawn to sporting and hunting; I'm drawn to doing good. My mission is to spread education across this territory.** He traveled months, by boat and by train, by horse and by cart, to build this shining new school on a hill. A charity school for miners' children.

Teacher Leigh sits taller when he tells this part. His voice is sonorous, vibrating the fine thin panes of window glass. He surveys his audience—friends who gather to him on Sundays. And then, from that height, he looks fondly at Lucy.

Imagine my delight when I found Lucy. She and her family have a unique role in my book, and it's my responsibility to record them correctly.

Lucy tingles, her eyes downturned and fixed on the saltcellar.

You see how these miners insist on drinking and gambling their coin away. And those Indian camps that resist civilizing . . . this family, however! They're different. Lucy's mother is of great breeding, you can tell.

"We're not miners," Lucy says, softly, so that she doesn't interrupt Teacher Leigh.

Shopkeepers and mine bosses, kept wives and ranchers riding from the surrounding plots of land—they come chattering into the parlor, through the door that Teacher Leigh props open when he isn't working on his monograph. **Has it really been— Come, Leigh, I must tell you— How's that mare of yours? I heard—**

Lessons in how other people live.

From afar, Lucy couldn't grasp it. Always from a distance she saw miners' wives flitting between shacks, borrowing washboards, thimbles, recipes, soap. **They don't know self-sufficiency**, Ba said pityingly. He taught Lucy silence was better than gossip. He taught her to stand under the yawn of sky and listen to the wind through the grass. **Listen hard enough and you can hear the land.**

But now Lucy hears the baker talk about the butcher, who talks about the girl working at Jim's store, who talks about a miner's wife run off with a cowboy. Their talk a bright thread stitching the town together, rich as the tapestry Lucy saw hung from a porch. Its owner hurried it away, as if Lucy meant thievery. Lucy wanted only to look. To touch, maybe, and let it drape around her, like these honeyed Sundays with the glass windows and the talk, the bodies, heating the room.

Unseen, mouth watering with words she can't contribute, Lucy puts out a finger. Licks up fallen granules of salt. How bright the sting on her tongue. How fleeting.

At home, dusk, Lucy waits for the private moment when she and Ma stand alone at the stove. Another dinner of potatoes, of marrow and cartilage stewed to sludge. It's only midweek and Sunday so far off, yet Lucy is tired of it: the brown taste of unsalted meat, the dirt floor that roughens her heels, the scrimping and saving when gold clamors all around them.

"Ma? How long will it take us to save up for that parcel of land?"

Even to Lucy, Ma won't say. Ma smiles the smile of secrets.

Lessons in wanting what she can't have.

Best of the Sunday company are the real ladies. Not the women of the town but those from the teacher's old life, come visiting with no sign of the West stamped as sun-lines in their skin. They bring news of the velvet seats on train cars, of the flowers planted on their green lawns. These ladies sometimes beckon Lucy close. **Tell me**, they say.

For these women Teacher Leigh and Lucy play a game. He asks and she answers, batting her education back and forth like a colorful ball. **What's thirty-eight into fourteen thousand eight hundred and sixteen? Three hundred eighty-nine and thirty-four remaining. How long ago was the first civilized outpost founded in this territory? Twoscore years ago and three.**

This Sunday, an older lady sits on the horsehair couch.

"Meet my own teacher," the teacher says. "Miss Lila."

Miss Lila looks Lucy over. A severe face, out of which comes a voice harder than the red lines drawn around her lips. "She seems clever. You always did have an eye for that. Clever's easy, though. Far harder to teach is character. Moral fiber."

"Lucy has a fair share of that too."

Lucy tucks the compliment away, to relay later to Ma. Miss Lila's gaze rests on her, like the gazes in the schoolhouse when Lucy walks to the chalkboard. Wanting her to fail.

"Let me demonstrate," Teacher Leigh says. "Lucy?"

"Yes?" She looks up. Belief makes handsome the teacher's narrow face.

"Let's say you and I are traveling the same wagon trail. We start out with equal provisions. One month into the journey, you lose your goods in a fording. It's the hottest time of the year. The river is foul, not fit to drink from. The next town is weeks away. What do you do?"

Lucy nearly laughs. Why, this question is easy. The answer comes quicker than math or history.

"I'd butcher an ox. I'd drink its blood and continue on till fresh water."

This lesson is burned into Lucy's skin. She's stood on that bank, inhaled that foul water. Watched Ma and Ba argue as thirst stuck her tongue to her mouth. But Teacher Leigh has frozen, and Miss Lila's hand covers her throat. They both of them stare as if Lucy's got food on her face.

She licks her lips. Sweat beads over them.

"The answer," the teacher says, "is of course that you should ask for help. I would offer half my provisions, and therefore spread goodwill. So that the next time I myself have an accident, I'll receive assistance in return."

The teacher pours tea for Miss Lila, coaxes sweets into her hand. His back to Lucy is rigid with disappointment. Lucy listens to their crunching. Remembering the crunch in her own teeth, that night on the trail when Ma sifted the last of the flour and found the wriggling bodies of weevils. They baked biscuits anyhow, and ate after dark so as not to see what they chewed. All those miles they traveled, and not once did another wagon offer help.

Lucy reaches, unseen, for the salt.

Lessons in agreement.

Lessons in trickery.

Lucy waits for Ma to look away from the pot. In one deft movement, Lucy opens her handkerchief and sprinkles salt in.

Ba declares the oxtail extra-fine that night. Oxtail on Sunday, porridge on Monday, potatoes on Tuesday, trotters on Wednesday, potatoes potatoes potatoes again. Lucy doesn't use much. Just a hint. Salt expands the tired taste of the food. Close her eyes, and as she chews the house expands too, many-roomed. A taste to stretch her till Sunday.

"Lucy," Ma says, catching Lucy's hand before the

stove's red heat. The handkerchief sticks out from between Lucy's fingers. A few grains of salt trickle free. "Where did you take this from?"

"He gave it to me." The teacher passes the salt-cellar every Sunday, anyhow. Lessons in near-truths. "Besides, you took the cookies." Lucy yanks the handkerchief back. "It's not fair. You—you—it's not **fair**!"

She crouches, shaking a little from fear. Ma's anger is rarer than Ba's, but more precise. More liable to hunt out tender spots. Ma knows to pinch Lucy's earlobe where it's thinnest, to forbid what Lucy loves most.

But Ma doesn't move. "You shi," she says, her gaze skipping over Lucy's face, "I wonder if we shouldn't have left home."

Lucy turns. There's only blank wall where Ma stares. She tries to see the home Ma sees. From the dry soil of rememory she digs up this: grass rustling, streaked and dusty light. A familiar path underfoot, and Ba's shadow with its dowsing rod, and somewhere the call of Ma's voice, and dinner-smoke in the air—

"We always had salt," Ma says. "Mei tian. And fish from the ocean, Lucy girl. Wo de ma—your grandmother—the way she steamed them—"

Oh. Ma doesn't mean their campsites, their prospecting days. She means a home Lucy can't see. Across the ocean.

"You're a good girl, Lucy. You don't ask for much. Try to understand. I'm saving, dong bu dong, every bit we can. Though sometimes I think—you and Sam might have had a better life there. **He** might."

Lucy tries to picture Ma's mother, Ma's father, the family Ma speaks of crowded into a room. All she conjures is Teacher Leigh's parlor, full of voices on a Sunday.

"Ma—are you lonely?"

"Shuo shen me. I have you, Lucy girl."

But not during the day. For the first time Lucy considers Ma alone in the house, considers the long dim hours Ma rocks by the window while Lucy reads in the schoolhouse, while Ba and Sam dig gold. How quiet it must get. The only sound the leak of other wives' talk when the wind blows just so from far across the valley.

Ma pats the handkerchief in Lucy's hand. "You can use this for now, nu er. I suppose he did give it to you."

Under Ma's gaze, this time, Lucy tips salt into the stew. No word this time about beholdenness as Ma's spine bends over the pot. Lucy is jolted to see her own hunger in Ma's face.

Her hand slips. A heap of white lands on the surface, dissolves. Surely it's too much. No one else appears to notice. At dinner they gulp their portions and scrape their bowls, ask again and again for more. A ring of dark stew forms around

Ma's mouth. She eats so quick she doesn't pause to wipe.

Lucy herself takes two bites and puts her spoon aside. Her tongue burns. Another taste mixes in with the salt, unwelcome and bitter.

Lessons in shame.

Gold

Then comes the day that Ba takes Lucy to the gold field.

It's morning when they set out, yet they turn from the sun and slip beneath the plateau's shadow. Lucy drags her feet in protest. It's a school day. She shouldn't be tramping the hills—this is where Sam belongs. But Sam took sick and it was Ma, forever counting coin, who insisted that Lucy go.

They reach the valley's edge, where grass gives way to rock and a ridge rises like animal hackles: **Turn back. Beware.**

Ba steps over.

The plateau is bare and gray. Not even desperate miners venture out here—not even those who lost jobs in the fire and spend their days restless as starving dogs, scrounging for food, work, anything to keep busy. Yet Ba keeps his prospecting tools hidden in the fiddle case all the same.

Rock walls rise higher and higher on either side, shutting out the sun. "The river carved this path," Ba says, a line of shadow splitting his face, and Lucy nearly laughs at the boldness of the lie.

The path deepens, widens, ascends. At its very top Lucy sees that the plateau isn't flat. It's scooped hollow. They stand at the bottom of an empty bowl. High up, a circle of sky. Her legs tremble. Is this what they came for? This nothing rock?

Ba points to a line of green far off. It gains complexity as they approach. Cottonwoods, reeds, blue irises and white lilies. Thirsty plants, all. Yet no water in sight.

"Take a look," Ba says, that glitter in his eyes. "This here's the lake."

———— ◦ ————

A long time ago, Lucy girl, a river ran through this land. Started right here in what used to be a lake. If we looked up a hundred hundred hundred years ago, why, we'd see water more'n a mile deep above us, and underwater forests taller than any forest on land, and fish swimming so thick they blocked the light. This lake was the birthing place for the creek that runs below.

Don't look so surprised. Plenty of things in this land that used to be grander, just like the buffalo.

It was cold back then. Snow most of the year. I've reason to believe it got warmer with time, the animals smaller. The lake shrank some, and the fish shrank to fit, and all the salt and the dirt and the metal in that big bowl of water filled a smaller bowl.

That's right. The gold too. It was always there.

There was no man alive back then to see it, but something must've happened to disappear the lake. You want to hear my thoughts, I figure it for a big quake. The ground must've leapt up like your ma when she saw a rattler, and when it fell back down it cracked. The lake leaked through.

Now, most of the fish and the salt and the gold flowed downstream, following that same path we just climbed. They made a river through town. That's why this town grew up, in fact. Before it was a coal mine, it was a prospecting site. Men picked the river as clean as your ma picks bone. And they ruined that water.

I tell you the creek used to be wider, and clearer, and filled with fish. It's not right, that way of doing things. I don't see how you can claim to own a place and treat it so poor, there are methods of getting what you want without tearing at the land like a pack of wild dogs—but I'm getting away from my story.

I heard tales of the lakebed from Indian traders and got to thinking: Gold's heavy, right? The water down below had to come from somewhere, and if that somewhere was up, then maybe all the gold hadn't washed away. Maybe some of it stuck. Your ma dislikes me associating with Indians; smart though she is, she hasn't come round to how their knowledge of this land runs deep.

Anyhow, the lake is why there's gold here, Lucy girl, and the bones of fish if you care to look. You'll see it today, all around you. Sometimes when I'm up here at night and the wind's blowing powerful strong and I hear a rustle, I'll turn thinking to see Sam. But nothing's there. Sometimes I feel like a sea leaf is brushing my face, or I hear a wet sound though the ground's dry. Sometimes I think leaves and fish and water could haunt a man as much as anything else . . . but that's ghost talk. Point

is, there's always been gold in these hills.
You just had to believe.

———◇———

What's the name for this feeling? This being parched
and quenched all at once. Lucy's mouth is dry, her
lips cracked. But inside her is a sloshing—**water**,
Ma calls her—a sense that the world Ba speaks of is
close. Move quick enough and she might puncture
the thin skin of the day. Might feel the ancient lake
flood her.

Because this land they live in is a land of missing
things. A land stripped of its gold, its rivers, its buffalo, its Indians, its tigers, its jackals, its birds and
its green and its living. To move through this land
and believe Ba's tales is to see each hill as a burial
mound with its own crown of bones. Who could
believe that and survive? Who could believe that
and keep from looking, as Ba and Sam do, always
toward the past? Letting it drag behind them. Letting it make them into fools.

And so Lucy fears that unwritten history. Easier
to dismiss all Ba's tales as tall ones—because believe, and where does it end? If she believes that
tigers live, then does she believe that Indians are
hunted and dying? If she believes in fish the size of
men, does she believe in men who string up others
like linefuls of catch? Easier to avoid that history,

unwritten as it is except in the soughing of dry grass, in the marks of lost trails, in the rumors from the mouths of bored men and mean girls, in the cracked patterns of buffalo bone. Easier by far to read the history that Teacher Leigh teaches, those names and dates orderly as bricks, stacked to build a civilization.

Still. Lucy never quite escapes that other. The wild one. It prowls the edges of her vision, an animal just beyond the campfire's glow. That history speaks not in words but in roar and beat and blood. It made Lucy as the lake made gold. Made Sam's wildness, and Ba's limp, and made the yearning in Ma's voice when she speaks of the ocean. But to stare down that history makes Lucy dizzy, as if she peers from the wrong end of a spyglass to see Ba and Ma smaller than her, Ba and Ma with bas and mas of their own, across an ocean bigger than the vanished lake.

Lucy takes a breath and looks up. That circle of sky, blue as water. She gives in. She imagines the glint of fish, the sea grass taller than trees. If she is water, then let her be water. Let her slosh.

Ba walks the green and Lucy follows. Where bedrock cracks open, mud shows through, and ancient river pebbles, and the plants that draw from the lake's last dregs. They fill their panning trays with earth. Swirl and stare, looking for a gleam.

The sun sears; water leaves Lucy at an astonishing rate. Where did it go, all that lost water? Can a lake, without proper burial, become a ghost? Can a place remember, and hurt, and rage against what hurt it? She thinks it might. She thinks: **Not me. I didn't hurt you. Help me.**

She finds the fossil of a fish. She finds a big lump of quartz. She finds that hoping hurts worse than not hoping. Ba outpaces her—she wonders if Sam was able to keep up. In her hurry, Lucy trips and spills her pan, so that Ba sees her sprawled in failure.

She picks up the worthless quartz and throws it at a tree. It breaks into two halves, sinking to the mud.

Ba picks it up. Rubs it. Taps his chisel against it, knocking flakes free. "Lucy girl."

She chokes back a sob. But his hand is moving toward her with gentleness. In his palm, the cracked quartz shows its yellow center.

"How did you know?" Lucy whispers. She would have left it buried for another century.

"Why, Lucy girl, you feel where it's buried. You just feel it."

He passes the gold to her.

The nugget is heavy and sun-warm. The size of a small egg. She turns it. There's a hollow through its center. It slips over her middle finger.

"Take a corner," Ba says, squeezing his forefinger and thumb together to show how much. Lucy looks at him, disbelieving. "Try it, Lucy girl."

It has no taste. No juice. Her mouth floods anyways. She was parched and quenched, and now only quenched. Does it change her, that fleck she swallows? Does it glimmer just under her skin, settle between stomach and heart? Years later, she will probe herself in the dark, wondering if she can see the difference.

"You're a proper prospector now. That in there will call other riches to you. Ting wo."

Descending that evening, Ba hoists Lucy over the rock wall and pulls himself up after her. He points out the inland mountains to the East, the coast to the West. On clear days, he claims Lucy could see fog from the ocean. Ships' sails riding the air like wings.

"Your ma thinks there's nothing more beautiful than a ship. I prefer real birds. Look at them two goshawks."

Two forms wheel and dive, landing atop an oak.

"See that there?"

Lucy sees nothing. Sam's eyes are sharp from days in the sun; when Lucy looks up from books, the edges of the world are blurred. Another of her disappointments.

To her surprise, Ba brings his face to her level, puts his stubbled cheek against hers. This close, it's as if his smell is hers, too: tobacco and sun, sweat and dust. He turns their heads together and Lucy sees the nest with two small mouths, gaping.

"The moment those hatchlings are big enough, I mean to climb up and get chicks for the two of you. You can train them to hunt, with no need for gun or knife. Did you know?"

Ba's voice is washed with wonder. Today, Lucy can see what he sees: those two chicks grown bigger than their parents, wheeling free. Before Ba takes his face away, Lucy asks, "I did good today, right?"

"Sure you did." Both of them consider the nugget in Lucy's hand. It looks larger now, brushed clean of dirt. "That's three or four months' work in a day, I'll wager. Your ma'll be pleased. Now, you want to know what's the biggest help?" Ba pulls back and narrows his eyes. "Keep quiet about this place. Ting wo? What we do here . . . well, it ain't wrong. This land's unclaimed. But many a man might think it wasn't right, either. People are jealous of us, dong bu dong? Always have been. Because we're adventurers. What are we, Lucy girl?"

"Special," she says. Up here she even believes it.

Ma's in bed when they return. Five months on and her ankles have swollen, the baby a perpetual ache on her back. Usually Ba handles her as if she's made of gold herself. Today he dives to the mattress, making it bounce. Sam, feverish beside Ma, groans.

Ma pushes Ba off. She yanks her dress straight and sits. "The mine boss came around. He said we can't live on mine property if you aren't working. Lei si wo, that little man."

Ba and Ma whisper about the mine boss at night. But never this loud, and never in front of Lucy or Sam. Ma's eyes have a fierce look. Something like the goshawks.

"Did he say when?" Ba asks.

"I talked him down." Ma's mouth twists as if she's bitten something bad. "Begged, more like. He'll give us another month. Dan shi payment next time is double."

"What'd you say to him?"

"Bie guan—"

"What'd you promise him?"

"I smiled and talked sweet. Told him we'll pay extra." Ma gives an impatient flick of her head. "Men like him are easy to handle." Ba's hands clench behind his back. He starts to speak, but Ma talks over him as she does when Sam throws a tantrum. "That's not important. Gao su wo, what will we do? We haven't saved enough. And the baby's on his way. What's next?"

What's next? Ma has asked at the end of their time at each prospecting site, at each mine, when hope and coin run low. Ba blusters sometimes, other times goes sullen, other times stomps out to clear his head and return the next morning reeking of remorse and drink. He's never answered straight. Until now.

"We'll go," he says, slipping the nugget onto Ma's finger.

Ma's hand drops from the weight. She lifts her trembling fingers to her face.

"Our Lucy's a genius for gold," Ba says. "We'll be gone in a month if we work quick enough. And settled on our own land, bought free and clear. All five of us."

Ma weighs the nugget in her palm. Nestled there, it looks more like an egg than ever. Her lips move, counting.

"I've got my eye on a piece of land eight miles toward the ocean. Between two hills, forty acres, plenty of trails for riding, and the prettiest little pond—"

"We'll have horses?" Sam says, rousing.

"Sure. Sure. And—" Ba turns to Lucy. "Close enough that you could ride to school if you get up early on a fast horse. Though I don't figure why—" He stops himself. Says, simply, "If you want."

Lucy knows the effort it took him to say that. She reaches for his hand.

"And for your ma—"

Ma's head shoots up. She's finished calculating. "Gou le. This is enough."

"Now hold on there. I know you're excited, qin ai de, but we've got a few more weeks of work yet. I asked about the price—"

"Not that land." The secret smile is curving Ma's lips, stretching them wider than Lucy's ever seen. Ma's mouth parts. Behind, a glisten. "Somewhere much better. This is enough for five tickets on the ship."

Ba was always the storyteller. Ma delivered instructions, reprimands, quizzes, calls to dinner, lullabies, facts. She told no stories about herself. Now, at last, she gathers them around her on the mattress.

The story Ma carried inside her is bigger than a baby, bigger than the West, bigger than the whole of the world Lucy was born to. Inside Ma is a place of wide cobbled streets and low red walls, mists and rocky gardens. A place that grows bitter melons and peppers so hot they'd set fire to this dry grass. **Home** is the place. Ma's voice so accented with longing that Lucy can hardly understand her. **Home** sounds like a fairy tale that Ma reads from a secret fourth book, written on the backs of her shut eyelids. Ma speaks of fruit that bears in the shape of stars. Green rocks harder and rarer than gold. She speaks the unpronounceable name of the mountain where she was born.

Lucy's hands go clammy. The old feeling of being

lost. In Ba's stories she recognizes the land she grew up in. The hills in Ba's stories are these hills, but greener; these trails, but thick with creatures. Ma's place is unknowable. Even Ma's names slide or knot on Lucy's tongue.

"What about school?" Lucy asks.

"Mei guan xi." Ma laughs. "There'll be schools there. Bigger than this provincial little place."

Ma calls on Ba to tell too. About the fruit called dragon's eye, and the mist on the mountains, and the fish grilled at the harbor on a summer's day.

Instead, Ba says, "Qin ai de, I thought we agreed to stay here. A piece of land for our own."

Ma shakes her head till blood muddles her cheeks. "Gold can't buy everything. This will never be **our** land. Ni zhi dao. I want our boy to grow up among his people." She presses the nugget between her breasts, as if it's truly an egg she means to hatch with the heat of her conviction. "Zhe ge means we can leave as soon as he's born. We'll get there before he's off milk. Xiang xiang: his first taste will be the taste of home. You promised." The crackle in her voice rises. "Cong kai shi, you promised we'd go back to our people."

And Sam, voice thick with fever, says, "What people?"

"People like you, nu er," Ma says, brushing hair from Sam's sweaty face. "Going across will be like—like—a dream. Water's easier than traveling by wagon, bao bei. You'll be like princesses falling

asleep under an enchantment. Waking up somewhere better."

But Lucy read that story as nightmare. She asks
again about school. Sam asks about horses. Lucy
asks about lessons, and trains, and Sam about buffalo. Ma winces as if cut.

"Girls," Ma says. "You'll like it."

"If this place is so wonderful," Lucy says, "then
why did you leave? Why'd you come here alone?"

Ma's face, which has opened wide, closes. She
pulls her arms to her chest, so quick her elbow clips
Lucy's shoulder. "That's enough for tonight. Lei
si wo."

"Ow," Lucy says, more astonished than hurt. But
Ma doesn't apologize.

Lucy doesn't like how Ma licked her lips at the
memory of star fruit, which Lucy hasn't tasted. She
doesn't like how Ma, speaking of the tiled roof of
her childhood home, damns the roofs of Lucy's.
Well, sometimes the rain against tin or canvas can
make a music as pretty as the two-stringed fiddles
Ma talks about. Sometimes the dust that Ma hates
so much furs the hills a tender gold. Lucy demands
to know what makes Ma's streets prettier, Ma's rain
nicer, Ma's food tastier. She asks and asks, her voice
swelling, and gets no answers as Ma shrinks back
into the pillows with every question. As if Lucy's
words are a violence.

Then Ba is saying, **Da zui**, and he is lifting Lucy
away. She screams into his shoulder as he carries

her, kicking, up to the loft. By the time he's carried Sam up too, the sloshing Lucy felt on the plateau has come to a boil.

"I won't go," Lucy says to him. "I don't want to live with those other chinks."

Straightaway the taste of wrongness. Like the mud pies the boys shaped in the schoolyard, forcing Lucy to lick them. She deserves a slapping. Ba only looks at her sadly. The taste is hers to swallow.

"That's no word for you to learn, Lucy girl. Maybe your ma's right to take you from here. This is the right word."

He tells them.

Lucy cups it on her tongue. Sam does the same. It tastes foreign. It tastes right. It tastes the way Ma said the food of home tastes: sour and sweet, bitter and spicy, all at once.

But they're kids. Nine and eight. Uncareful with their toys, their knees, their elbows. They let the name for themselves drop down the cracks in their sleep, with a child's trust that there is always more the next day: more love, more words, more time, more places to go with the shapes of their parents in the wagon seat, the sway and creak of travel lulling them to sleep.

Water

Lucy wakes dry-mouthed to the sound of water. A patter on tin, echoing: the season's first rain has come. Her bladder throbs as she climbs down. The wet thickens to a suck and slap, as if the shack has flooded. The moon is thin and the end of the month nigh and the tin warps the light, so that shifting silver waves lap the walls. The house is an ocean. And the ship? She freezes on the bottom rung. The ship is a mattress and on it a sea creature, many-armed and terrible, with skin slick and wet. Her throat is too parched to scream. And then she sees: not one creature but two. Ma sits astride Ba, her belly crushing him. Her nightgown falls over them both, and her legs hook his, pressing him into the mattress. She's hurting him. His breaths come quick and shuddering. —**ets**, Ma says. She rises up, bears down. Her weight makes him groan. **Tickets.** Ba puts a hand to her chest to stop her. **Beauty is a weapon**, Ma said, and Lucy thinks she may begin to understand. Ma's power a night-time power. Sweat gathers on Lucy, in those places where skin rubs skin: the crook of her elbows, the space between her thighs. A wet heat in the room; the rainy season is coming. Ba's eyes roll back. And still Ma hurts him, till his head goes loose and a single word escapes him: **Yes.** Only then does Ma lift off. Lucy is aware of the sting of her own urine down her leg. Shamefaced she climbs upstairs. No need for the outhouse tonight.

Mud

Once, Ma guarded her trunk so fiercely. She rationed its contents and most of all she rationed its smell. Inside her trunk lives a musky perfume, bitter and sweet. A smell not of this land, diminished each time the lid lifted.

Now that same trunk gapes, dresses and medicines spilled free. No need to hoard when they mean to set out for the harbor next week, leaving the trunk behind. Ma, her belly big and the baby weeks away, says they won't need extra weight. Soon they'll be living where that smell is common.

"Hao mei," Ma says, handing Lucy a pair of delicate white shoes, beaded, long-coveted. "They suit you."

Lucy spins as Ma bids her, then slips the shoes off.

She refuses to admire the beadwork. Runs barefoot into the rain.

"Don't forget to thank him," Ma calls.

There was a time when Ma's praise quenched a thirst in Lucy. Now praise arrives like this season's rain: too much, too early. The mine is flooding. More men are out of work. With the swirl of brown water rise rumors, and tempers. Last week the mine boss visited unannounced to collect rent. He burst inside, gaze darting. Lucy was glad, then, for how Ma had hid the pouches. Ba stood by his pistol, but Ma was undisturbed. She smiled at the boss and stepped over the puddle he left. Only said they'd best get used to wet before sailing.

Storm encroaches on the order of Teacher Leigh's house too. His coyote brush is bedraggled, bent this way and that by wind. A puddle laps his porch. Nellie whickers uneasily, and Lucy stands stroking the mare's nose. Practicing goodbyes.

The mood in the parlor is prickly, the light low. A shattered lamp sits in one corner, and there's wood nailed over a broken windowpane. The other guests—the butcher and Miss Lila, whose return East was delayed by weather—sit discussing the latest mine accident. A flood swept away supports and collapsed three tunnels. Eight men are dead.

"There's no worse year for rainfall on record," the teacher says. "I've even had some miners approach me, asking for assistance." He shakes his head mournfully. "I had to turn them away, of course."

"Those poor miners," Miss Lila says, heaping sugar into her tea. "I hear there are more trapped belowground. They say those walking above can hear screams. Imagine living like that, at fortune's whim." She turns to Lucy. "Your poor family!"

"We're not miners," Lucy says, Ba's words leaping to her mouth.

"There's no shame in it, child." Miss Lila pats Lucy's arm. "What else would your father do?"

They watch her, their kindness oppressive as the weather. Lucy wants to tell them about standing on that plateau, the nugget a small sun in her hand. She bites her lip, still pondering what to say as the mine boss enters the house and greets the teacher. Then the boss sees Lucy.

"You," he says, striding over. "Aren't your folks packed yet? Your mother told me you were on your way out any day now."

"There must be some misunderstanding," Teacher Leigh says, putting a protective arm in front of Lucy. "Lucy is my star pupil. She's not going anywhere. I'm in contact with her mother."

Swallowing, Lucy says, "Sir, I need to tell you something. In private, please."

Ba swore them to secrecy, but Ma permitted Lucy

to tell the teacher about their leaving next week, if not about their gold. Out on the porch, Lucy explains the ship as the teacher's face pinches.

"I thought your mother would have more respect for your education. We're accomplishing great deeds here, Lucy."

"She says thank you." Best not to repeat what Ma said about better schools across the ocean.

"One week isn't near enough time to complete my research. You know how important this monograph is. Though perhaps, if your mother herself were to come, and lend her answers as well—"

Lucy shakes her head. Nothing can distract Ma from her vision of the land across the ocean. As the teacher rails against the rashness of this move, Lucy bites her lip. She agrees. But she can't explain it properly without mentioning the gold.

"You may go," the teacher says at last. "All the work we've done is useless now." His voice is bitter. "You understand I'll be removing you from the history—there's no value in a half-finished chapter. And, Lucy? There's no point in your coming to school this week, either. If you're going, then go."

All that week the shack eddies with preparation, as messy within as the world without. Clothes and medicines are strewn round, and Sam's toys, Ba's tools, blankets for the baby, cloth torn and resewn into diapers, the three worn storybooks Lucy fought to take though Ma said there would be new, and better, stories.

Ba comes stomping in with sacks of flour and potatoes. Supplies for their journey to the harbor, and then, after the baby is born there, supplies for the ship.

"Bu gou," Ma says. "Where's the salt pork?"

"We'll get the rest at the coast. Prices have gone up. Some of those inland roads are flooding. Jim's charging an arm and a leg."

"We can afford a little more," Ma says, putting both hands to her stomach. "What's a few coins to us? The baby—"

"People are starting to ask questions."

That stops her.

"I don't know how," Ba says, fingering his pistol. Too wet for hunting, yet he cleans the barrel nightly. Sometimes even twice a night, sitting by the door and pausing at every sound. "Someone today asked me where I was headed—"

"Xiao xin," Ma says, laying a hand on his forearm. She inclines her head toward Lucy and Sam. Ba quiets. Whispers move through the shack late that night, guttering along with the rain on the tin.

No trace of them is meant to remain. Their footprints in the dirt floor will be swept, their clotheslines taken down, their garden left to drown or rot. Another set of miners will be given this house, or maybe another flock of hens. It was never their house, or their land, to begin with. The wet season will wash away every imprint, shoe print, hair, fingernail, mark, chewed pencil, dented pan, drawn tiger, voice, story.

A fresh horror surges through Lucy as she listens to rain soften the land, swell the creeks, chill the air. A recurring image of the family tossed out like Ma's pail of muddy brown dishwater. What proof will there be that they existed at all in these hills?

Surely she can leave something behind. Something that lasts.

And so Lucy sneaks out alone on the morning of their last day in town. A long day ahead: Ma and Lucy are to pack the rest of the house while Ba and Sam rake the gold field one final time. They'll set out for the harbor that evening, under cover of dark. Safer this way, Ba said strangely, though the roads are treacherous and waterlogged.

Lucy heads to the place that's secret from Ba and Sam—and secret, today, from Ma too. Something tight in her fist as she hurries over the swollen creek, up the teacher's path. A bright fleck in this grayness. The smallest bit of gold.

It's not stealing. She wants only to show it to her teacher. Anyhow he doesn't care for riches—he chose to give up his family's wealth. He's a scholar who prizes evidence. She'll gift him this bit of gold, along with new information for his monograph, a piece of the Western territory recorded in no other book. He can preserve the dead lake—and them—in ink.

At the top of the path, she stops. A field of poppies has sprung up overnight.

Golden, some call these poppies, but Lucy has seen the real thing and these flowers are richer by far. Sunset caught in the petals. She plucks one, another. She'll bring a bouquet and watch the teacher praise her discernment. As she moves through the field, a figure slams out of Teacher Leigh's house, its stiff-legged stride projecting fury—not the fair teacher but a dark-haired man, hat jammed low, maybe the mine boss or Jim, or even one of the miners come begging. Lucy hurries away, downslope, aiming for a patch of coyote brush that'll keep her discreet. Her foot catches a rock hidden by the mass of flowers.

Slow, slow, and then fast—she's falling. Downhill, tumbling, body pulled into a ball for poor protection. Mud slams into her, breathing suddenly a violence. She's stopped. Her mouth, her chin, blaze pain. She rolls onto her back, vision wavering. Is the figure approaching? To help her up? The last thing she sees for certain is the petals waving, innocent, beside her cheek.

———

She comes to some time later. Taste of copper. Her chin and tongue gone numb. She turns her head left, right. Sees her own hand, outstretched.

Empty.

Lucy scrabbles through the poppies, heedless of how many roots and stems she upturns. The field is returned to mud by the time she sits back on her heels, panting. Blood drips off her hurt chin. Torn petals wink, but there is no gold. There is no gold. Surely she didn't drop it. She clenched her fist so tight as she fell that there are marks from her fingernails on her palm. She didn't drop it.

Unless it was taken.

Halting, dizzy, she drags herself to Teacher Leigh's porch.

"I'm sorry," she mumbles when he opens the door. "I brought it—I did—for your research—I, I don't know where it is. I know where it came from—the plateau. It has a history. We found it. The water. You can write about it—please. We're leaving, and—and you can write about it."

"What do you mean?" the teacher says. She's half-fallen on him and he pulls back, horrified. Her blood on his clean white shirt. She gives a gurgling laugh. Sprays fresh pink. She was right. His clothes would never last on a trail.

"The gold," she slurs. She hopes he understands through the mud and blood in her mouth. "I, I mean me. Us. You can write about it . . ."

Exhausted of words she holds her empty hand up

to him, again and again, as if he could see on it the precious imprint.

She wakes again with the smell of Ma around her. The light's changed. Outside the small window, the rain has stopped.

She's on Ma's mattress, face pressed into the pillow where Ma's face usually rests. A stain spreads from Lucy's mouth. Pink, now browning. Jackal hour, colors going blurred and dirty. Hard to tell what's real and not. How did she get here? She recalls the teacher's hands lifting her, gray hair, the warm column of Nellie's neck—the teacher must have brought her home.

She hears his voice. Precise, cutting clean through the dim shack.

". . . worried," he says. "About all of you."

"I appreciate the offer," Ma says. Her arms are crossed, hands tucked into armpits. Hidden, her bare palms with their calluses and scars. She never leaves the house ungloved. "Staying with you would be an imposition. We're safe enough on our own."

"But what's next?" Odd to hear Ma's question in the teacher's mouth. "You and Lucy deserve more than this." He glances around—a quick glance, sufficient to take in the cramped room. "Lucy has told me how she was raised from nothing. I can read between the lines. Your influence is obvious.

In all my years I've rarely met an individual of your moral fiber, especially among the fairer sex. Lucy may have told you about my monograph. I've made it my life's work to study and record the extraordinary. Your daughter is impressive, but I suspect I may be focusing on the wrong primary subject."

No, Lucy wants to say. Her mouth is swollen shut with pain.

"I'm nothing special," Ma says. "I do it for my children. That's why we need to leave before this next one comes."

"Surely the roads aren't safe. Stay a little longer. Assist me in my work. It requires no more than answering some questions. I can pay you a fee. Three more months, I should think. And if you ever feel unsafe—well, my doors are open to you. I've a spare room. Not for all of you, perhaps, that might not be quite comfortable, but you and maybe Lucy. And when the baby comes, I'm good friends with the doctor in town."

The teacher steps closer, his eyes so earnest. Ma refuses his gaze. She looks around the shack as he did. Lingering not on the hidden gold but the leaking window, the blackened tin, the half-washed dishes. Lucy knows where Ma will look—the same spots Lucy looks to each time she returns from the neat schoolhouse, the sunny parlor. All their dark and dirty places. All their shame.

"You're still very beautiful," the teacher says. Ma's eyes quit their roaming to fix on him. He clears his throat. He's a man who insists on precision. "You **are** very beautiful."

Lucy's bloody mouth goes dry. She is aware of her thirst—not quite. **A** thirst, then, gathered in the damp house.

Is there color on Ma's cheeks? Hard to tell in the dusk. "Thank you. I've a good deal of packing left, and I'm sure you're a busy man. I appreciate your bringing Lucy here, but we're not fit to entertain today. You see the state of things—"

Ma's hands swing over their half-packed belongings, then freeze. The exposed blue flecks on her palms are like an animal's strange spotting. She snatches her hands back and laughs a thin, nervous laugh Lucy has never heard.

"You must be wanting to get back," Ma says, as the teacher says, "May I touch?"

Ma moves to open the door as the teacher reaches forward. A confusion of limbs. Over the teacher's shoulder, Ma locks eyes at last with Lucy. Her mouth parts in surprise—whether at the teacher's actions, or at the sight of Lucy awake, Lucy can't tell. Hour of the jackal and shadows are confused, edges running together. It's Ma's hand that the teacher touches, Lucy is almost certain, Ma's hand on Ma's belly—but for a moment it could be a different softness.

When the teacher has left, Ma comes with the washbasin and dabs at Lucy's chin. Crusted blood loosens from the cut, mixes in with Lucy's tears. Ma bends to wring the rag, and Lucy catches sight of herself in the mirror. Her unlovely face is even more misshapen.

Ma straightens and reappears as reflection. Her white neck, her sleek hair, a rebuke.

Lucy says, "The teacher likes you."

"Guai," Ma says, wiping a tear from Lucy's cheek. "It'll stop hurting soon."

"He's right. You **are** beautiful." She looks nothing like Ma, or Sam. Them with their shine.

"You heard us?"

Lucy nods.

"He's a kind man. He was frantic about you. Zhi yao make us feel welcome."

But he sent Lucy away last week. "You mean he wants to make **you** feel welcome."

"And who do you think is responsible for taking care of you? Ni de Ba?" A string of spittle flies from Ma's mouth. "Fei hua. He'd have you girls starving alongside him while he digs your graves in the hills."

"He found gold," Lucy says, trying not to let her dismay show.

"Mei cuo. Can he keep it, though? Lucy girl, I care for your father, but luck isn't something we have. Not in this land. I've known that for a long time."

Ma's eyes dart once more round the house, quick

as the birds that sing out at sunset, so that you never see them—just the quivering grass where they alit. To the stovepipe with its pouch, the pallet with its pouch, the cupboard with its two pouches so small and thin they fit between the hinges. Last of all Ma looks down at herself. She squeezes something between her breasts: a pouch previously unknown to Lucy. It must hide a big piece, to judge by its size.

"We may not need your teacher's help. But I intend to hold on to that option. Ni zhi dao, Lucy girl, what real riches are?" Lucy points to the pouch, which Ma tucks back in her dress. "Bu dui, nu er. I could spend this gold tomorrow and it would belong to someone else. No—I want us rich in choices. That's something no one can take." Ma sighs, long and low, and later Lucy will recall that sigh every time she hears the wind moan through a too-small opening. "Mei guan xi, you'll understand when you're older."

Ma's said this before. "I don't think so," Lucy snaps. "I think I'd understand if I was prettier."

Ma smiles. Lips, white teeth. And then the smile changes. Ma's lips curl back to show gums, and two canines, one chipped, and the tip of a tongue between. Ma's shoulders hunch, her eyes going slit—Ma still smiling, but transformed.

Then Ma lets her face relax. Once more it's the face that Lucy knows.

"Ting wo, Lucy girl. What I meant to say that day was that beauty's the kind of weapon that doesn't last so long as others. If you choose to use it—mei cuo, there's no shame. But you're lucky. You have this too." She raps Lucy's head. "Xing le, xing le. Don't cry."

Lucy can't help it. Like the rising creek, what's in her has been weeks, months, in the gathering. The tears come harder. In the mirror she sees that the blood is gone from her chin, in its place this fresh wet. A drop falls to Ma's hand. Lucy doesn't look like Ma. Doesn't have Ma's beauty. And yet, in the warping mirror, there is resemblance. An answering sorrow on Ma's reflection though she sheds no tears of her own. Ma brings Lucy's salt to her mouth, and sucks it clean.

Wind

Ma instructs Lucy to say she fell against the stove while packing. It hardly matters—when Ba and Sam return that evening, they're too preoccupied with trotting the new mule out from its hiding place behind the toolshed, with loading the new wagon.

As Sam carries Ma's rocking chair over the threshold, wind blasts through the door. Nearly bowls Sam over with its fury. A wind from inland, with a sound like the slap of water.

They head out anyhow, bent against the gusts. Between the miners' shacks, down the main road, people stare frankly. When they reach the road out of town, they find it flooded. Muddy water stretches wide as a river. An ocean.

For weeks they've heard rumors of entire valleys flooded inland, the once-dry land birthing a
hundred hundred lakes. Now wind has blown the
brown water here, cutting off the trails in and out
of town. They're trapped.

"It'll go down tomorrow," Ba reassures them after
they've returned to a shack even more dismal than
usual. A candle stub flickers over the bare table—
they've left the tablecloth, the plates, most of their
belongings packed in the wagon. "Next week," he
says when tomorrow comes. "This weather isn't but
a run of bad luck. It'll pass."

Ma's eyes go blank as a caught rabbit's. She averts
her face from the mention of luck.

Jackals follow the floods. Soon they circle the
town, howls braided into the wind. People say
the creatures are drawn to the mines, parts of
which are burning again even as other parts flood.
A charred breeze. Ba alone doesn't blame the jackals. He rails against the clogged rivers and cut-down
trees, the small game overhunted to extinction, the
mines that destroyed hillsides till the soil runs like
ink. **Bi zui**, Ma snaps. Tells him to quit stirring up
trouble.

Lucy can't sleep. When she does she dreams of that
lost fleck of gold. It appears each night in a new

location: in the yawning mouth of a jackal, pinned to the mine boss's hat, above a drawing of her own face reading WANTED, studded in Ma's neck, winking from a bleeding gunshot hole where Ba's eye once was. She wakes, whimpering, and spends the rest of the night watching the door.

No flesh-and-blood people arrive. The threat of beasts keeps the town indoors. The mine closes indefinitely, all its tunnels flooded now. Ba and Ma argue about what to do. Ba wants to set out and swim their wagon across the road—but Ma points out that wind has toppled several oaks and is liable to blow them off course. Ma says, **The baby, the baby, the baby**. He's due soon now. Any day.

They settle down to wait with everyone else. The valley a brown bowl, starting to froth.

Signs are posted.

WANTED
Jackal hides
$1 bounty

Packs of men roam the hills at night, former miners desperate for any pay. Sam petitions to join the hunt, pestering till Ma cries, shaking Sam's arm, **Why can't you be a good girl?**

For all that the men go hunting, the number of jackals only grows. Howling thrums their ears. Clouds so dark they look like pieces of sky cut out, wind whipping them along, the air like a drum about to burst—though rain is still withheld. Children are warned from outdoor chores.

The air in the shack goes soupy. Sam, cooped up, is prone to sudden fits of motion, thudding heels against the walls, chasing nothing round and round for hours. Ma quits scolding—there's no stopping Sam, and anyhow the baby is kicking too. Ma spends her days laid flat, talking to the baby. She coaxes him to stay sleeping. To stay inside.

Ba returns with news of food prices gone skyhigh, people sickening on dirty creek water. Miners form grim lines outside the hotel, whose owner posted about the bounty. No one's been paid for their hides yet.

And then a child is taken.

Ba and Ma whisper. Won't share details. They

say it isn't fit for children, say they don't want to give Lucy and Sam bad dreams. Lucy doesn't explain that her dreams are bad enough anyhow.

That night a man howls, and the jackals join in. So mournful that a body might think they were the ones who've lost.

Blood

Lucy knows they can survive the jackals because they have before.

There was a night between one town and another, between one mine and the next, when the family came to a line of dung laid across the road like a missive. So fresh it steamed. The ancient mule stumbled. The crack of its leg split the night.

From the mule's throat came a mewling. Three years they'd had this gentle beast and never heard her cry. Her rolling eye found Lucy.

They went on. Their one remaining mule panted, made quicker by fear and a lightened load. Their extra provisions were tossed out in the grass. The noise of jackals grew closer, then paused. The silence more terrible than howls. The family hurried on.

———

The jackals who finally enter the shack on the first day of storm, on the day the clouds open and the bones of a child stir up from the swollen creek, aren't the jackals Lucy expected.

They look mostly like men. One has a brown beard, the other red as the hair of the girl who was taken. Half-familiar—Lucy must have seen them a dozen times in the low light of those early mornings at the mine. Only the hides on their shoulders are of the beast, giving off a wet, rank odor.

Like men, they carry guns.

They crash through the door before Ba can grab his pistol. The pounding rain hid their approach till too late. The brown one orders Ba into a chair. The red jackal herds Lucy and Sam to the stove. Ma, on the mattress under a heap of extra blankets, goes unseen.

"We'd like a bite to eat," the brown one says.

Strange that a wild thing can speak so polite. He sounds like a guest in Teacher Leigh's parlor. Ba cusses as the red one bats pans and plates off the stove. He plunges hands into the cold stewpot and crunches a mess of cartilage, spitting a long splinter of bone to the floor. Gobbets drop from his lips onto Lucy and Sam.

Out of Sam's small chest, a warning rumble.

Lucy holds tight to Sam's arm. Keeps Sam from rashness.

"It looks like you've more than enough to share," the brown one says, poking through their supplies. The potatoes, the flour, the lard, all damning. "Doesn't seem right when most of us are starving. Doesn't seem right that you sat snug and rich while the rest of us were out of work. Why, we had to send our families out looking for gold to buy food. You'd know something about that, I think."

Ba's cussing subsides.

"My little girl went out there," the red one screams, his voice like breaking glass. He flings his arm toward the half-open door. The long-awaited storm is gray froth, spitting in angry globs like schoolyard kids. Like the redheaded girl once spat at Lucy before she tired of bullying. The red jackal's gaze bores through Lucy, as if he reads her mind.

"A real shame," the brown one says, pressing his rifle into Ba's bad leg. "This could all have been avoided if we'd known where that fleck of gold we found came from. My brother's girl wouldn't have had to wander willy-nilly."

Ba's mouth stays shut. The stubbornness that Sam inherited—he'll never tell.

"I'd say a trade seems fair," the brown jackal says. A confused silence, and then Lucy understands as the red one locks mad eyes on Sam. Sam who shines.

Lucy's voice is mute, but her legs move. It was her fault. She took what was precious from the house. She takes a step—half a step, stiff with dread. It's enough. The red one seizes her instead.

Ba's face is torn between fury and fear as the red jackal drags Lucy to the door. She wonders which will win, whether Ba will speak. She never knows. Because Sam lunges for the red jackal, stabbing with the spat-out bone shard.

The jackal howls, releasing Lucy. Grabbing for Sam.

Sam is small and wily, brown and strong from days on the gold field. As the red jackal slashes with his knife, Sam ducks and dances. The brown jackal waves his gun, can't shoot for fear of hitting his partner. Sam catches Lucy's eye across the room. Impossibly, Sam grins.

And then the red one takes hold—not of Sam's arm, but Sam's long, grown-back hair.

Ba yells. Lucy screams. But it's the third voice that the jackals attend to. A voice like a sweep of fire, hot in a house grown cold.

"Stop," Ma says, standing by stages. Blankets shed from her. Her huge belly like a piece of the hills come alive. And then she speaks to Ba, only Ba. "Ba jin gei ta men. Ni fa feng le ma? Yao zhao gu hai zi. Ru guo wo men jia ren an quan, na jiu zu gou le."

It's a language the rest can't decipher. Words so quick they might as well be the senseless patter and shriek of rain. For the first time Lucy understands that the language Ma shared with them, in bits and pieces, was only a child's game.

Ba's face slackens, Ba's shoulders puddling as the red jackal strides to Ma and slaps her so hard her lip splits open.

"Speak proper," he hisses.

Calmly, Ma puts a hand to her chest. She draws a crumpled handkerchief from the pouch inside her dress and holds it to her bleeding lip. When she drops the soiled cloth, her lips are sealed, her right cheek squirrel-swollen from the blow.

Ma says no more. Not when the men ask where the money is hid, not when they contemplate cutting out Ba's tongue, not when they slash the bundles and tear the clothes, shatter the medicine bottles in the trunk. That sweet, bitter perfume mingles with the jackals' stink. Ma says nothing even when they find the first hidden pouch, and tear the shack and the wagon apart in search of the rest. Ma doesn't look at them, doesn't look at Ba or Sam or Lucy. Ma looks out the open door.

At the last, the jackals herd the family together and search their bodies for gold. Stripped and patted, Ma is once again the sun, the moon, her naked belly casting a horrible light around which the day turns. The jackals take the pouch from between

206 C Pam Zhang

her breasts, turn it inside out—empty. Ba closes his
eyes, as if the sight could blind him.

"There's more in these hills," Ba says that night as
they sit in their own wreckage. No mattress left
whole, no blankets, no pillows, no medicines, no
plates, no food, no gold. The new mule and the
new wagon were taken. Near on six months in this
town and they're poorer than when they arrived.
"We'll find more. All we need's time, qin ai de.
Might be another six months. Maybe a year. He'll
still be young."

Still Ma is silent.

They sleep all four together that night, two torn
mattresses dragged to make one. Lucy and Sam
cling together in the center, Ma and Ba at either
side. Ma faces out from Lucy, her back a long oc-
clusion. That night there are no whispers.

The next day, as the storm grows fiercer, Lucy fits
together what parts she can, sews what she can,
makes meals of what she can—the pork rinds re-
trieved from a dark corner, the flour painstakingly
scooped though it bakes up gritty.

Sam helps. Unasked, Sam cleans and stacks, dusts
and sorts. The sound of Sam's body a sturdy speech.

Otherwise, the shack is silent. Ma lies prone, un-speaking though her swollen cheek has deflated. Ba paces and paces.

And then again, the pounding.

This time Ba opens the door with pistol in hand. There's only a piece of paper tied to the knob. Dark shapes hurrying away in the rain.

Lucy reads the words aloud. Her voice shrinks with every sentence.

It's a proclamation of new law. Approved already in town, and soon to be proposed to the rest of the territory. Ba rages pointlessly through the reading, tearing again what's already been torn.

The jackals' power isn't in the gold they stole, or in their guns. Their power is in this paper that takes away the family's future before it can even be dug up. The hills may run flush with gold but none of it will be theirs. Hold it in their hands, swallow it down, and still it won't be theirs. The law strips all rights to gold and land from any man not born in this territory.

How did they survive the attack on the wagon all those years back?

They didn't. Leastways not all of them. They left the mule and didn't shoot or bury her. Ma made no mention, then, of silver or water.

"Bie kan," Ma instructed as they ran. But Lucy

looked back. A dozen pinpoint eyes stung through the dark as the pack closed in. The living mule a distraction. A sacrifice. All that Lucy could bear— she'd seen dead things in plenty. What made her shudder was how firm Ma held her head. Where the rest of the family looked back at the faithful mule, only Ma heeded her own command. She bit her lip, and blood pinked her teeth. Likely it pained her. But Ma showed no pain, and never looked back.

Water

He is born that third night of storm.

That little creek, descended from ancient lake, remembers its history and rises. At the first wet touch, the sleepers in the valley dream the same dream: Fish so thick they block the light. Sea grass taller than trees.

At the edge of the valley, on higher ground, Ma thrashes on a ruined mattress. For six months Ba has praised the baby for its headstrong nature. For what made it a boy. Now he curses it. He takes Ma's hand. She stares at him with eyes so shiny with pain, it looks like hate.

Ba leaves to fetch the doctor. After a look at Ma's pulsing belly, Sam leaves too. Saying something about gathering tools from the shed.

"Lucy girl," Ma growls when they're alone. Her eyes roll back, teeth a rictus. These are her first words since the jackals left, though her cheek healed so quick it's as if it were never injured. "Talk to me. Distract me. Anything." Her stomach ripples. "Shuo!"

"It was me," Lucy says before she can lose her nerve. "I took gold out of the house—just to show the teacher, for his research—I was going to bring it back—it was just a speck—and, and, I fell and I lost it."

As she has countless times before, Ma holds Lucy's secret in silence.

"I mean," Lucy whispers into the terrible quiet, "I think those men who broke in took it. I saw someone. When I fell. It was all my fault, Ma."

Ma starts to laugh. Laughter that's closer kin to rage than joy, laughter like a consuming. Lucy thinks again of fire. But what's being burned?

"Bie guan," Ma says. She catches her breath, throat spasming as it did when she first took sick with the baby. "It doesn't matter, Lucy girl. What does it matter who it was? They all hate us. Bu neng blame yourself for our bad luck. That's what passes for justice in this gou shi piece of land."

Ma points to the wrecked door, and past—to the hills with faceless men lurking in every house, from every lit window. Ma's hate is big enough for all of it.

"I'm sorry," Lucy says again.

"Hen jiu yi qian, I did worse without intending. When I was young, I thought I knew what was right for everyone. You remind me of myself. Belly-ful of anger."

But that's Sam. Lucy's not angry. She's good.

"Gao su wo, Lucy girl, my smart one, why didn't your ba listen to me when the men came? I've been trying to figure. Zhi yao give those men a few pouches, they would've left us alone. I know their kind. Lazy. You heard me tell him, dui bu dui?"

Ma wrings Lucy's hand. Lucy can only say, mis-erably, "You spoke too quick, Ma. I didn't under-stand you."

Ma blinks. "You didn't—understand me? Wo de nu er. My own daughter and she can't under-stand me."

Another wave of pain curls Ma's body like a fist. When she loosens, her voice is less certain.

"Mei wen ti," Ma pants. "Not too late to learn. Yi ding get you into a proper school. Back home."

"Or—Ma, what if we went East instead? Teacher Leigh says there's better schools there. It's civilized. And I've already learned some of the books . . ."

Lightning flashes. Once, twice in quick succes-sion. When it passes, Lucy blinks dazzled eyes. The room is left dimmer, as Ma's face is dimmer. Gone the anger. What remains is the sadness that stalks Ma's beauty. The ache of her.

"It's got its claws in you," Ma says. Her fingers dig into Lucy's hand. "This land's claimed you and your sister both, shi ma?"

That's what Ba says. The jackals and their law say different. How's Lucy to know when she's never lived any other place? She can't answer.

"You're hurting me, Ma." Ma's hand is smaller than Ba's. Delicate when gloved. But its grip is stronger. "You're hurting me!"

"Ni ji de, what you said when we went to visit your teacher?" Ma lets go of Lucy. She squeezes the pouch inside her dress. Though it must be empty now, though the jackals found nothing inside, Ma seems to draw from it some comfort. "You wanted to go alone. You said, you didn't need—" Ma's voice breaks. She brushes Lucy's cheek. A touch so familiar that Lucy can, and will for years, call it up by closing her eyes. Ma holds Lucy a long moment, then lets go. They hear thudding from the toolshed.

"Go help Sam," Ma says. "Li kai wo, nu er."

Those are the last words she speaks to Lucy.

By the time Ba returns without the doctor, Ma has lost all words. Lucy and Sam kneel by the mattress, dampened with sweat and strange water, but Ma doesn't see them.

Ba roars. He drags Lucy and Sam out to the shed

and tells them to stay put. They fall asleep entangled for warmth. The wind shrieks through their dreams, and Ma—

They wake to an impossible sun.

Lucy stands. The roof of the shed is missing. Below, the valley has birthed a lake. Gone the creek, gone the other miners' shacks. On the South side only roofs poke up. People huddle atop. Their shack, cut off from the rest, pushed to the edge of the valley on undesirable land, is the only place untouched.

And then Ba is striding over, reaching down for them. His chest: a red smell. Mud, and blood.

"The baby was born dead. I buried him. And your ma—"

Lucy opens her mouth. This time Ba doesn't call her **da zui**. Doesn't tell her to hush. He claps a hand to her lips. Both of them go still as the lake water. His calluses scrape her teeth.

"Not another word. None of your damn questions. Ting wo?"

Ba leads them to the edge of the lake. His hands are hard as he pushes them into the water. There is panic on Sam's face, a foamed thrashing. Lucy floats easily; she is hollow. She helps Sam. Ba isn't watching either of them. He himself stays under the water a long, long time, teaching some kind of lesson. About survival, most like. Or fear. Or waiting. He won't ever say.

The Ba that surfaces at last, wet sluicing off him, is a different man. Lucy won't quite grasp it for a few weeks more, when the fists come out.

What they lose in that three-day storm:
The roof of the shed.
The dresses.
The baby.
The medicines.
The three storybooks.
Ba's laugh.
Ba's hope.
The prospecting tools.
The gold in the house.
The gold in the hills.
All talk of gold.
Ma.
And though they don't know it for years, they lose Sam's girlhood. Swept out, scoured clean. Disappeared the way Ma's body disappeared. The Sam who swims out of the lake doesn't wring that long hair dry, doesn't brush it a hundred careful strokes. Sam cuts it. **Mourning**, Sam says, though Sam's eyes glitter. The washed-clean sun fierce off Sam's shorn head. One brother lost, another gained: that's the night that Sam is born.

PART THREE

XX42/XX62

Wind Wind Wind
Wind Wind

Lucy girl.
Sun's sinking down these hills and here you are sinking too. I know the sort of bone-deep tired you and Sam must feel these days as you run. I know what it is to flee with your past panting behind, claws extending in the dark. I'm not a cruel man, whatever you think.

Lucy girl, there were plenty of times I wanted to give you a soft, easy life. But if I did, the world would gnaw you down like these buffalo bones.

Night's the only time I got now, and this wind the only sort of voice. I have your ear till sunup. It's not too late, yet.

Lucy girl, there's only one story worth telling now.

———

Every soul in this territory knows the year a man pulled gold from the river and the whole country drew up into itself, took a breath that blew wagons out across the West. All your life you heard people say the story starts in '48. And all your life when people told you this story, did you ever question why?

They told it to shut you out. They told it to claim it, to make it theirs and not yours. They told it to say we came too late. Thieves, they called us. They said this land could never be our land.

I know you like things written down and read out by schoolteachers. I know you like what's neat and pretty. But it's high time you heard the truth story, and if it hurts—well, at least you'll be tougher for it.

So listen. Tell yourself it's the wind in your ear if you must, but I reckon these nights belong to me till you bury that body of mine.

That history in your books is plain lie. Gold wasn't found by a man, but by a boy the same age as you. Twelve. And it wasn't found in '48 but back in '42. I know because it was me that found it.

———

Well, it was properly Billy that touched gold first. Billy was my best friend, a grown man of forty or so, though it was hard to say and he sure wasn't saying. People today'd call him mutt: his ma was Indian and his ba one of those small, dark vaqueros come from across the Southern desert. They left Billy with two names—one most people couldn't pronounce, and one most could—plus skin the color of fresh-peeled manzanita bark. His arm shone in the river as he tickled a fish.

Something flashed against Billy's dark red, brighter than scales. I shouted.

What Billy handed me was a pretty yellow rock. Too pliable to be of use, and me too old for trinkets. I let it fall back through my fingers. It caught the sun as it tumbled, a shard of light that lodged in my eye. For minutes after, I saw spots across the hills.

I swear that gold winked at me, like it knew what I didn't.

This was the year of '42, though the camp where I grew up didn't call it '42. Just as we didn't call our hills the West. West of where? It was just our land, and we were just people. We ranged between ocean to one side, mountains to the other.

The camp I grew up in was full of Billys. By which I mean old men, quiet, many with more than one name. They didn't like to talk of the past. Best that I could piece together, they were the remnants of three or maybe four tribes now jumbled up, old men and cripples too stubborn or tired to leave when the rest did for better hunting grounds. There'd been a priest when many of them were boys, who'd given them new names—and a pox that killed half their people. The priest had also given them a common language, which they taught me. That camp was all outcasts and stragglers, what your Ma considered the wrong kind of company. And sure there wasn't a clean handkerchief among them, but there was kindness, or at least a kind of weariness that looked nearly the same. Too many had seen destruction.

Still, the hills were good for plenty when I grew up. Poppies in the wet season, fat rabbits in the dry. Manzanita berries and wild sorrel, miner's lettuce, and the paw prints of wolves in streambeds. Never a shortage of green. As to how I got there—I knew as little about myself as about the old men. They'd found me on a foraging trip down the coast: a newborn, hours old, crying alone, my ma and ba dead beside me. Saltwater stains on their clothes.

I asked Billy, once, how he knew it was my ma and ba on account of their being dead, and the dead not speaking. He touched my eyes. Then touched the edges of his own and pulled them out till they narrowed.

Here's the thing, Lucy girl: like you I never grew up among people who looked like me. But that's no excuse, and don't you use it. If I had a ba, then he was the sun that warmed me most days and beat me sweaty-sore on others; if I had a ma, then she was the grass that held me when I lay down and slept. I grew up in these hills and they raised me: the streams and rock shelves, the valleys where scrub oaks bunched so thick they seemed one mass but allowed me, skinny and swift, to slip between trunks and pierce the hollow center where branches knit a green ceiling. If I had a people, then I saw those people in the reflecting pools, where water was so clear it showed a world the exact double of this one: another set of hills and sky, another boy looking back with my same eyes. I grew up knowing I belonged to this land, Lucy girl. You and Sam do too, never mind how you look. Don't you let any man with a history book tell you different.

But I'm getting carried away. No need linger on the pretty stories, the kind I've always fed you because you were a child.

Well, things are different now. You thought me hard? You see the truth of it: the world's a good deal harder. It ain't fair, but you and Sam won't get years for growing. Just maybe these nights. Just maybe what I can tell you.

Years went by and I hardly remembered that yellow rock. Until a day in '49 when we woke up to a boom, then dust clouds, then the river by our camp running brown, running black. We woke up to wagons of men, and trees coming down while buildings went up. The old men in my camp turned their backs till it was too late. Till there was nothing to fish or hunt or eat. They slipped away rather than fight. Some went South, some over the mountains, some to cool grass wallows to wait for death. Too much destruction, you see.

Billy alone stayed with me. And just like in '42, we waded looking for gold.

Too late, though. The easy gold was picked clean. What remained required whole teams of men, and carts of dynamite. We got jobs washing dishes, sweeping the saloon. Helped that Billy had taught me writing.

Seemed I woke up in '49 and all my dreams were of gold: the wink of it slipping through my fingers seven years back. I panned when I could. Found a few flecks amounting to nothing.

I saw how hard the gold men worked their miners. Men lost legs to dynamite, got crushed by rock. Men shot each other, stole and stabbed, starved in lean weeks. Dozens of 'em turned around each month and headed back East. But hundreds replaced them. And a few struck it rich, became gold men themselves.

There came a night in '50 when the gold man who owned the biggest mines—the fattest and richest of the lot—called across the saloon.

"You. Come here. No, not you. You, boy—with the funny eyes."

Billy wouldn't come along. I kept going.

"Are those eyes real, boy? Or you some kind of half-wit?"

Up close I saw that the gold man, for all his fatness, wasn't so much older than me. I told him I was no half-wit, kept my fists behind my back. I'd learned that year about talking with fists instead of words when people looked at me funny. It saved me repeating myself. But the gold man wasn't alone. A hired man in black stood behind him with a gun.

"And you write? You read? Don't lie to me."

I told him Billy had taught me. Called Billy over, but the gold man didn't even look at him. The gold man said he had a job for me. Young and soft that I was, I didn't think to ask why he chose me. Let that be a lesson to you, Lucy girl. Always ask why. Always know what part of you they want.

The gold man explained that there would come a time when the hills were scraped empty. When men would bring families to settle. They'd need supplies. Houses. Food. The gold man planned to lay railroad track through the West, joining plains to ocean. For that he needed cheap labor. And he'd gotten a whole shipful of it.

Sure, I told him, I could go to the coast and train his workers. Sure, I could talk to them on his behalf.

Truth is, I hardly understood half of what the gold man said. I'd never seen a train, didn't know the ocean route he spoke of, or where the workers came from. But I understood his power. I didn't ask questions. He had a gold watch the size of my palm that he flicked as he talked. He was fat enough that I could cling like a tick to his wealth. Through him I could claim what had slipped from my fingers as a boy, what was always mine—didn't me and Billy touch gold first?

I asked for Billy to come along too. I told that gold man about Billy's loyalty and his circumspection, his strong arms and his tracker's knowledge. I had the gold man near convinced, I could tell—but it was Billy himself who ruined his chance. Billy said he'd rather stay behind.

I never properly got an answer why. Billy wasn't big on talking. All he said was he was staying. That it was better for me to go on alone. When I asked why, he touched my eyes. I never saw him after that night.

Lucy girl, I told you. I learned a long time back: family comes first. No one else matters.

Two of the gold man's hired men rode along with me to meet the ship. That was my first horse, Lucy girl, and I pretended I knew what riding was. Bled for days till I hardened.

Wagonloads of railroad track set out behind us, going slower. They'd meet us at the coast after some weeks. The gold man said I was to teach the two hundred while we waited. I didn't ask what I was meant to teach.

The hired men wore black and spoke mostly to each other. They camped a distance away at night and never invited me to join, not that I cared—I liked my solitary bed. I hardly recall those two weeks of travel to the coast; all I saw was the wealth in my future. My eyes were so dazzled, it took me a moment to see what came off that ship:

Two hundred people who looked like me.

Eyes the shape of mine, noses like mine, hair like mine. Men and women and some hardly more'n kids, dragging their trunks and bags, wearing funny robes. I started to count them.

And then I saw your ma.

You know your ma. So I won't say how she looked. What I'll tell you is the feeling that welled up in me as she passed, a feeling akin to striking groundwater when you've wandered hot all day and thirst is a knife at your throat. That promise of quenching to come. Same feeling I expect you had as a girl after playing all day in the grass, arriving home to a plate of dinner kept warm. That feeling of knowing someone will call your name—that's the feeling I got when your ma met my eyes. I knew I was almost home.

I kept my head screwed tight and kept counting. Got to a hundred and ninety-three people before they quit coming. The two hired men looked at me; I looked at a sailor. The sailor went in and pushed six more onto the dock. Said one died on the way over.

The last six were ancient, bent like trees. God knows what work the gold man expected to get out of them. One fell on the gangplank. And guess who ran to help the old woman up?

That's right. Your ma.

Your ma looked right at me. Under her gaze, I got a sailor to load the six into a wagon along with the trunks and satchels the two hundred had brought. I nudged the sailor along with a coin from the wallet the gold man had given me for buying supplies.

They tried to load your ma onto the wagon too, but she walked with the others. When the two hired men mounted up, I got down and walked too.

Lucy girl, you always thought it was your old ba pushing the family, wanting more. But the push came first from your ma. Because that day of the ship, she saw me wrong. She mistook me for the gold man who ordered other men around. She mistook me for someone who'd paid for a ship and jobs. She mistook me for something bigger than myself. By the time I understood what your ma believed, it was too late to correct her.

That first night, I learned we didn't speak the same language.

The gold man had found a barn for the two hundred to stay in. I stood first watch outside and heard them jabbering in confusion. Some of them pounded on the door, angry, and yelled at me through the cracks. Maybe they hadn't expected locks, or straw beds.

The two hired men were already camped way down on the beach, but they came over on account of the commotion.

"What's the matter with them?" the taller of the hired men asked. "Tell 'em to settle down."

I was younger than him, and had two good legs back then. I could've knocked him down. But he had a gun, and I didn't.

"Do your job," he said. "The one you're paid for."

That cleared the red from my eyes. I swallowed my questions. I told not a soul that I didn't understand what the two hundred spoke. I tucked that secret down deep, deep, in the same soft spot where I was once a boy so stupid I let gold slip between my fingers.

I went inside the barn and rang a cowbell.

You know what makes a good teacher, Lucy girl? Not nice words or pretty clothes. A good teacher is a firm teacher. Ting wo. The first lesson I taught was that they couldn't use the words they'd brought over. Not here. The first man to speak, I clapped a hand across his jaw. Held it shut. You need force to accomplish anything, Lucy girl.

Mouth, I said, pointing. **Hand**, I said, pointing. **No**, I said. **Quiet**, I said. And we began.

That first night: Teacher. Speak. Barn. Straw. Sleep. Corn. No. No. No.

The first day on the road: Horse. Road. Faster. Tree. Sun. Day. Water. Walk. Stand. Faster. Faster.

The second night: Corn. Dirt. Down. Hand. Foot. Night. Moon. Bed.

The third day: Stand. Rest. March. Sorry. Work. Work. No.

The third night, when we got to the place we were meant to build a railroad: Man. Woman. Baby. Born.

I was off my watch on that third night when your ma came and found me alone. How she did it I never figured; when I asked later, she just laughed and said a woman needed her secrets. I don't know how she slipped past the hired man who stood guard. I guess she has—had—her ways. Her smiling ways. I didn't think on it that night, though I've thought about it many times since.

We'd settled to wait for the wagons on a pretty piece of land not far from the coast. We smelled salt when the wind blew, and in the distance were cypress trees bent at unlikely angles. The two hundred slept, locked in for the night, in an old stone building up on the ridge. Rusted bell tower above and a stream out front. Half a mile beyond that were grassy hills where the hired men set up their own camp. And out in the other direction was a little lake, pretty if you ignored the bugs and marshy grass. That lake I claimed for my own.

Your ma came up to me as I stood looking into the lake. I was hoping for a glint in the water.

"Teach?" your ma said, startling me so that I nearly fell in. She didn't say **Sorry** like I'd taught them. She smiled, wickedly.

Your ma was eager to learn. Not like those among the two hundred who looked at me sullenly, who saw me as the enemy. Those sorts hated me more'n they hated the hired men, who whipped their ankles with green branches. I expect they took me for a traitor, saw my eyes and my face like theirs and hated me the worse for it. Those sorts whispered about me. Of course, I had no idea what they said. So I had to punish them for any words. All words. Otherwise my discipline would've fallen apart completely.

Which meant the two hundred watched me as carefully as the hired men watched me, and I worked to make my face a mask. No one could learn how much I didn't know.

"You," your ma said. She pointed to me. Then she cupped her hands over her stomach. Over and over she did this. I shook my head. She made a kind of frustrated growl and grabbed my hand.

I'd thought her lovely and mild. She was kind to the old people. Laughed easily. Had a high, clear voice like some little songbird. But the hand that grabbed mine could do more than hammer railroad ties. I remembered what the hired men said to each other when they traded watch: **Don't turn your back. They're savages.**

Your ma's hand was strong, but her waist, when she made me touch it, was softer than anything since I lost my rabbit-skin hat from Billy. She made me trace around her waist, then drew me close till the sides of our bodies touched. She traced that touching line. Cupped her hands again over her stomach. Pointed at me.

I still didn't understand.

Your ma put a hand on my chest and a hand on her own breast. She trailed down my chest, my belly. Stopped at my pants. I'm sure she could see my blush.

"Word?" she said, pushing at her breast. "Word?" she said again, two fingers lightly tracing my pants.

I taught her **man.** I taught her **woman.** As she

cupped her stomach, I taught her **baby**. When again she pointed to me, I understood her original question.

"I was born back there," I told her. There was still blood in my cheeks. I was half-dizzy with it as I pointed toward my hills. Your ma's face lit up.

It wasn't till after she'd left me alone that I cooled down, and realized I'd pointed in the wrong direction. Toward the ocean. She thought we came from the same place. And I didn't have the words to explain otherwise.

I know you think me a liar, Lucy girl. But don't you ever think me stupid. Don't think I missed how you looked at me those nights I came back drunk. The sheer arrogance of you, looking at me like you knew better. Looking at me like you were disappointed.

That look so like your ma's.

Your ma was like you in a whole lot of ways. She believed that dressing right and talking right could set the world right around her. She studied me and the hired men. Asked us the words for **shirt** and **dress**, asked what women wore in this land. Always looking to better herself, your ma.

You see, your ma had come seeking fortune. All the two hundred had. Back home your ma's own ba was dead, her ma's hands ruined gutting fish. She was promised to marry an old fisherman, till she boarded the ship.

Golden mountain, she told me the same night she told about the mother, the fisherman, the man at the harbor who promised this place over the ocean would make them rich. We were lying out that night in the grass beside my lake. I laughed fit to die when I heard: some poor teacher had blundered the word for **hills**.

Lucy girl, I regretted that laughter all my life.

I couldn't tell your ma why I laughed, of course. Couldn't tell her why it was so funny, the idea of the two hundred getting rich. She still thought I could make it happen for them. That it was my ship, my man at the harbor making promises, my railroad we'd build when the wagons arrived.

So I said something stupid. I said I laughed on account of how she pronounced **gold**: thick as syrup, half-swallowed. Your ma flushed and left me alone that night.

Later on I caught her practicing the word. **Gold gold gold gold gold.**

Your ma spoke prettier than me by the end. Looked prettier too. People thought me hard, and her soft. We made a good team. Had a balance, same as you and Sam. But believe me, Lucy girl, when I say that your ma was even more fixed on making a fortune.

———

Your ma got the two hundred to trust me. She had a quality that made people listen, never mind that she was young, and a woman. She was—well, Sam might call it bossy. Like you, Lucy girl. She was smart so she figured she knew best. Most of the time she did, and convinced everyone else of it.

I started taking meals with the two hundred at your ma's insistence, listening to them chatter in their own language in the corners. I pretended not to hear. So long as they didn't speak it to my face, I let it pass.

Plenty of time for chatter, anyhow. The wagons of railroad supplies were late in coming. Couldn't get through on account of the horizon being lit up by the worst fires these hills have seen.

Turns out that when you dig up streams and clog rivers, when you cut trees and their roots no longer hold the soil back, that soil goes dry. Crumbles like left-out bread. Like the whole land's gone stale. The plants die, the grass bakes—and when the dry season comes, a spark can set it all aflame.

The hired men swore and paced. They polished their guns like they meant to rub through the metal. But there was nothing to be done. At least we were by the coast, with damp in the air. The fire didn't seem like to reach us. We waited.

Animals started to show up one day. They darted over the stream, past the walls of the stone building, heading to the coast. Rabbits skinny with terror, mice and squirrels and possums. Flocks of birds blocking out the shrunken red sun. Once a young buck leapt clear over me with antlers ablaze. There was quiet for a while, then the slower creatures came: snakes, lizards. For a day and a night no one could step in the grass for fear of being bitten. Even the hired men abandoned their own camp and slept in the building.

And last, but unseen, the tiger.

I woke up one day to paw prints around the marshy edge of the lake. Too big for wolf. Hard to tell with the sky so red, but I swore I saw a flash of orange in the reeds.

Your ma came up to me yawning. Her hair was mussed, but she was never lovelier than in the morning, smelling of sleep and the people we were at night. I rarely saw her that way. Made idle by the fire, she'd started to fuss with her hair. She'd braid it and pin it and curl it, asking endless questions about how ladies here wore it. Same with her clothes. Your ma took thread from her trunk and stitched and hemmed that robe of hers into different shapes. She got other women to join her too. I didn't have the heart to say those dresses would have no place once the wagons arrived, when they'd be sweating all day over railroad ties.

Your ma wanted to make me friendly with the

rest of the two hundred. She poked fun at my quiet, teased me for being so solitary. Some people are born solitary, no less happy for it—I was, and I suspect you were, too, Lucy girl, but your ma didn't understand. She pestered about my family till I told her they were dead. She made me talk dresses to the women, dragged me to join the circles of men gambling with straws. She bossed me.

Truth is, the faces of the two hundred didn't warm me. Their language and gossip were strange, as was the easy way they called each other fat and picked loose threads from each other's sleeves. What did it matter that we looked alike? I came from the hills, and the two hundred spooked at the sound of jackals. They were soft people who'd believed a pack of lies, and I didn't need them. I sat down with the men just to please your ma, and, given how often I won, I suspect the men let me play just to please her too. I suspected your ma'd had a sweetheart among the two hundred before they reached shore. There was a certain man who argued with her constantly, and another who always tried to give her extra food. She didn't say and I didn't ask; all that mattered was that she'd brought her trunk to my lake and slept there most nights.

All that mattered, Lucy girl, was that there was a time when your ma had eyes only for me.

I forgot plenty of things in my life: Billy's face, the color of poppies, how to sleep gentle so that I didn't wake up with fists clenched and an ache already started in my shoulders, the word for the smell of earth after rain, the taste of clean water. And there's other things I'm forgetting in death: how it felt to swing my fist and feel the knuckles crack, how mud squelched between my toes, how it was to have fingers and toes and hunger. I expect there'll come a day when I forget everything of myself, after you and Sam bury me—not just my body but what little of me is in your blood and speech. But. Even if there comes a day when I'm no more than a wind roaming these hills, then I expect that wind will still remember one thing and whisper it to every blade of grass: the way I felt when your ma looked only at me. So bright a lesser man might fear it.

In any case your ma stood that morning looking at the paw print. I put an arm around her, figuring she was scared. **Tiger**, I taught her, and started to describe the beast.

She threw my arm off and laughed. "Don't you know?" she said, mocking. Then she bent and put her hand in the tiger's print. Her eyes dared me. You might not believe this, Lucy girl, but she kissed that mud.

"Luck," she said. "Home." With her finger she drew a word in the mud. As she did she sang a tune I'd learn was the tiger song. **Lao hu, lao hu.**

Your ma shone with pure mischief. Fearless. She hadn't broken my rule about speaking her language, but she'd stalked the edge of that rule as the tiger stalked the lake. She'd written it, sung it. She laughed at me as I tried to figure out what to do about her.

Fire behind her, the sky hot with the world's burning, her muddy mouth and snarled hair, the print of a beast come so close it could have taken us in the night—all this and she laughed. Wilder than all this put together.

Something moved in my chest. As a child I'd awoken in the night to a shake in my bones. Billy said it was a tiger's roar: from far off, they can't be heard, only felt. My chest roared that morning beside the lake. What had stalked me since the day the ship arrived, what I'd feared some nights as I held your ma close, that day pounced. Sank claws into my heart. After weeks of rules, I spoke my first words of your ma's language.

I'd listened to the two hundred. Their cusses came easiest. But I'd heard lovers too.

Qin ai de, I said to your ma. It was a guess. I didn't know its proper meaning till I saw it in her eyes.

Softness took me over as rot took over the oaks one year when I was a boy. What looked a harmless fuzz weakened the trees from within. Years later, they split and died.

I'd grown up solitary, needing only shade, a

stream, and from time to time a chat with one of the old men. My growing had made me strong enough to survive.

But your ma—she stroked my brow, made me lay my head in her lap as she cleaned out my earwax. She studied my eyes, a lighter brown than the rest of the two hundred, and declared the color contained liquid. Concluded I was water, and not wood as she'd once thought.

I let myself speak more of your ma's words. Pet names, cusses. Giving them as little gifts to her. But only I was allowed to speak them—I still frowned on her using her own language. And I was still stern with the two hundred. They weren't permitted to speak freely, or to go outside unaccompanied, save for an hour at dusk and dawn.

The rules were to protect them too. I saw the hired men getting more restless as the fires kept us trapped. Their hands itching at their guns.

And then one evening I came back from my lake, hand in hand with your ma. We'd found a grove of oaks much like my boyhood grove, the branches making a green room in the center. Your ma danced around me singing the last word of the tiger song: **Lai. Lai. Lai.** Calling as she'd called me to come beneath the trees.

There was a hush around the stone building as we arrived.

The hired men dragged a body around the corner. It was a man I'd gambled with, always clever at avoiding the short straw. Well, his luck had run out. It was that man, but his chest was a bloody hole.

"He was trying to run," the taller of the hired men said as he shucked his bloody gloves.

But the bullet had entered from the front.

Your ma flew at the hired men, her right hand flashing out. "He don't run! You run!"

The hired man was quick, and your ma's hand whistled over his ear. She might as well have hit him. I saw the look on his face.

So I grabbed your ma. Harder than I would've otherwise, on account of the hired men watching.

Thing is, your ma spoke true: the hired men often wandered from their posts, sometimes with a woman from the two hundred trailing behind. Too often truth ain't in what's right, Lucy girl— sometimes it's in who speaks it. Or writes it. The hired men had guns and I let them say what they said.

"Tell them," your ma said to me. "Your men. Tell them."

The taller one told me to control her, and went down to the stream to wash.

Your ma cried against me as I led her back to our lake. Her tears were hot enough to melt me, and after months of tucking it deep, I started to tell her the truth.

I told her they weren't my men. I told her I owned no ship, no railroad. I told her the railroad jobs would be hard and hateful and wouldn't make them rich. As a boy I'd stripped a baby bird of its pinfeathers till it was a raw pink thing, till I threw up in the grass. Speaking truth made me feel just as sick.

As I spoke, your ma went stiff. She pushed me away. That strength in her arms—she could snap me like I was nothing.

"Liar," she said. I'd taught that word in the first week. "Liar."

I'd made myself detestable in your ma's eyes. Took her two days to speak to me again, two days while she prepared to bury the dead man. Even then she only acknowledged me because I gave her two pieces of silver for his eyes and paid the hired men for the right to wash the body in the stream.

And then I—

No.

No, no. Alright now, Lucy girl. I said I'd tell a true story, and there might be no time left. So here's the truth. Sometimes you pay in coin. Sometimes you pay in dignity.

Alone outside the building, the two hundred locked up inside and only the dead man to watch, I got on my knees and put my lips to the hired men's boots. Just as your ma'd kissed the tiger's print. I begged them to let her do her burying. I begged them not to punish her for trying to hit them. Can you imagine, Lucy girl? Me?

Later on, I kissed your ma's feet too. Then her ankles, her thighs. I begged her to forgive me. She kept her spine straight and looked down her nose.

"Hao de," she said.

Those words changed us. She'd broken my rule against speaking her language, and I couldn't stop her. From then on she'd use more and more of her words, and I'd muddle through, piecing their meaning together, mimicking them. I'd always had an aptitude for birdcalls; this imitation was similar enough, and if I had an accent then it could be excused by my isolation. But from then on I would live in fear.

"Don't lie again," your ma warned me.

That was when I realized I could never tell her the rest of the truth. Elsewise she'd leave me. I tucked my story, my true story, deep, deep down in that last layer of me, where I was still a boy running free in these hills. I resolved never to tell her where I came from. I resolved that it wouldn't be lying if I didn't speak of it.

Can you blame me, Lucy girl?

It's a funny thing, how easy it was to keep this lie. No one suspected me, because no man seeing my face believed I was born here. Haven't you seen that for yourself, Lucy girl? Those jackals with their paper law. They didn't care about the truth. They assumed their own truth.

That night your ma made me answer question after question. About the railroads and the gold man. About how hard he worked his miners, and how much he paid, and where they lived, how big their houses, how well they ate. How many of them died. At the end of it, she made a plan.

Do you recall, Lucy girl, that night you found your nugget, and brought it to your ma, and pestered her to remember?

There was a reason I put you to bed that night. Rememory can hurt. I've got my leg to show it, and your ma—well, you can't see the mark on her, but she has one all the same. She got it in the fire. We all have stories we can't tell. And this story about the fire is the one your ma buried deepest.

The thing is, the fire was her idea.

From the beginning your ma and I shared a sense of fairness. I taught **liar** the first week when a girl among the two hundred tried to sneak double rations. It was your ma who caught that girl by the hair and marched her to me.

Your ma nodded as I laid out punishment: two meals less for that girl the next day. Your ma deemed it fair.

You remember, Lucy girl, the way your ma listened when you and Sam fought? How she weighed every word before judging? How she believed in honest work? Well, the night she planned the fire, she weighed the cost of the two hundred's passage against the dead man buried by the stream. She weighed promises told at a distant harbor against the truth of the gold man's dealings. In the end she judged it fair that the two hundred should escape their railroad contract. It was built on deception, after all.

She talked so well. She was so smart. And maybe I let her boss me, on account of how I feared letting her down.

Her plan was simple. To escape, we had to get rid of the hired men.

To get rid of the hired men, we would set a fire.

I don't scare easy, Lucy girl. And I don't pretend to be blameless. I've hit many a man when my blood boils. But the way your ma talked was different. Chilly. A life for a life, she said, adding the old woman who'd died on the ship to the shot man. She has—had—a passion for sums, your ma. Tallied up grievances as if they were coins, and paid them back without a second thought. That's why she was the one to handle our gold, those months before the storm. That's why, the night of the storm—

But I'm getting ahead of myself.

Justice was the word your ma had me teach her that night she planned the fire.

Soft as your ma'd made me by then, I couldn't sleep after we decided on our plan. The hired men's lives were a weight on me no matter how I lay. I left your ma sleeping—her face placid as the lake—and went for a walk. I nodded to the shorter hired man on watch as I passed—the younger one, who hadn't shot the dead man.

He lifted his pipe in greeting, then kept it lifted. Offered it to me.

Who knows why these people do what they do, Lucy girl? I've turned that moment in my head time and again and still I can't figure. Was he acting on some wager from his partner? Was he tired of tobacco and looking to get rid of it? Was he like the dumb animal who comes to the edge of the snare and stiffens, suddenly wary, instinct pricking its hairs? Was he the jackal who, cornered, lowers its ears slyly and cries like a human baby? Was he lonely? Was he foolish? Was he kind? What moves in the heads of these people each time they look at us and size us up, what makes them decide on one day to call us **chink** and the next day to let us pass, and some days to offer charity? I don't rightly know, Lucy girl. Never figured it out.

On that night I took the pipe, not wanting to rouse the hired man's suspicions. He seemed restless. Eager for talk. Said something about the moon being pretty, which it was, and the wildfires dying down, which they were. He said something about a kid sister back at home that made my gut clench so that I was almost ready to wake your ma, take my promise back, tell her the whole truth about me and accept whatever judgment she passed, till the hired man said:

"Where do you come from? Same as them?"

I was half-mad that night, sloshing with pent truths. For some reason I told him. "I'm from this very territory. Not so far from here."

And that man laughed.

I put his pipe in my mouth. I sucked down his tobacco. Fires still burned on the horizon beyond the glow of the bowl. Animals were fleeing, and they might never return. I sucked and glowed and thought about saying what was funny was how he and thousands of others came only last year to ravage this land and now they claimed it, when it was my land and Billy's land and the Indians' land and the tigers' and the buffalos' land burning—and then your ma's word lit in my mind. **Justice.** I bid the man good night.

Only your ma and myself acted out her plan. The two hundred were stuck in the building, and your ma said we didn't need to tell them anyhow. Said it'd be hard on their conscience. Said we should let them sleep easy. Said—with an impatient toss of her head—that anyhow she knew this would be better for them. Said they'd thank her.

She asked me the word for it. Not **lie**, or **liar**. The kinder word. I taught her **secret**.

We slipped out holding hands. Nodded to the man standing watch. We went out, to the hills that huddled around the hired men's camp. There we filled our arms and wove dry plants into a track, which we laid down for the fire to follow. We surrounded the hired men's camp with scrub, with grass knotted tight enough to burn long, with thistle heads crackling menace. The high grass hid our intent as we built a circle, a fence, a prison of combustible stuff that would raise flames higher than walls. All it would take was a spark.

And as we did this deadly work? We lay on our bellies. We whispered softly. From a distance, if the hired men bothered to look, they'd see only the grasses swaying above us, as they do to mark the passage of lovers.

When it came time for my watch, I took my place by the building. The two hired men returned to their camp. They started dinner. Hidden from them, at the start of a long track of tinder, your ma struck a piece of flint.

This story's hard to tell, Lucy girl. Even for me. Got no flesh and rightly I shouldn't hurt, but rememory hurts me.

We meant to trade two lives for two. The fire had its own idea. That fire reared up like it wasn't fire but something living: an enormous beast lofted into the sky, orange flames striped black with smoke. A thing born of the hills, born of the rage that the land should feel. Certainly not a tame thing. You ever corner an animal, Lucy girl? Even a mouse will turn and bite at the last, when it believes itself dying. Amidst the crackle and the smoke—Lucy girl, I swear those hills birthed a tiger.

I saw the fire follow its track downhill. I saw the black forms of the hired men run. Not fast enough. The flames found the dry circle we'd laid, and swallowed the hired men's camp.

I whooped then. Saw your ma racing from her hiding spot, heading for our lake.

The fire, finished with the camp, went toward the stream as planned. We meant for it to die in the water. A quiet death.

But a fickle wind blew up, stronger than either of us had figured. It stoked the flames higher. I saw the beast raise one long, flaming limb—and step over the stream.

The fire split in two. One part roared forward, toward me and the building that held the two hundred. The other part lunged to the side, licking the grasses, pursuing your ma.

Like your ma I believe in fairness. But more'n than, I believe in family. Ting wo, Lucy girl. Your family comes first. You stick by them. You don't betray your family.

I'm not a cruel man, Lucy girl. There were three horses tied up by the building and I left two. I unlocked the door and screamed at the two hundred to run. I gave them as much a chance as I could give them, and then I rode after your ma.

It turned out that building wasn't stone through and through. Whoever built it built lazy, and inside those stones hid a center of straw and dung. A secret heart that dried out over many years in the sun. That caught the fire and fed it.

Half a mile away, holding your ma waist-deep in our lake, I saw the building go up in flame.

It blazed so big and hungry I felt the blast of heat from that distance. It caught any stray people who'd started to run. Your ma was unconscious from breathing smoke; I'd dragged her onto the back of the horse and crashed right into the water. She didn't see it, or breathe the awful smoke of cooking flesh. But I did. I watched, knowing she'd want me to witness the two hundred as they died.

I never did take to meat again after that, though your ma liked it plenty.

A question that's followed me for years, Lucy girl, is this: can you love a person and hate them all at once? I think so. I think so. When your ma first woke in the ashfall, she smiled at me. No—grinned. The wicked grin of a girl who'd pulled off her prank. She was bold as anything. So certain we'd done right. So certain she knew best.

Then she coughed, and when she sat up—she saw what stretched behind. Our lake of fire, reflecting the sky. The spooked and lathered horse I'd saved. The flames still flicking along the ridge where the building was charred black rubble.

Your ma cried as an animal cries, rocking back and forth in the shallows. She tipped her head back and howled. Night came and still she scratched me if I approached, and bared her teeth. The cracking, hissing sounds from her smoke-torn throat—they weren't words.

You've heard me tell stories of transformation,

Lucy girl. Men into wolves. Women into seals and swans. Well, your ma transformed that night, though her face and body looked the same.

Twice she ran to the far edge of the lake and looked out at the ruins of the two hundred. Her whole body quivered, pointed toward them. Away from me. I could see in her the wildness. I could see her desire to run. I left the horse where it was. Let her leave if she wanted.

And then, in the smeared gray dawn, I felt her burrow into my side. Her fingers sharp enough to rip my belly, my guts. I wouldn't have stopped her. All she tore was my shirt, my pants. Her howls didn't stop so much as turn into moans, grunts. At last she curled against me and asked me, over and over, in a scratchy, smoke-ruined voice, not to leave her alone.

The weeks that passed while we waited for the fire to die, for your ma's throat to heal—they went this way: Sometimes I'd catch your ma staring at me with hate. Other times, love. I was the only person left to her. I suppose I had to carry both. She raged and beat my chest, but lay quiet to let me rub poultices on her throat.

Her throat never did heal proper. Just like your nose, Lucy girl. That voice of your ma's, that scratch and rustle of it—that was something made.

———

I've told you before that I met a tiger, and came away with this bad leg. You never believed me. I saw the judgment in your eyes. Sometimes that made me furious—my own daughter practically calling me a liar—and other times I was pleased. Didn't I tell you, Lucy girl? That you should always ask why a person is telling you their story?

The truth, now: here's how I met the tiger.

This was some weeks on and us two still the only two in a blackened world. No animal or man had set foot over the burnt hills—and no wagons of railroad supplies. If the gold man had heard of the fire, likely he thought us perished with the rest.

When the ground cooled enough, your ma wanted to look.

First we went to the hired men's camp. Your ma kicked through, ignoring their charred bones and the remains of their guns. We panned the ashes for their gold and their silver. Lumpen things that were once coins. She spat on the campsite as we left.

And then we took what we'd found to the remains of the building on the ridge.

"Word," your ma said as she used her hand to cover a piece of bone.

I taught her **bury**, and she taught me how. Silver. Running water. Something to remind of home. She'd brought cloth from her trunk—a small miracle that its contents smelled of perfume and not smoke. Your ma bundled bone into scraps of cloth. Laid the silver on top.

"Better?" she asked me.

I said I reckoned the two hundred were in a better place. In a way, they were. I didn't know what kind of life they could have had in this land.

Your ma shook her head. For the first time since I'd known her, she spoke with doubt. "Better if not us?"

I soothed her. I told her, over and over, it wasn't her fault.

Her voice healed some, and some of her confidence came back, so that she would become a mother who could say right from wrong. But I tell you, Lucy girl, that day in the ashes she lost her convictions. I saw the guilt and the wondering eat at her worse than flames.

Which is why I waited for her to fall asleep before I returned to the building alone.

Night in those burnt hills was eerie. Darker than any night before or since. Nothing to reflect what little moon showed through the smoke: an unchanging dark. I stole into the burnt building. I found those bundles of bone. And I took back the silver.

We needed it more than the dead did, Lucy girl.

As I walked back I got the sense that something watched me. I walked quicker. Halted. It halted too. Seemed footsteps were matching mine. Soon I was running, the earth thudding under a weight greater than my own. I heard a roar behind me, louder than fire or wind. A sharpness reached from the dark and sliced my knee. I stumbled onward, bleeding, so scared I never once looked back.

This is my story, Lucy girl. My truth. And I'm telling you, the tiger that marked me and caused my limp—I didn't see it. But I felt the truth of it in my bones. Your ma cleaned my wound and dressed it the next morning. I didn't want to saddle her with more guilt—she was shaky those days—so I said I'd cut myself walking to the latrine in the dark. Just bad luck.

But was it? The cut, though shallow, went through the tendon, severed it so neatly that I never walked true again. The skin healed, but something essential had been nicked from me. Did chance make that clean cut? Or the claws of a canny predator, a beast that still guarded these hills after everything else was gone and dead? Was it punishment for the secret in my pocket, clanking silver? I never saw the tiger's face, but does that make my story any less true?

Not much more to tell, Lucy girl. Morning's coming.

I promised your ma we'd build a fortune all our own. I promised her there was still gold in these hills so long as we looked. Just over the horizon, I promised her. The next place will be better. And I promised her, on those nights she cried till she went stony, that if it didn't work out I'd take her back. To that place beyond the ocean.

She didn't talk near as much as she had before, on account of her throat paining her. Some nights as we traveled through the prospecting sites, I felt her rise from our bed. She stood beside the horse, looking out, pointed away, that wildness in her.

But she didn't run. And she didn't run. And her throat healed a bit, and soon you swelled in her belly. She started sleeping through the night. She smiled once in a while. When you were born, Lucy girl, you were like an anchor dropping on the ship your ma used to tell about: holding us down, holding us together. Holding us to this land. For that, I was always grateful.

Your ma after the fire was never quite the same girl who'd come off the ship bossing two hundred and kissing tigers' prints. She grew wary—you saw, Lucy girl, how prospecting spooked her. How she was fearful of luck.

The new Ma had love and hate in her both. She sang you songs and sewed you dresses and rubbed my bad leg and teased. And she fought me over the gold, over the raising of you and Sam, over my dislike of rich men and my preference for Indian camps where I gambled and traded—over the right way to be, the right people to be. Once she'd mistaken me for a man with power, and ever after she was careful to track who had it, who to speak to, who to avoid. If I was a gambler, then she was a clerk. That hating part of her never stopped measuring what was fair. Never stopped counting up my sins, my rare successes.

But she stayed with me. I figure it was on account of the two hundred, in the end. They'd made her doubt herself, and I was cowardly enough to use it. I'm not proud to say that sometimes I reminded your ma of what had happened to them, out of spite.

And then, the storm.

Sure, when we were robbed of our gold that night, your ma saw my worth drop lower than ever. Sure, we lost our supplies. But I figure it was the baby that decided her.

We'd wanted him so much. When you were born, when Sam was, you knit us—I figure we counted on the baby to do the same. And when he was born dead, that tiny blue body, when I cut the cord on him—something else was cut too. Your ma looked at him the way she'd looked at those bundles of bone in the ash. That same guilt. I saw her tallying the decisions we'd made over the years—the meat we didn't have for so long, the jostling of the wagon, the coal dust down her lungs—and I saw her see the baby as judgment passed on our living.

Years ago in that burnt building, she meant to say those people would've been better off without us. Maybe she figured that you, and Sam, and that dead baby, would be better off without her.

She didn't die, Lucy girl. I went out to bury your brother and came back to an empty house. Your ma was always strong. As to where she went, I never wanted to know. If questions rose up in me, why, I drank them down. I drowned them as the storm had drowned most other things.

When you get to be older, Lucy girl, you'll learn that sometimes, knowing is worse than not knowing. I didn't want to know about your ma. Not what she did, or with whom, or how she felt looking into some other man's face. I didn't want to know the precise spot on a map that could hurt me.

It seems that to tell you the whole story, I got to tell as well the story I wish was true.

Here's the truth: until the night your ma took off, I believed that under my hardness there still hid a softer man. I figured that one day when we were rich and comfortable, when your ma didn't have to stand on her feet to work, let alone think of running—then I'd take the shining nuggets from the shelves of our own house on a piece of land so big we never saw another body. I'd put those nuggets in your hands, in Sam's hands, in the boy's hands. Soft hands all. And I'd tell a story. About how, as a boy, me and Billy found the first gold in these hills.

There, Lucy girl. Now you've heard what you always wanted to know. I told Sam years back. Why didn't I tell you? Well, maybe it was on account of shame. Maybe fear that you'd run after your ma. I know you loved her best. I saw how you looked at me by the end, and it was what I'd seen in your ma: love and hate both.

It was hard to bear, Lucy girl. Because truth is, I loved you just as well as Sam, though it was Sam I spoke to on account of Sam being tough enough to hear me out. Maybe I even loved you better, though that's a shameful thing to say. Shameful to love just because you needed the loving more, soft that you were. I remember the morning you were born. Your eyes opened and they were my eyes. Light brown, nearly gold. Not like your ma's or Sam's. Too much of my water in you.

Maybe I treated you hard on account of you growing to look more and more like her.

It's likely you'll hate me after this telling. Come morning, if you remember, I wouldn't be surprised to see you tumble my bones into a ditch and leave me for the jackals.

Lucy girl.

Bao bei.

Nu er.

I looked for a fortune and thought it slipped between my fingers, but it occurs to me I did make something of this land after all—I made you and Sam. You turned out alright, didn't you? I taught you to be strong. I taught you to be hard. I taught you to survive. To look at you now, taking care of Sam, trying to bury my body proper—I don't regret that teaching. I got no need to apologize. I only wish I'd stayed and taught you more. You'll have to make do with bits, as you have all your life. You're a smart girl. Just remember: your family comes first. Ting wo.

PART FOUR

XX67

Mud

Summer comes, bringing rumors of a tiger.

The air is close and sweat-sticky. Cicadas, crickets, sighs, a dark ratcheting. A time for lingering after lamps are lit, for windows swung wide— a languorous heat in ordinary times, a loosening.

But this year the tiger presses its claw against the vein of the town, and all Sweetwater shivers. A few chickens went missing three days back, and a side of beef. A guard dog was found with its throat slashed. Yesterday a woman fainted while hanging laundry and woke gibbering about a creature behind her sheets. A print left in the mud. Fear is this summer's excitement, as hoops were last summer's, and syrup over crushed ice the summer before's.

Anna, of course, wants a taste.

"Don't you think," Anna says, tipping her head back as Lucy untangles her curls, "that a baby tiger would make a lovely pet? I could train it to come when called. Maybe I should ask for one."

Lucy raps Anna's forehead with the comb. "I think you should quit squirming. Turn around."

"Or maybe a wolf pup. Or a little jackal. Those I know Papa can find."

Lucy remembers jackals, and what those teeth can do to a girl. But she only smiles at Anna, her face kept clear and sweet.

Anna talks of the tiger as Lucy buttons the thirty pearl buttons down the back of Anna's linen dress. Anna talks as she does the same for Lucy: same buttons, same dress, same boots excepting that Lucy's have three extra inches of heel to make her match Anna's height. Lucy's hair takes longest—her curls must be set and heated. Anna goes quiet at last, tongue poking out in concentration.

But as they leave for the station, Anna strokes the orange throat of a flower in her garden. "I've decided to call it a tiger lily," she says, her green eyes even wider in pleasure. Last week the baker renamed his two-color loaves **tiger bread**, the dressmaker a striped fabric. "Isn't it clever?"

The flower on its stalk nods along with Lucy.

The streets stand eerily empty as they pass through Anna's side of town, those mansions themselves sprawling wide and lazy as sunning cats.

People are sparse, moving in nervous knots when they do appear. A group of three or more, it's said, and the tiger won't dare approach.

A rumble jolts the street, and shoulders tense, faces draining. It's only a carriage with its wheel stuck. Movement returns as a gust of nervous laughter.

Anna presses close to Lucy. "Maybe . . . maybe it isn't safe to go to the station today."

There's a jump in Lucy's heart that even the rumored tiger couldn't incite. She tamps it down, as she's learned to tamp down so much else. "Don't be silly, Anna. You have to meet your fiancé."

Yet Anna wheedles, coaxes, cajoles, her capacity for speech a marvel—an endless, carrying current that flows past all obstacles. Seventeen like Lucy, there are times when Anna seems a child. She begs for one stop.

Long before they see it, they hear it: the house of the woman who claims she was visited by a tiger. A crowd's gathered, chattering, on her lawn. "It came right up," the woman says. "I heard it growl."

Anna tugs Lucy to the front. Two slight girls, and yet people part around them because they're really three. Anna's hired man follows. Gossip says that all of the hired men employed by Anna's father—taciturn, stealthy men outfitted in non-descript black—carry guns under their coats. Ordinarily, Anna rolls her eyes at the notion.

Today Anna's too transfixed to notice. She hunkers in the mud, seeming ready to kiss the print, or ask of it some benediction. So alive with hope and possibility that envy snaps in Lucy with the sudden, cold teeth of a steel trap. What she'd give to feel that.

Lucy steps closer. The print's half a print. Two toes, a partial paw pad, hardly bigger than a saucer. Some lesser cat left it—lynx or bobcat, or even a fat domestic tom.

Anna says something about her heart racing, and Lucy echoes it, as if her own heart isn't flat and sluggish, as if the old disappointment doesn't rankle. She could turn and tell the crowd the truth of this print, watch their faces fall. But. She's told her story in Sweetwater. **Orphan. Left on a doorstep. Don't know who my parents are. No one but me.** That girl doesn't know tigers.

"I think that if you were an animal," Anna says, "you'd be a tiger. The very sweetest, most beautiful kind."

Lucy kisses the top of Anna's head. Flowers, warm milk. A soothing nursery scent. She puts a hand out to help Anna up.

"Of course," Anna says, taking the hand, "we'd have to get you declawed."

Heat makes sap, and blood, rise faster. Lucy's

hand so sweat-slippery around her friend's. Who could blame her, on this hot day, for losing her grip? Not even the hired man would know the difference if she let go, sending Anna sprawling into the mud, brown eating up the clean white field of fabric.

Lucy pulls Anna up so fast that their shoulders knock together. As Anna turns back through the crowd, Lucy hangs behind, wiping her sweaty palm. There's a second print some distance from the first. Not a paw—a pointed boot.

"Your sister's leaving," a man says, glancing over. That first glance quick. The second protracted. It takes Lucy apart, eyes and nose and mouth and hair. Counting up her differences. By then Lucy is past him, slipping her arm through her friend's. From behind, they're identical.

So there is no tiger, no terror, no crisis to avert what Lucy's dreaded all week long. Right on schedule the train comes ripping. Its whistle pierces the station. Track trembles, cottonwoods shedding loose leaves. Anna says something the wheels drown out.

Lucy mouths the words she hopes to hear: **I've decided not to get married.**

What? she sees Anna say as the smell of chicken shit enters the station.

A part of Lucy stays on the platform where a freight car halts, feathers puffing from between its slats. Another part staggers back into a dim shack at the edge of a valley. She feels Anna propping her up, asking if she's unwell.

Lucy swallows back bile. **I'm quite well, excepting this train reminds me of living in a hen coop. Likely the shit got in my food and bed.** "I'm only thirsty."

Anna offers to call a carriage. Today even that kindness is souring, spoiling in the summer heat. Summer is Lucy's least favorite season. How heavy it drags. How damp. After five years in this town, a longing still fills her for the clear-cut world of two seasons only: dry or wet. She stands, brushing Anna off. Says she'll walk back alone.

"You can't!" Anna cries. "Sweetheart, the tiger. I won't do a thing except worry if you leave. You shouldn't—you can't—"

It's too hot to protest, and pointless anyhow, as Anna will get her way. Lucy sits. "Look. Here. I'll wait right on this bench." She resists a strange compulsion to purr.

In that thronged station, Anna manages to be first at the train door when it opens.

Charles's light hair is a fit to Anna's dark curls, his chin a fit to the top of her head, his gold watch a fit to her gold rings, his hired man a fit to hers. Most of all they fit in how they stand. At the center, unconcerned with the passengers forced to step around, unconcerned with tucking in their elbows, shrinking the circle of their feet. Anna throws her head back all the way in laughter, and a woman jumps away from the swing of those curls—which are doused, Lucy knows, with rose water.

Soon it's just Anna and Charles talking on the empty platform, and their hired men, and Lucy. Time creeps. Sun slants over the bench. The creases of Lucy's dress grow limp with sweat.

A last, lone cart drives into the station. The butcher's boy has come for his chickens. Red-faced, collar askew, he stands too close to Lucy as he struggles with the freight car's door. She edges away, intending to unpair herself—and then the door slams open. A gritty wind swallows her dress.

Down the platform, Charles's hand has fallen to Anna's waist. Neither notices the commotion.

Lucy beats at herself, but it's too late. Dirt and sweat mix into a muddy paste that clings to white fabric, dirtying her dress as, earlier, she imagined Anna's dress dirtied. She must look as filthy as the butcher's boy. Anna's voice carries on, and on, and when Lucy leaves, only the hired men take notice.

Water

It's a swollen orange sunset by the time Lucy wades into the river.

Rumor has emptied the banks. No one around to see as she damps her skirts, pauses. As, very carefully, she contorts herself to undo all thirty pearl buttons. She floats naked beside her dress. The water rushes over flesh and fabric alike, dispassionate in its cleansing.

If Anna is her second friend in Sweetwater, the river is her first.

Five years ago she first crossed into town. Carts banged into her, a crowd spun her round. She was lost. The sky no help—look up as she'd learned to do in the hills, and buildings crowded her view.

Clouds didn't circle. She was the center of nothing and the land didn't speak. She was no one.

She found her way to a restaurant kitchen. A relief in what she knew: greasy dishes, low ceiling, ache in her bent neck. Three other girls stood at the sink. One pale, two dark. Lucy murmured: **An orphan. Left. Don't know. No one.** The pale girl lost interest. The dark girls were persistent, whispering together till they approached Lucy in the alley.

"Who are you?" the taller asked.

"An orphan."

"No," said the shorter, stepping closer. Lucy looked them full in the face: Indian, most like. There were a number of Indians, people of all stripes, in Sweetwater's streets. "Who are your **people**?" The short girl pressed a hand to her chest, spoke the name of her tribe.

Another long-ago name, spoken to her in a loft, whirled across Lucy's memory, broke apart like dust. **This is the right word.** Gone. Taste of her own dry tongue. If she'd had a people, she could no longer name them. The taller Indian girl put her hand on her chest, too, and Lucy realized that the two must be sisters.

The girls kept looking at Lucy, kept asking, kept inviting her to share their strange, wrapped lunches. Kept pestering till one day Lucy turned and said something about skin. About water. About filth.

The Indian girls never spoke to her again. Lick of shame, consuming, then an emptiness that she learned to see as lightness. Deliberately this time, she let the name of the girls' people drop between the gaps in her memory, gone where her own name had gone. At least they left her alone.

She wasn't completely alone, not yet. Noon and night she returned to the river with kitchen scraps that Sam wrinkled a nose at. Sam offered those two silver dollars, Lucy pretending deafness till the offering stopped. Other talk stopped too. Sam grew more picky, more fidgety, more absent. Gone for hours, Sam acquired food some other way.

Finally came the trade fair the mountain man had spoken of. Cowboys and trappers and cattlemen, games and shows, blew through Sweetwater like weather. When the fair lifted away, Sam was gone too—and Nellie.

For a week more, Lucy waited alone with the river. So clear up top. So much rubble at its bottom. At last she threw her belongings—threadbare, dented, tattered and mean, sun-stained and stinking of the long road from the Western territory— into the water. She moved with just the dress on her back into a boardinghouse.

Her first year, she scanned Sweetwater's crowds. Thousands of faces, more types than she'd seen before. None familiar.

Her second year she quit seeking disappointment, hurried head-down through the streets. Sometimes voices called. Never those she knew. Men, mostly, and mostly at night.

Her third year she said **Orphan, Left, No one**
so often the words made a lacquer over the truth.
A blank story to suit this town where she learned
what civilization properly meant: no danger, no adventure, no uncertainty in a place so bled of wildness that a false tiger could be an event.

Three years of suds, wrinkled hands, cobbles,
neat corners, green leaves then brown leaves then
no leaves then green again, sharp-creased dresses,
coins slid over the grocer's counter, white curtains, starched sheets, salt, sweet water, heavy air,
streetlamps, cricked neck, dish suds turned to laundry suds, a new job at the hotel with higher pay, the
Indian girls left behind in the kitchen where Lucy
heard they were indentured to work eight years
more to pay a debt, salt, sweet water, aching hands,
air so hard to breathe, glint of fork and knife at a
table set for one, and no touch on her own skin but
for the touch of river water.

And then at the start of the fourth year, Lucy
met Anna by the river.

"What are you doing with that?" a voice asked
that day from behind. A hand shot over Lucy's
shoulder, pointing at the stick in Lucy's hand. A
strange girl stepped forward on the riverbank. She
held a dowsing rod just like Lucy's.

"I'm Anna," she said. Her voice broke the solitude.

Up till then Lucy had come to the river alone.
On days off she swam, or scrubbed her skin, or
searched the water for glimpses of her own face:

slash of cheek, wing of hair, an eye's narrow line. She picked up objects—long gray rocks, pebbles black as bullets, a branch forked into a Y like a dowsing rod—and held them to her ear as if they might speak to her as no one did.

And then, Anna.

I hear it'll rain tomorrow.
I like your hair.
I like your freckles.
Will you teach me to swim like that?
How old are you?
Sixteen.
Me too.

Lucy came to suspect that her new friend, too, had something to hide. They never spoke of the past. Anna had interest only in the future. A train she wanted to ride, a dress she wanted made, a fruit she wanted to eat come autumn. Life as a bloom of possibilities, just waiting for to ripen.

One Sunday the bank was white with frost and Anna carried three of the autumn apples she'd talked about for weeks—so red that Lucy's eyes smarted. Anna spun her dowsing rod in rare silence, then said, "My father was a prospector."

Lucy's mouth was full of juice. Sweetness loosed her tongue. "Mine too."

To her surprise Anna didn't let the words lie between them as usual. "I knew it," she said, gripping Lucy's hands. Lucy tried to slide back. Tried to divine what the girl knew, and how. The gun, the bank, the jackal-men? "I knew you were the same as me. Papa said not to tell people, he said I'm too naïve, he doesn't like when I come here without my hired man—but I knew I could trust you. The moment I saw you, I knew. We're going to be the very best of friends."

Anna is a prospector's daughter, but there the likeness ends. Because when Anna's father took gold from these hills, he kept it. He has deeds to prove his claim, and men who work under him. He hoarded mines, hotels, stores, trains, a house in Sweetwater far from the hills he'd emptied of riches, a daughter.

Fool's gold is a thing Lucy learns of in Sweetwater. A cheap stone, it deceives the untrained eye. **Fool's gold** has become a saying about that which imitates truth. Prospector's daughter Anna may be, but she looked at Lucy and was deceived.

Lucy amended her lie. **An orphan. Don't know. No one. But I suspect my father was a prospector.** Anna forgave. Anna forgives easy, laughs easy, cries so easy that Lucy, who does none of this easy, who has packed so tight the grave of her girlhood that little feeling trembles through, marvels. And still Anna insists, **We're just the same, deep down.**

In Anna's house there are twenty-one rooms and

fifteen horses, two kitchens and three fountains. Velvet and damask, silver and marble. And in the largest room, its vaulted ceiling so high that the blue tiles mimic sky, is a deed in a frame. The frame is solid gold. The deed is mere paper. Dusty edges, one corner torn. Anna's father's signature a snake across the bottom. This is his most precious thing, this that gives him claim to his first prospecting site. **Are you hurting?** Anna asked the first time she brought Lucy to see the deed. **Your face—it looks—** Likely Anna had little practice with the word **despair.** Anyhow Anna fussed over Lucy, fed her sweets, led her across the marble floors and pressed onto Lucy silver boxes of salt, velvet dresses. Anna saying all the while, **The same.** Those words echo through the mansion where emptiness lurks despite the maids and grooms and gardeners—Anna's mother dead, her father always traveling—and Lucy thought she heard what sounded behind them.

It is as if Anna waved a wand over her friend— only the wand was a dowsing rod, and the rod held by Anna's father, and the magic only gold. Transformation into the same girl.

It worked, for a while. They even tricked the half-blind gardener. Same dress, same curls. Lucy repeated Anna's words, repeated her carefree laugh. Anna filled Lucy's vision so that, passing a mirror, Lucy was startled at the face within—not green-eyed, not round. A strange, grave face with crooked nose and guarded eyes.

The gardener said, **Yes, little madam**. He cut the flowers that Lucy asked for.

The spell broke at midnight, two months back, when Lucy stayed longer than ever in Anna's room. They lit a candle, sneaked cold biscuits though the cook could've whipped up a feast. A vase of cut roses heady. Pressed close on Anna's bed, the rest of the enormous house darkened, insignificant. Anna turned in midgiggle. Her face close and flushed. She asked if Lucy would like to live in one of the twenty-one rooms. Said, **You're like a sister to me.**

For the first time since returning to an empty riverbank, Lucy imagined waking to the certainty of another. That animal smell of a second body. Truth welled up in her, muddy. She was ready to speak.

And then the gas lamps flared on. A man stood in the doorway, asking, "Who are you?"

Anna's father had returned from his business trip. Lucy brushed crumbs from her dress, dipped her head to hide her exposed nose.

Anna was born in this soft green place, but her father was of the hills. He knew true gold and wasn't deceived. As Anna hugged him, he asked where Lucy came from. Said he'd heard of people like her from his colleagues. He listened to the lies— **Orphan—Don't know—No one**—and then he asked Anna for a private word. Lucy gathered her things and left. No one called her back.

———

Since then, Anna's quit talking of their shared future. The train they'd ride to its last stop in the East, the picnics they'd eat in her father's orchards, the rivers they'd swim, the dresses they'd buy with her father's money. No mention of Lucy living in one of the twenty-one rooms.

After that night beaus were sent to the mansion. Anna mocked them, complained of them, compared them to animals and furniture. But she picked a man with his own family mansion, his own wealth in gold.

Now Anna speaks of a house with Charles, a garden with Charles, travel with Charles. Of course Lucy is invited along. Anna so pleased by her best friend and her fiancé arrayed around her that she doesn't see how Charles's fingers loiter at Lucy's waist, how Charles calls Lucy **our very close friend**, how Charles sends gifts to the hotel where Lucy launders clothes and shows up at Lucy's window stinking of a saloon.

Lucy accepts invitations to dinner and sits at the table set for three. She praises the delicacies. The flowers. The kindness. Never mentioning Charles's whispering, when Anna leaves the room, that they should take a walk alone. The place beside Anna— once wide enough to accommodate a sister—has narrowed.

And so Lucy soaks in the river, alone as she was before. Her skin puckers into damp ridges. Still she floats. Imagining a future in which she is as wrinkled on land as she is in water, and still sitting, smiling beside her friend. What other future can there be? She's become what she said: **Orphan. No one**. No fortune, no land, no horse, no family, no past, no home, no future.

Meat

Lucy walks back dripping. By twilight people startle at her tangled hair, the slap of her bare feet. On the steps of her boardinghouse, three girls cross her path. Fear of the tiger makes them jumpy. One flinches at the sight of Lucy, who is possessed of an urge like instinct—to move not aside but **forward**, leaping straight at their silliness. She could teach a lesson in real fear, the thing that snaps girls' spines.

She smiles, lets them pass. The air's too still. Restless twitch at the corner of her lips. Maybe a meal will settle her.

The landlady catches her just inside the door, saying there's a visitor in the parlor. It must be an anxious Anna. Lucy sighs, thanks the woman.

"A **male** visitor," the landlady says, moving to block Lucy's path. Her spit flies. After five quiet years at the boardinghouse, this rage is surprising. "Keep that door open, mind you, and no bringing him upstairs. I'll be watching."

Full dark has fallen. A stalking hour. It must be Charles.

It was night the first time she met Charles, too. Three years ago, long before Anna. A time when Lucy still woke in the dark with her feet itching, loneliness a dry scratch in her throat that no amount of water could quench. And so she walked all the way across town.

By day decent people avoided the streets nearest the station, grimy with saloons and gambling dens, where vaqueros, gamblers, Indians, drunkards, cowboys, charlatans, disreputable women, and other unsavory types were known to congregate. By night, those same streets called to Lucy. A familiar defeat in the postures of the people there. Looking soothed Lucy as thirteen, fourteen passed. Her limbs outgrew their gawkiness, her hair smoothed, and she found people beginning to look at her too. Men, especially.

Those dirty streets cracked open after dark like the spines of schoolbooks. **You'll understand when you're older**, Ma used to say. Lucy learned to call

Ma's glide into her step, Sam's swagger. Playing a game that thrilled and scared her both. She learned to ignore, to respond, to spit and flee unpunished. Poor men, desperate men, rough men—and then a man who was none of these.

He fell into Lucy as he was thrown out of a gambling den. Cusses pursued him, his expensive clothes were torn—yet he laughed, unfazed. Promised he'd be back with more to spend. **Where did you come from?,** he said to Lucy. Unlike the rest, he didn't rage or sputter at her rebuff. He kept smiling. He kept coming back.

Poor men gave up, disappeared, ran out of money and pride. He had the arrogance of wealth. One night he offered a handful of coins and Lucy turned away, shivering. Not fear—more like how a man's hands shiver after firing a gun. She looked over her arms, her breasts, her belly. Trying to see where in that softness lay her weapon.

She quit those streets soon after. She'd learned to angle her bonnet, control her walk, brush hair over her face. Learned to deny the ghosts that haunted the silhouette of a broken man limping down an alley, or the momentary shape of a woman turning, long-necked, in the window of a bedroom above a saloon—how to seem an ordinary girl, the one who met Anna.

And then he reappeared beside Anna. Neatened, still smiling, named. **Charles**, Anna said as she introduced her fiancé, **this girl is very important to**

me. **Don't you forget her.** Charles pulled Lucy a hair too close in greeting, leaving just enough space between them to accommodate the narrow alley, the dark night, the secret they shared from Anna. He said, **How could I ever forget you?**

The man who waits in the parlor is black-haired, brown-skinned. He turns toward Lucy with narrowed eyes.

Her hand flies to her nose. It's Ba.

Though there's no grave soil on his red shirt, no maggots crawling from his boots, something long-buried breaks open. Lucy feels the heat, the choking dust. All the years and the distance and the cleanness of her living disappear as Ba walks toward her. It's not the Lucy of Sweetwater who stands in the parlor. It's a younger Lucy, slight and shoeless, so much of herself laid bare. A Lucy she figured buried in that Western territory.

She wants to run, but the tight dress constricts her ribs. She can't breathe. And Ba's too quick besides—the haint's come in a younger guise. No limp, no missing teeth. Long-legged, his cheek-bones could cut. He stands before her, grinning.

And he says, "Pow."

That voice. Not low enough for Ba. A husky quality like Ma's. Close-up the face looks its sixteen years.

"Your hair," Lucy says, voice breaking. "It's gotten so long."

Last she saw, Sam had shorn that hair to the scalp. Now it falls into Sam's eyes, curling just under the ears. Half a lifetime Lucy spent tucking that hair into a braid. She reaches for it now. Then remembers.

"What are you doing here?" She snatches her hand back. "You left me."

Sam's smile drops. Sam's chin lifts. "You weren't hardly around. You left first."

"I checked on you every day. And not one word—don't you have any consideration? I thought you were hurt, or dead. I didn't ask you back here. I can't believe—"

Some things can bring her back in an instant. Chicken shit. A dead man's face. And this stubbornness in Sam that's resisted the passage of the years. What Ma called sullenness. What Ba called **boy**. What Lucy called, with a mixture of admiration and envy, Sam's shine.

The door creaks wider. It's the landlady, her disapproval shrill. Lucy turns to reassure the woman, drawing politeness over the twelve-year-old's hurt.

When she turns back to Sam, she feels only weary. How can she explain the way it was when Sam left? Something went out of the world. A whole piece of her was tamped down and buried so deep that no one in Sweetwater can see it. She's changed. No longer the sister Sam knew.

"I think you'd better go," Lucy says.

And then Sam says, "I'm sorry."

The apology chases Ba's ghost from the room. It's Sam alone who stands there, extending a hand.

"Truce?"

A common hand. Rough, calloused, and quivering, making Lucy wonder what Sam buried too. Sam holds that hand out as seconds tick by. For the first time, it seems, Lucy has something Sam wants. How long will Sam stay to get it?

She leaves the hand hanging. "Let's get some dinner. You're buying."

Lucy chooses where they won't bump into Anna. A grease-spotted place by the station, where Sam orders without consulting the menu. Two steaks, a sour cook, and Sam aiming a smile so wide the woman walks away stunned, her own mouth turned up seemingly against her will. Meanwhile Lucy's appetite slunk out the door at the sight of the flypaper. She asks for water. Sam watches her wipe her dirty fork, then calls across the restaurant.

"Miss?" Diners turn. "Miss, you with the beautiful curls." The cook, graying hair in a twist, looks up from onions in astonishment. "We'd appreciate fresh cutlery. If you've got it. Thanks greatly, miss."

"Don't make a fuss," Lucy hisses, adjusting her hair over her face.

"They'll look no matter what."

Sam, as usual, makes that true. Drapes over the rickety chair as if it's a lounge in Anna's parlor. If Lucy learned to go unseen, then Sam spent five years polishing a natural shine brighter. Sam's walk is bolder, Sam's shoulders straighter. A new bandana at the throat hides Sam's lack of Adam's apple. Look hard and Lucy can see remnants of the pretty girl-child: long lashes, smooth skin. But it's like trying to fix on an animal moving through the grass at the jackal hour. Your eyes make you question.

What most people see is a man. Handsome as Ba must have been before life cut its marks in him. All Ma's charm and grace. Likely that's why the two steaks come so quick, why the cook flashes another gummy smile.

Sam falls upon the food with an old ferocity. Lucy spins her water glass, remembering starvation. Damp on her fingers, a matching damp in her eyes. What Sam stirs up is unwelcome. Murky.

Sam mistakes Lucy's gaze. "Do you want the second steak?"

"I can't. I'll ruin my dress." Lucy brushes the white fabric, imported special by Anna's father. She doesn't want to explain its cost, or Anna, or Anna's father. To distract she says, "Tell me where you've been."

Sam takes another bite, leans back. At sixteen, Sam's voice is unaccountably deep, with a singsong rhythm. Easy in this heat to imagine Sam spinning these tales by a campfire. They have the cadence of practice, like Lucy's orphan story. These—Lucy's eyes prick—are stories Sam shares with strangers.

Sam fell in with cowboys to lead a great cattle drive North. Traveled with adventurers to a lost Indian city in the South. Trekked up a mountain with a sole companion to see the world laid out from the peak. Sam chews and talks, swallows and boasts, and hunger roams in Lucy. A hunger for wild places, for paths that twist so you can't see their ends, for fear of the kind missing along with wildness in Sweetwater. A hunger for the trail that makes unsalted oats and cold beans into a feast, the trail that sears the body awake, not this sluggish place, this orderly place where all the streets are mapped and known.

"Where will you go now?" Lucy asks when Sam stops. The restaurant's gone quiet, yet an echo remains—a kind of ringing inside Lucy, as when one glass strikes another and sets it in motion too. She almost doesn't recognize it for hope. "With who?"

Sam scrapes a fork over the empty plate. "I'm going alone this time. Had enough of traveling in packs. I'm planning to go pretty far, and I figure I won't come back. So I figured—I figured I'd say goodbye."

The hunger in Lucy is grown so vast, she fears she might collapse into it. She calls for her own steak. Intends just to nibble. But the meat occupies her mouth and eyes so she doesn't have to speak or look at Sam, doesn't have to fear the keenness of her disappointment showing through. She lifts her plate to hide her face, and laps the bloody juices.

Sam pushes the other two plates across. Lucy licks those clean too. Only then does she look down at her dress. It's ruined, spattered with small pink drops.

Sam says, "It suits you."

Anger clarifies. This is Sam mocking again, come through town to upturn everything—selfish through and through. She reaches for the bill when it arrives, intending to call this a goodbye gift.

But Sam's quicker. Like some magic trick, Sam's brown hand slaps down—and when it lifts, there remains a flake of pure gold.

Lucy throws both hands, a forearm, over the sight. "Have you been prospecting?" Fear hums through her. She looks around, but none of the other diners have moved. The rest of the room seems suspended in torpor. "You know you can't. The law—"

"I didn't prospect for it. I was paid by some gold men I worked for."

"Why in the world would you do that?"

"Didn't you ever wonder?" The swagger leaves Sam's voice. For the first time Sam speaks softly, conscious of the other diners. "We weren't the only ones wronged. There's others, Indian and brown and black. None of us think it was right, what got took from us. Didn't you wonder what the gold men did with what honest folks dug up?"

Up this close, Lucy sees what she missed under Sam's charm. Beneath is the same mix of violence and bitterness and hope that killed Ba. That old history that Lucy orphaned herself from.

"Those gold men really think this land belongs to them," Sam says, scornful. "Isn't that the greatest joke?"

Lucy can't locate her laughter. What she can locate is the precise spot on a wall, in the biggest house in town, where a deed hangs in a frame that, if melted down and sold, could feed a hundred families. Sam may scorn it, but there it is in a place Sam could never imagine. Lucy pretends to dab at her dress. She knows the answer to Sam's question, and it shames her. She's seen where the gold goes. She is a guest in its house, she wears its gifts, she is its friend and walks arm in arm with it through Sweetwater.

Something lunges at them as they step from restaurant to dark street. Lucy jerks Sam back. It's only a kid, running by close enough to jostle their elbows. Legs flash in the streetlamps' orange light. Raggedy kids, most of them some shade of brown, play at tigers.

The littlest chases the others, his fingers hooked

to claws. They laugh at his thin yowl and scramble away. Soon he sits alone in the street. His face puckers.

And then from behind Lucy comes a growl that shakes her bones. A surging, uneven sound that rises and recedes, rises and recedes, till the very air rends around it. Into that suffocating night comes a cool breath of terror. The laughing children freeze. Down the block a drunkard rises, starts to pound at the nearest door. Only the littlest sits with eyes full of wonder.

Lucy turns. There's dread in her heart, and something else too. The growl set off another ringing.

No beast stands behind her. Only Sam, withdrawn into shadow. Sam's long throat ripples to produce that sound, far lower than should be possible. Bit by bit Sam quiets.

When Lucy can speak again, she says, "There's rumors of a tiger."

"I know." Sam stays in shadow. Eyes and grin show through. "A tiger with a taste for beef."

Lucy looks down at Sam's boots. The toes are pointed, just as the second print in the woman's yard was pointed. "You can't have . . ."

Sam shrugs. "I did."

The children have slid away, the drunk admitted into the saloon. The street returns to quiet—but it's not as it was. Something vital lacking. There is no tiger. Summer makes Lucy sluggish, stupid. What a fool she was. Here there was never even the possibility of tigers. Thousands of faces and none of them can shiver her. Except this one, and it's leaving again.

"They wouldn't survive one, would they?" Lucy says.

"Not like us." Sam's words come out singsong. "Nobody like us."

Lucy takes Sam's hand, as she didn't in the parlor. It's bigger now. Unfamiliar. Yet there, high up, tucked under sleeve, is the delicate wristbone. A rhythm recalls itself to Lucy as she swings their clasped hands. The old tiger song.

Lao hu, lao hu.

Sam joins in. It's sung as a round, their two voices chasing each other as the two tigers do in song. In singing Sam's voice is higher than in speaking. Almost sweet. When Lucy arrives at the end of her verse, she waits so that, with a pounce, they land on the last word together.

Lai.

Anna steps out as if summoned. "Lucinda? Is that you?"

Anna brings noise back to the street. She hugs Lucy around the neck, chatter spilling down Lucy's ears, flooding the nooks and alleys. Anna babbles her relief to see Lucy safe, scolds about the tiger, recounts her own night—how they left the hired men behind and Charles took her to a gambling den as a lark, how terrible and wonderful and marvelous it was inside.

"Guess how much money I lost," Anna says, giggling. She whispers the amount into Lucy's ear.

Behind, Sam's gaze on Lucy like a hot Western sun. Lucy knows what Sam must think. She lengthened her name—what of it? Sam was once Samantha. Neither quite what their parents intended. Why, then, this shame? Lucy wishes back the quiet. Wishes Anna away. She wants to think.

"Who's your friend?" Anna remembers to ask.

Sam steps fully under the streetlamp and Anna takes a breath. She looks between Sam and Lucy. Disassembling Lucy's face as others do—seeing not Lucy but eyes and cheekbones and hair.

"You must be—" Anna says.

"Sam." Smoothly Sam takes Anna's hand. "Pleased to meet you." No space left for Anna to repeat her question without rudeness. Sam is all teeth, roguish charm.

Anna laughs. "The pleasure is mine."

They're still clasping hands when Charles says, "And how do you know Lucinda?"

"Who?" Sam says in exaggerated confusion. "Oh, **Lucinda**. We only just met."

"You met **here**?" Charles says, his eyes going to the gambling den where Lucy saw him years back. "You mean—"

"No," Lucy says. "Sam comes from the same

orphanage where I was raised. They asked me to show Sam around Sweetwater."

"It's a fine town," Sam says. "Very—safe."

"Then you two aren't . . . ?" Anna looks between them. "We thought—" She smiles, uncertain. Her eyes flick to Sam's hand, which hangs loose.

A strained silence falls. The lamp above sputters, striping their faces. Anna, Charles, Lucy—all uneasy. Only Sam still grins. As if this is all some game played by Sam's rules. The orange light flatters Sam's cheekbones, Sam's dark eyes. Easy to imagine Sam a few years out. Gaining bulk, filling up on steak, becoming precisely who Sam wanted to be. Eleven years old and Sam declared, **An adventurer. A cowboy. An outlaw. When I'm grown.** After five years missing, five years lost, five years without place or person to box Sam in, the sibling who returned seems more familiar rather than less—Sam more **Sam**.

"I have an idea," Anna says to break the silence. "Why don't we show Sam a nicer part of town? Charles and I were on our way home for my cook's hot cocoa. Won't you join us? Lucinda, I know you love sweets."

Lucy wants only the empty street, and the aftermath of Sam's roar, which set off a reverberation that has yet to stop, one leading like a narrow, overgrown track to a place beyond words. But Sam is saying yes.

Skull

The cocoa is cooled by ice, garnished with fruit from Anna's garden, set beside biscuits and cream and a porcelain bowl that holds more sugar. Lucy's stomach revolts to see it. Her teeth hurt. Sam heaps spoonful after spoonful.

Charles draws a flask from his pocket. "This is as good as gold," he says, tipping the whiskey toward Anna. "Like my fiancée."

Sam's neck swivels, hawklike.

Only Lucy declines a pour, though Charles presses till Anna tells him to quit being a bully. Liquor signals ruination to Lucy. She watches Sam for slurred words or a quicker fury. Sam grows only more dazzling. Sam tugs at the bandana, blazes golden down the long brown column of neck, tells a story about tracking a wily silver fox. Anna, flushed from drink, gasps as Sam recounts tumbling into a hidden cave.

"And inside," Sam says, reaching into a pocket, "I found this."

A tiny skull sits on Sam's finger, bone polished to a luster like pearl. Anna leans closer.

"Dragon," Sam says, sliding the skull to Anna's palm. She protests: too small, too round, and where are the teeth? "**Baby** dragon. The runt of the litter."

Why, it's a lizard skull. Any child raised on the wagon trail could see it, but Anna is fooled. Her awed exclamations fill the room, setting Lucy's teeth on edge. Sam winks at Lucy over Anna's shoulder.

"Do you really trust him?" Charles says, coming to perch by Lucy's chair. His liquored breath coats her ear, followed by his damp lips. She jerks away. Drink makes him sloppy. Ordinarily she knows how to evade him, but the day has left her off-kilter too. "You know how Anna's father is about strangers."

"I do," Lucy says.

"The two of you are awfully familiar for having just met."

Sam's telling another tall tale. Anna laughs so hard she chokes, and Sam thumps her. The parlor feels cramped with four, as it didn't with three. Lucy stands. She asks Charles to join her for a walk.

For his daughter's sake, Anna's father ripped plants from their native soils. Vast territories were plundered to fill the garden. Some plants came with their own names, now discarded. Anna renamed them according to her fancies. **Tiger lily**, **serpent's tail**, **lion's mane**, **dragon's eye**—a menagerie of creatures with thorns trimmed and roots safe-buried. The garden is praised as a triumph by those who don't see the plants that fail to take.

Last week the grounds rang with blossoms. This week they're fading. Lucy and Charles crush petals underfoot until they reach the garden's center. Plants teem, thick enough to soak up sound.

"You're acting foolish," Lucy says. "It's not what you think, anyhow." Here there's space to step back, to look at Charles and judge how best to handle him.

Drink puffs his face, shines his cheeks, brings out the spoiled child in him, the one who pursues Lucy like a new toy he'll discard the next day. Once he's married and Anna in his bed, his restlessness will settle. It must. Till then, he's Anna's fiancé while she's looking—and Lucy's burden while Anna isn't.

"Don't instruct me." Charles is in a mood. Sometimes Lucy can freeze him out, or deflate him with a well-aimed tease. Today his face is petulant. He won't quit till he's extracted something from her— a favor, a compliment, a peek of her ankle. Easier to concede a favor than to watch him skulk for days, face a thundercloud and Lucy dreading the burst. And so, since he's bound to keep her secrets as she keeps his, she gives him a truth.

"I'm Sam's sister."

"So you admit you were lying about him." Charles punches a fist into his hand, triumphant. "I suspected you were up to something."

Lucy sighs. "You were right, Charles."

"So you and I can still be friends?"

"We can."

"Give me a kiss, then." Lucy pecks quickly at his offered cheek. His head snaps up, mouth seeking, but she expected this. She's stepped out of range.

"None of that." At his sulk, she teases, trying to shift back to lighter ground. "Behave, now. Don't take Anna to any more gambling dens."

Charles grabs the bush at the garden's center. A tall thing with fleshy, five-fingered leaves. **Mother dearest**, Anna named her favorite and thirstiest plant. She tends it herself despite the army of gardeners. Lucy couldn't believe the first time she saw Anna coo into the leaves. Only a girl so rich could lavish affection on a plant that drinks in one week what a whole family uses in the dry season. And only a man so rich could shred that plant like scrap paper.

"I was settling an old debt," Charles says, stiffly. "I meant to go alone, but you know how Anna can be. I told her it was on behalf of a friend. I trust you'll say the same if she asks."

"Of course. I only want the best for you two."
The next words stick, but Lucy gets them out. "I'm
looking forward to the wedding."

She thought the flattery would placate him,
but Charles says, with a viciousness that stops her,
"Don't pretend you care about my feelings **now**.
We saw the two of you holding hands. Tell me the
truth. You owe me at least that much."

A gathering thickness in Charles's voice, in the
humid garden with plants crammed close. Lucy
tries to pierce it by laughing. "I don't believe I owe
you anything."

He grabs her. Not his flirtatious touch, the one
that evaporates when Anna looks over. Charles
digs into the meat of Lucy's arm. Splotches spread
under his fingers. "Don't be coy. Haven't I sent you
nice gifts? Haven't I been sweet to you? You play at
demureness, but now? Why him? Why not **me**?"
Charles's voice thins to a child's whine. He drops
his face into Lucy's chest. Says, groaning, "I've
never met a girl like you. Please, Lucinda, you don't
know what you do to me."

But she knows. She's heard men say similar things,
always followed or preceded by, **Where did you
come from?** Spoken with marvel or spoken with
rage, it's all the same to her. She unpeels Charles's
fingers, pushes his face away last. She lets him linger. She doesn't like it, and a small part of her does.
What she does to him is the only thing she has, and
she won't give it away. Anna has everything else.

"He doesn't care for you," Charles yells as Lucy leaves. She keeps walking. "He's only using you to get to her. Just like the rest of them, your tailors and bakers and hobnobbers—they pay you heed because of Anna."

There is, if you dig through the muck, a steel-toothed envy at the bottom of her.

Lucy turns. She lets despair show, and shame. Lowers her eyes so Charles can't see them narrow. "You're right, Charles. How did I not see it before?"

Alone Lucy reenters the mansion. The hurt radiates, sharp, as she presses her arm where Charles pressed. Once, a mine door bit her in the same place. Now she pinches the skin redder. For the first time since Anna's father came to chase her out, Lucy sees a future open again.

Possibilities.

Charles, arrogant, imagines only a petty Lucy, a jealous Lucy, a cowed Lucy chasing Sam out with a story in Anna's ear.

What Lucy sees:

Anna sending Charles away once Lucy shows her arm as proof of his attack. Charles tumbling down, his footing lost—Charles the discarded one. Lucy sees, with a twinge, how Anna will despair. For a while. Soon enough Anna's head will lift at a joke Lucy makes. Anna will laugh that rippling laugh.

Anna and Lucy will take the train far, far from here. Long after Charles and Sam have left, Anna and Lucy will have their own adventure. And if the tamed land along the railroad tracks is softer, its beauty declawed—well, it's good enough.

Oddly, the parlor doors are shut. Lucy pulls them open.

Two bodies twist against the wall. Anna whimpers as if in pain, her right hand still holding that lizard skull. Sam grips Anna's other arm as Charles gripped Lucy's. A flush down Anna's arm, and her chest, and her throat—all the way to her lips, under Sam's lips.

Lucy makes a sound.

As the bodies part, the skull drops between. Unharmed till Anna steps back, blushing, unaware of the bone she grinds to powder. Sam doesn't blush. Sam grins.

Plum

Anna has always taken Lucy for sweet. **Sweetheart, sweet pea, sweet friend.** Last week Anna gifted Lucy with a crate of the year's first plums. Nausea brushed Lucy at the sight of the fruit, so ripe the skin was splitting.

Those colors like bruise.

Turned out, Anna had recalled a story Lucy told about gathering plums as a child. But the story was Sam's, the love for sweetness Sam's. Too late that day to explain how Lucy preferred the fruit dried and salted. She forced down one cloying bite after another.

Lucy thinks of the sickly plums she vomited as she holds back Anna's hair. The other girl spills her stomach into a cut-glass bowl. Sam is gone, sent to the garden with Charles.

"Shhh," Lucy says.

"You must think terribly of me," Anna sobs, turning her head up to be stroked. "I'm sorry."

"It's not your fault. Sam was in the wrong." Sam she'll deal with later.

Anna's sobs falter, then double. "I don't know what came over me. I shouldn't have taken so much whiskey. It's just that . . . it's just . . . Lucinda? Do you ever wish you could be someone else?"

Lucy's hand halts. The metal teeth graze her heart. She resumes stroking. She says, "No."

"Sometimes I wish I were **you**."

Lucy bites her tongue. Tastes salt.

"I'd give half my fortune to go around without Papa looking over my shoulder. You can go anywhere and no one cares. You could leave town tomorrow with Sam, if you wanted. You're **lucky**."

If Sam weren't going alone. If Lucy didn't know Sam would refuse her. She thinks of saying so, but the envy that Charles dug up in the garden is still snapping. Lucy says, "Let's trade, then. I'll stay in your rooms and you can run off."

Anna smiles weakly. Blows her nose. "Your jokes are such a comfort to me. I know I'm being silly. I'm sure it's only wedding jitters. Where is Charles, by the way?"

Lucy says, "I have something to tell you."

She tells. About the gambling den three years

back, Charles's hands and his offers. She shows the mark on her arm. She speaks gentle and hides certain facts—like the one time Charles kissed her off guard and for a moment she kissed back, the pulse in her throat a pounding power. She doesn't want to wound her friend. Maybe just scratch her. Maybe draw just enough blood to prove that Anna has something in her veins besides gold.

Anna doesn't wail or gasp as she does when she hears of the tiger. A single line forms on her brow, then smooths.

"I forgive you," Anna says.

Lucy stares.

"Papa's warned me that jealousy makes people act strangely. There's no need to tell lies about Charles. Sweetheart, we'll still have plenty of room in our life for you once we're married."

Lucy's voice is so clotted she can hardly speak. "I don't—I don't want—"

"Besides," Anna says, laughing her rippling, carefree laugh. "What would Charles want with **you**?"

Lucy tastes metal. Her teeth haven't let go her tongue.

Anna smiles at her.

Lucy could speak and she could scream and she could spit her bloody tongue to the rug and still Anna would see what Anna wants to see. Anna who thinks tigers are pets, or decorations to mount beautiful and glassy-eyed on her walls beside a deed that diminishes the land even as it claims it. Anna

304 C PAM ZHANG

wants Lucy docile beside her, the third seat in their train car, wearing their clothes, lapping their cocoa, sleeping near their bed and maybe even allowing the scratch of Charles's fingers at night. Anna wants a domestic thing, a harmless thing—Anna's tigers as different from Lucy's tigers as Anna's Charles is different from Lucy's Charles.

Anna is right to dismiss Lucy's story. She has nothing to fear from Charles. She's untouchable, protected by her hired man, her father's gold.

Lucy steps back till the parlor door is at her shoulders. She puts her hand to the knob.

"Come now, dear," Anna says. "There's nothing to be angry over."

Lucy looks down at herself. The white linen dress reaches high, up and around her throat as is the fashion. Laces bind tight her ribs. Thirty buttons down the back, requiring a good quarter hour to undo unassisted. Unless. She reaches a hand behind and tugs as hard as she can.

The pearl buttons, ripping free, ping sweetly against the door.

Lucy steps out of the ruined dress. Out of the high boots. She stands in the doorway in her shift, three inches shorter. She feels cooler already, the air less heavy, inviting Anna to look and see: no longer the same, no longer Anna's poorer reflection. Lucy herself, barefoot as the day she came to Sweetwater.

———

Down the stairs and out to the garden. Lucy's feet thump to match her heart. Flowers strike at her cheeks, pollen chokes her, the five-fingered leaves of the bush pull her hair limp. She'll never curl it again. **Lai**, she calls into the stinking greenery as she hunts for Sam. She wishes all the plants razed by drought. She wishes for the honesty of dry grass.

The face coming through the dark is savage. And then Sam blinks, taking in Lucy's bedraggled state.

"Did you change your hair?" Sam asks, squinting. "It suits you. You look like your old self."

Earlier, Lucy bristled. Now she hears the words as Sam means them: a compliment. Something rustles, and she shudders. "Did you see Charles?"

"We chatted. He ran off. I'm tired of this place. Can we go?"

With effort, Lucy says, "Don't you want to—to say goodbye to Anna?"

"Not especially." Sam walks off, voice spreading through the leaves. "I thought she'd be more interesting, being so rich. She's awful dull."

Lucy laughs so hard she stumbles against Sam's arm. She presses into that arm, that sturdy back, her laughter condensing to hiccups against Sam's red shirt. Once they rode Nellie pressed together this way and saw half the world. Warily, Sam says, "What's so funny?"

"Did you know," Lucy says, muffled, "she wants to declaw a tiger."

"Idiot," Sam snorts. "I hope she enjoys being cursed for seven generations. What kind of a place is this? Don't they know—"

"—the stories? Not a one. Let's go back—to my boardinghouse."

She almost said, **home**.

Wind

On their way back Sam stops at the deserted town pump. The usual crowds are dispersed tonight, leaving only the squeak of the handle. The gush of water. The hiss between Sam's teeth as Sam puts a fist in the stream. As the dark stain on Sam's knuckles begins to wash free.

That color—impossible to see it true in the dark. Lucy touches a smaller stain high on Sam's sleeve. She puts her wet fingers to her nose and smells a jangling.

It's blood.

"It ain't mine," Sam reassures her. "I only bloodied his nose."

"You said you **chatted** with Charles."

"He said things about you. I was protecting you." Sam's chin lifts. "I did right."

"You can't—" Lucy begins. But Sam **did**. Sam who doesn't bend to the world's rules but bends them. Sam came to town and became the impossible tiger. "I hope you broke it."

Sam doesn't recoil from that ugliness. Only says, "She's not a friend to you, either, you know. However rich or pretty."

"I know," Lucy says, in a small voice.

"I hope you picked your other friends smarter."

"You don't have to worry about that." Lucy sits down, exhausted, right there on the wet flagstones. Damp creeps up her shift. She stretches her legs out, lies all the way back with a hand pressed to her eyes. She feels rather than sees Sam bending, hovering, lying down too. For a while, there is quiet.

"Don't you ever get bored in this place?" Sam says. Lucy stiffens. The sting goes out of the question as Sam adds, "Don't you ever get lonely?"

All day it's been stifling hot. Now Lucy perceives a faint breath of wind. A Westerly wind, the kind native to the hills and born at the coast. They might be laid out in the long yellow grass and looking at the stars. The best thing about stars is that you can see in them any shape you want. Make any story. Better, even, when the person beside you doesn't see them the same way.

Lucy sits up. "Take me on your next adventure."

"It'll be hard going."

"I've been resting for five years."

"Your feet look awful soft."

"You wouldn't say that if you tried wearing boots three inches high."

"If you do . . . it won't be easy to turn back."

"Why not?"

And Sam says, "I aim to go across the ocean."

When they arrive at the boardinghouse to collect Lucy's belongings, a man in black is pacing the porch.

Ignore them, Anna said of her hired men the first time Lucy saw one and stopped dead. **Papa and his friends keep them as a precaution, but they mean you no harm. They don't mean anyone harm—not good people, at least—I've never seen my men do worse than push a drunk aside or ask a debtor for money. They're glorified errand boys. Here, watch this. I'll ask him to pass the tea.** And because Anna laughed, Lucy laughed too.

These silent men grew as invisible to Lucy as their purported guns. It's true she never saw one do more than menace. But there's something different about this man—and then it comes to her. She's never seen a hired man without Anna to command him. He's eerie as a shadow without its caster.

The man turns. Sam drags Lucy back around the corner, a firm hand over her mouth.

"It must be a misunderstanding," Lucy whispers, humoring Sam. "Anna wouldn't—it's a mistake. Likely she sent him with a message." **Errand boys.** "I'll talk to him."

Sam lets loose a string of hushed, unfamiliar words. Lucy recognizes only the last cuss. "Ben dan. Anna didn't send him."

Lucy opens her mouth to correct Sam. Then she hears it. The man's pacing—an unerring, pitiless tempo. A long-buried part of her, stirring awake, says, **Hunting**. She looks at the blood on Sam's sleeve that wouldn't wash out. "You mean Charles sent him?"

Sam cuts Lucy a look she knows. In another life she aimed that same look at Sam—the look given to an exasperating child.

"This isn't some lovers' quarrel," Sam says. "He's here for me."

Fear strums Lucy in earnest now. Blown in on the wind is a part of her old world. The dangerous part.

"But why—"

"He thinks I owe some money."

Anna has spoken of how the hired men are sometimes sent to collect on debts. Lucy relaxes. "Is that all? So pay him back. I have some savings—"

"No," Sam snarls, and Lucy flinches. A coiled violence in that voice, like a pulled-back fist. For the first time she truly believes the stories Sam told at dinner. She can see in Sam the cowboy, the mountaineer, the miner. The hardened man unknown to her. "I don't owe anything. Never mind that. You'll be safe enough if I leave town alone."

"But **why**?" Lucy can ask, and ask, but the question is futile. That old stubbornness firms Sam's jaw. The years make no difference—even young and pudgy, Sam never broke a silence.

Lucy's gaze falls instead to Sam's swollen knuckles. They mark Sam's courage. Some things shifted tonight and can't be taken back: the cut on Sam's hand, the blood on Charles's nose, Anna. Where, the wind seems to ask, is Lucy's courage?

Her heart thuds, but Sam can't hear that. Lucy smiles a practiced smile. Tosses her head as if she has curls to bounce. "What do I care about safe? This town is safe, and just look at it. I'm coming."

"You don't understand. It won't be fun. It—"

"It'll be an adventure. Besides, if you get hauled off into some debtors' prison, you'll need someone to break you out."

She intended it as a jest, but Sam's gaze remains distant, following the hired man, whose pattern brings him closer and closer to the corner. Sam looks ready to bolt.

"Please," Lucy says. "I don't care about some stupid debt—I won't ask about it if you insist. Let's **go**."

"What about your things?"

"They're only things." As Lucy says it, she realizes

it's true. She thinks of the thirty pearl buttons scattered across Anna's rug. How the ping of them against the door was like claws, gently clicking. "What makes a family a family?"

She thought that, at least, would make Sam smile.

Blood

A safe distance from Sweetwater, Sam calls a halt. All night and all morning they've traveled. True to Sam's prediction, Lucy's feet have blistered. Her eyes are gritty. She half dozes, thinking of her feather bed. She wants a rest, a bite to eat. But Sam squats by the stream they've followed and sinks hands into the mud.

"This isn't the time to play around with war paint," Lucy says as mud slathers Sam's cheeks.

"It's to hide our scent. In case of dogs."

Morning's risen on the decision Lucy made in the dark. Swift clouds race overhead. Without buildings to shrink the sky, she's terribly exposed. This is the land freed of its frame, loosened from a deed, and it is huge and whistling and uncontainable.

She stands at the mercy of wind and weather. No longer brave or wild as she felt last night, but puny, sun-stunned, tired, hungry. She scurries behind Sam, whose stride loosens as they leave Sweetwater behind.

For five years Lucy let more and more of herself be buried. Sank into Sweetwater's slow life like a mule in quicksand, too stupid to notice till it was half-drowned. While Sam, wandering, grew only more into Sam. Learning how to run, how to survive, how to escape dogs, how to spot who means them harm.

"You can still turn back," Sam says.

Lucy glares. She slaps her hands into the mud. A familiar smell coats her, like the waters in mining country. Once she drank it down complaining. Now she makes herself breathe deep. She's choosing this mud, as she's choosing this life. She can no longer avoid the harder truths.

She asks, "Did you really aim to miss that banker?"

"No."

"Why'd you lie?"

"I figured you'd leave me if I told."

It's Lucy's turn to say, "I'm sorry." Words alone seem insufficient. Remembering what Sam did in the boardinghouse, she sticks out her hand. "Pardners?"

She half meant it as a joke, but Sam's grown-up face is solemn. Sam grips beyond Lucy's hand, at her wrist, fingers finding the vein. Lucy finds Sam's vein in turn. She waits till their blood grows peaceful, till their heartbeats match. They're starting over.

"I promise I'm not leaving," Lucy says.

"I know that now. Just—" Sam swallows. "I figured you'd run too. Because you look so much like her."

"Who?" There's a queer whistling in Lucy's head, though no wind stirs. Her hands and feet gone cold. She lets go of Sam.

"I tried to tell you, ages ago. By the river. Ba told me and I figure you deserve to know too. Ma left us."

Lucy laughs. Can't quite manage carefree. It's the old **ha-ha-ha**s of her childhood that heave up, the sound of cracked heat. Sam starts to speak, but Lucy puts her hands over her ears and walks downstream.

Alone Lucy pitches stones in the water. When tiredness makes her pause, her reflection in the still waters makes her start again.

She looks like her.

Lucy knew for years that Ba was a dead man walking after that storm. Now she knows what killed him, sure as whiskey, sure as the coal dust in his lungs. Ma put a wound in him that festered over three years.

"Sorry," Lucy says. If Ba's haint hears, it stays quiet.

Beauty is a weapon, Ma said. **Don't be beholden**, Ma said. **My smart one**, Ma said. **Rich in choices**, Ma said. Ma who split up the gold as she split up the family. Lucy remembers the pouch hidden between Ma's breasts. It was empty when the jackals got to it—but it wasn't always.

Slow and stupid, eight years too late, Lucy thinks of how Ma took a handkerchief from that pouch the night the jackals came. How she held it over her mouth. How her cheek was swollen on one side, and how she didn't open her lips again that night. How quickly that swelling went down—a swelling big as a small egg, big as a piece of gold tucked in the cheek of a woman smart enough to hide it there. The jackals never found Lucy's nugget, which was more than enough for one ticket.

All these years Lucy carried Ma's love like an incantation against the harder things. Now it's become a burden. No wonder Sam leaves certain truths unspoken. Lucy sinks her head between her knees. Why did Sam tell her now?

And then, as her blood whooshes between her ears, as her head droops heavy, she remembers Ma's trunk. The weight of it, which Sam lifted onto Nellie alone. Sam carried the burden of Ba's love too—and Lucy didn't help shoulder it that day. She should have. She should have stood her ground, should have stayed—that day, and the other day by the riverbank five years back, and this day. She should always have stayed with Sam. She stands. Throws a last stone into the water, breaking that image into fragments. It's just water. She runs back the way she came.

She's almost too late. Sam is packing up the campsite.

"I thought—" Sam says, the old reproach, the old guilt and old secrets and old ghosts rising. How to bury them?

Lucy pulls a knife from Sam's pack. Asks if Sam will cut her hair.

Lucy is afraid as she kneels with Sam behind her. Not of the knife—of herself. These last years, her wiry hair grew in smooth and sleek at last, as Ma said it would. What if she proves as vain as Ma? As selfish?

She closes her eyes so as not to see it. As the hanks fall free, a space opens on her neck. A lightness.

There is, she is coming to see, a place that exists between the world Ba pursued and the world Ma wanted. His a lost world, doomed to make the present and future dim in comparison. Hers so narrow it could accommodate only one. A place Lucy and

Sam might arrive at together. Almost a new kind of land.

Sam pauses midway. "Should I stop? I can't see."

Complete dark. The jackal hour, the hour of uncertainty, is past. Lucy can't recall what creature this hour belongs to.

"Keep going."

When Sam is done, Lucy stands. A great weight off her head. The last of her old hair slithers from her lap. She remembers: this is the hour of the snake. Her hair twists on the ground, limp, never half so important as she believed it to be. She makes to kick it. Sam holds her back.

Sam commences to dig.

Lucy joins once she understands. Ma wasn't wrong, just as Ma wasn't right. Beauty is a weapon, one that can strangle its wielder. It turned against Sam, and against Lucy. Down into the grave they lay that long, shining hair that Ma intended to pass to both her daughters. Before they tamp the dirt, Sam drops in a piece of silver.

Lucy wakes early. Springs a hand to her head. Warily, she approaches the stream.

Her hair's been shorn to an inch below her ears, the same length all around. Not a man's cut, not a woman's. Not even a girl's. A cut like a bowl turned upside down. Up till the age of five, this was the cut Lucy and Sam wore before they wore a girl's braids.

She smiles. Her reflection smiles back. Her face is reshaped, her chin looking stronger. This is the cut of a child, androgynous still, who can grow to be anything. She takes Sam's meaning.

Swinging her new hair, Lucy gets breakfast on. There's meat in Sam's pack, and tubers, dried berries. A few sticks of candy. And two surprises.

The first is a pistol, so much like Ba's that Lucy nearly drops it. She makes herself hold it out. Surprising how it fits to her palm, how it cools and quiets. She lays it carefully back.

The second thing she cooks.

Sam raises an eyebrow at the porridge made of horse oats, but doesn't complain. They pass the tasteless mush between them.

"I've been thinking about that land beyond the ocean again," Lucy says when they're done. "What makes a home a home? Tell me a story I can dream on."

If Lucy were a gambler, she'd bet their blood beat the same rhythm now.

"It's got mountains," Sam says, haltingly. "Not like these mountains. Where we're going the mountains are soft and green, old and full of mist. The cities around them are built with low red walls."

Sam's voice is rising, lilting. As if windows have

been cut in a room that previously had none. Once, Anna showed Lucy an instrument her father had sent. A tube that started out thin, opened at the end into a flower. Pegs and holes along its length. The first note Lucy blew screeched, as harsh as the train. But the second—once Anna fiddled with the pegs, pulled free a plug of dust—the second note was high and clear and singing. Sam's voice does that. It **opens**.

"They make lanterns from paper instead of glass. So the light on the streets is always red-tinted. They wear their hair braided long, even the men. They've got buffalo too, only theirs are smaller, and gentled, and used to carry water. And they've got tigers. Just the same as our tigers."

The Sam who speaks is high and sweet. A child emerging from beneath five years of grit.

"Why do you hide it?" Lucy says.

Sam coughs. Tugs at the bandana. Says, low and hoarse once more, "This **is** my voice. Men don't take me seriously otherwise."

"It's such a shame, though. You shouldn't have to hide yourself—not all men, surely, the good ones . . ."

"There aren't any good ones."

"What about the men you traveled with? The cowboys, or the adventurers, or the mountain man we met?"

"Not him, either. Not once he found out."

"Sam?"

"He only did what Charles wanted to do to you." Sam shrugs. "What men do to girls. I won't get mistaken again."

Lucy remembers the mountain man's hunger. The prick of his eyes on her body. She touches Sam's shoulder. But whatever windows opened when Sam spoke of the new land have slammed shut. There is the faintest of shivers through Sam, hidden by the motion of Sam leaping up to clear the breakfast things.

"Doesn't matter anyhow," Sam says, setting the pan down with a resounding clang. "We're going far away. I've been searching to settle all these years, across the territories, and no place has ever been right. Took me a long time to figure why. I'm ready for a piece of land of our own. Not a place where we'll have to look over our shoulders, not stolen, not belonging to buffalo or Indians, not used-up. This time, we'll go where no one will question our buying it."

Sam unbuttons the first few buttons of that red shirt. A flash of bandages over narrow chest— and then Sam takes out a wallet. Shakes its contents free.

Sam's secret, like all their family's secrets, is gold.

There are flakes like the one Sam used as payment in Sweetwater. Two nuggets near as big as what Lucy found all those years ago. And every size in between. Sam has more than enough for two tickets. To most, this gold would look like luck itself. Lucy shrinks back. She knows better.

"Where'd you get it, Sam?"

"Told you. I worked."

But they worked half their lives. Their bodies are still marked by it. The calluses, the blue flecks of coal. The hurt. That's what they got for half a lifetime of work.

"Sam, I know we said no questions, but this— I have to know—"

Sam looks away. No—Sam **flinches**. As if Lucy's words are blows. The shiver that started at the mention of the mountain man hasn't ended. Despite the clothes, Sam looks for a moment more like Ma than ever—that sadness running beneath strength, like the underground shush of an unseen river. Hasn't Lucy caused enough harm with her questions? She bites her tongue. Look at Sam's body now, and for all its height she sees only vulnerabilities. The bandana that hides the soft throat. The pants over the secret pocket, the shirt buttoned high despite the heat. How precarious Sam seems, hidden by mere cloth.

And so Lucy chooses quiet. By the time they set out, Sam's hands are once more steady. They leave that question buried, as they leave the other two graves. What difference will it make in any case, once they're far enough to make this land, and the story of how they left it, mere history?

Gold

West for the last time. The same mountains, the same pass.

And then the hills, the hills.

In reverse they chart their own course. The prospecting sites, the coal mines. Same and yet changed, as they are same and yet changed.

Old sites litter the grass like broken beads. Travel goes quicker than the last time. Maybe on account of what they've left behind, maybe on account of their longer legs. Maybe on account of their rushing toward a place they want to be. What makes a home a home? The bones, the grass, the sky bleached white at its edges from heat—familiar and yet not, as if, flipping through an old book read once upon a time, they find the pages disordered, the colors melted by sun and years, the story misremembered. So that each morning dawns both known and surprising: a smoking mine, a town no larger than one crossroads and two boys loitering, white bone, a town all ashes with tiger prints in its crust, another crossroads with two girls one tall one short, a choked stream, another crossroads, a mound in the sighing grass, a stream blackened yet running, a mound in the singing grass where something might be buried, a mine where wildflowers have grown over broken earth, another crossroads, another saloon, another morning, another night, another high noon with sweat stinging their squinted eyes, another crossroads, another dusk with the wind seeming to whisper over an unmarked mound in the weeping grass where something might be buried, another crossroads, another crossroads, another crossroads, gold, grass, grass, grass, gold, grass, gold—

Maybe the travel goes quicker on account of the two horses Sam steals. **Sister**, one is named, and the other, **Brother**. Sam swings in, then out, of the trading post. They've ridden half a day before Lucy sees the weight of Sam's wallet: as plump as before.

"They're ours," Sam calls back through the wind of their passage. "We've paid our dues."

Lucy lets loose a string of cusses. The grass swallows them, nodding assent. She knows what Sam means. How can they be beholden? How can they be any more outside the law? That law a treacherous thing, twisting to sink fangs into them however it can. Better to make their own rules, as Sam always has. Anyhow, they're leaving.

Gold grass gold grass gold grass gold grass gold

Maybe the travel goes quicker on account of their running from pursuers. At the horizon the dry heat shivers, as if trying to lift off. Sun-blinded, her shorter hair lashing her cheeks—Lucy sees shapes, not all of them real. At the corner of her eye: A wagon? A figure waving? A dark silhouette? Look straight on and there's nothing. Sam keeps a hand on the gun and squints for debt collectors in black. Twice they cross paths with Indian travelers and Sam dismounts to speak to them, learning that they, chased out, are searching too. Lucy does what Ma never would have: she greets them shyly, follows Sam in sharing their meager food. Their hands, dipping into one stewpot, are dusty, yes, hard-used, yes—but if at first Lucy flinches back, soon enough she sees that her own are no cleaner. In their weary faces a familiar exhaustion and hope. She eats.

At other times she hears the screams of children playing on the wind when she and Sam are quite alone. What makes a ghost a ghost? Can a person be haunted by herself?

Gold grass gold grass gold grass gold grass

Maybe the travel goes quicker on account of the stories Sam tells at the campfire. No longer smooth—Sam's adventuring stories peel back night by night. Sam tells of the Southern desert where the bite from a dragon lizard festered till a man died blackened like a weeks-old corpse. Of how men looted that ancient Indian city they found, smashed the pots and pissed in the graves, but out of a crevice in the cliffs Sam found white flowers that bloomed at night and woke the camp with scent. Of how in the North a freeze leapt down and iced half the cattle where they stood, and in the blinding snow some men went crazy and ran out stark naked and some men drew beautiful shapes in the drifts and some men called Sam **chink**. More rarely Sam speaks of the job with the gold men, where Sam learned the new ways of prospecting with weapons that blast hills to dust, and befriended men and women black and brown and red, and learned the names of their tribes and lands. But in the telling of these gold stories Sam's face darkens, Sam's gaze skitters as if fearing the boom of dynamite, till Sam's voice fades and Sam gulps whiskey.

Gold grass gold grass gold grass gold

Maybe the travel goes quicker on account of the two of them being more alike than Lucy remembers. Same and yet changed. On the day Lucy tears her skirt, Sam draws needle quicker than gun. Lucy admires the clever stitchwork that affixes the bandana at Sam's throat and keeps the buttons on Sam's shirt from popping. Sam attentive to clothes despite a disdain for skirts, as if saying, with each tug of the needle, **What people see shapes how**

they treat you. Meanwhile Lucy learns the hunter's trade. Hitches her shift high with no shame and no eyes around, and chases down rabbits, squirrels, partridges with flashing spots. A few times she pulls on Sam's spare pants. Run quick enough and she can shuck the weight of herself, as she once did by floating in a river. They catch so much game they eat only the good dark meat and leave the lean for the jackals. A grateful howling spools behind.

They both talk, slowly, of the life they'll have beyond the ocean. Laying their dreams out on the table, cautious at first, spooked as poker players showing their cards at the long game's end. Lucy intends to stay on their land with only wind and grass to talk to. Sam wants to venture into the crowded streets, taste the fish, haggle with the merchants. **Aren't you sick of being looked at? / But over there they won't just look. They'll actually see me.**

Gold grass gold grass gold grass

Maybe the travel goes quicker on account of the gambling games Sam teaches to pass the time. This should worry Lucy—Sam's love for a fortune that rests on a stroke of luck. But she puts the old fears aside. She learns poker and checkers, how to lean forward with cards held close so that the man across the table will watch her chest and not her bluff.

Gold grass gold grass gold

Maybe the travel goes quicker on account of the buffalo. One moment they're riding, next moment the light is half-gone. They look up through shadow. There it is. As if a piece of the hills has shifted, stepped close. Does either one breathe? Even the wind hangs still. Ancient thing with its pelt gone blond at the tips, brown body fringed with gold. Its hooves are wider than Lucy's hand. She raises hers to compare. Keeps it raised in greeting. And then the buffalo is moving, blowing its sweet grass breath, and its coat brushes her palm. At her side, Sam holds a hand up too. The buffalo passes, melting back into the hills that have its color and shape.

I thought they were dead. / Me too.

Gold grass gold grass

Maybe the travel goes quicker on account of the land growing more familiar, the shapes of the hills each morning better fitted to the shapes in Lucy's dreams. One day they hit a piece of trail and she knows with a force like a fist in her gut what will come round the bend: a rocky outcrop, wild garlic in the shade, a stream's crooked elbow where she once found a dead snake.

Lucy dismounts and makes Sam follow on foot, swearing and sweating, to the crest of a hill. She tells Sam to look up. The clouds begin to circle, them two at the center. Once, Lucy was taught to look from fear of being lost. But now she teaches Sam to look for beauty. As Sam's impatience shifts to awe, the land shifts too. Same and yet changed.

Gold grass gold

Maybe the travel goes quicker on account of Lucy feeling a sorrow kin to love. Because though these dry yellow hills yielded nothing but pain and sweat and misplaced hope—she knows them. A part of her is buried in them, a part of her lost in them, a part of her found and born in them—so many parts belong to this land. An ache in her chest like the tug of a dowsing rod. Across the ocean the people will look like them, but they won't know the shapes of these hills, or the soughing of grass, or the taste of muddy water—all these things that shape Lucy within as her eyes and nose shape her without. Maybe the travel goes quicker on account of Lucy mourning, already, the loss of this land.

But she'll have Sam.

Gold grass

Maybe the travel goes quicker on account of Sam's unease hurrying them along. Sam of two faces: bold and grinning straight-on; at other times twitchy, hard-lipped, glancing round. This second Sam looks at Lucy with a mouth that opens and closes, as if a man pushes uncertainly at the door of a room he fears to enter. **Tiger got your tongue? / It's nothing.** This second Sam starts at the merest rustle, the whuff of their horses settling down at night. This Sam sleeps little, sleeps sitting up. Enters a saloon only to dash out, pop-eyed, saying the man in the back—fat, bald, harmless—looks wrong. Lucy vows to ask, later—when words aren't quite so dangerous, so liable to make Sam shake—why Sam lives so cautious. But that can wait till they're on the ship with the ocean wide around them, and they have all the time in the world to learn a new language, one that hasn't hurt them.

Gold

Salt

The end of the West. Here. A fist of land that punches into ocean, atop which men have built a town so big some name it **City**.

This land like no land Lucy has seen before. Fog greets them, curling and obscuring, making of the coast a damp gray dream. Soft and hard all at once. The wildflowers, the wind-bent cypresses, the pebbles underfoot and the gulls overhead and the boom that Lucy mistakes, at first, for the roar of a beast—till Sam tells her it's the sound of waves against the cliffs.

If this land is like no land, then the water is like no water. Sam takes Lucy down to the wet edge. On foot they cross the sand. The ocean is gray. Ugly under its lid of fog. Look hard enough and there's blue, some green, a spark of distant sunlight. Mostly the water is unconcerned with beauty. Mostly it rages and beats the cliffs till they crumble, plunging unwary creatures to their deaths. The water eats at the posts of the docks, bends that wood to its knees. The water does not reflect. It is itself, and it spreads to the horizon.

Fog fills Lucy's mouth. She licks, and licks again: salty.

"All this time," she says to Sam. "All this time, I thought I belonged in **Sweet**water."

Later she'll learn how hard it is to live at the end of the West. Sometimes the ocean takes a life, sometimes the fog that hides lighthouse beams. Most often it's the hills themselves that are deadly, seven of them in this city, every few years shaking houses loose as a dog shakes fleas. Later she'll learn that down within the sea-foam are bones more numerous than the bones of buffalo. Later she'll learn that when the fog lifts, there comes the hard, clear light.

Sam's gotten only more jittery as they approached the city. Hurry set them down early—their ship won't launch till tomorrow morning.

The remainder of the day stretches before them. Lamps glisten through the fog, and Lucy thinks of the tales Sam has told of this city: the gambling dens like mansions, the shows where men dress as women and women as men and the music is a transformation. And the food.

"We've time to spare," Lucy says. "Let's get a bite to eat."

Sam frowns. Next thing Sam will be talking about taking care, keeping their heads down.

"Come on," Lucy coaxes. "You can't expect we'll spend this whole day hiding in some dark corner. Besides, no one can find us in this fog." She extends an arm to demonstrate. Her hand goes misty at the end. "See? How about we get some of that seafood stew? I could use hot food. Or a hot bath."

"You really want a bath?"

She didn't expect that this, of all things, would sway Sam. On the trail they washed in muddy streams, and never once did Sam spend more than a few seconds in the water. Sam bathed as if scared of wet—Lucy never even saw Sam unclothed.

Lucy nods. She senses another question under this simple one. There are secrets in the air, sharp as the salt.

"We shouldn't," Sam says. Something like yearning breaks through Sam's face. A softness that grew less and less frequent on the trail as Sam drove them faster, harder, onward. "But—"

"We deserve a rest," Lucy says, touching Sam's arm.

Sam gives a jerk of the head. Not quite a nod.

Then Sam is wheeling the horse around, heading down a valley so thick with fog it looks like a bowl of steaming milk. Lucy scrambles to follow.

Fog encircles them. Damp fingers of wind through their hair. The low world murmurs, remembering itself in snatches as fleeting as old dream: a house marked 571, a tree trunk where a marble glints, yellow flowers against a blue wall. A cracked door. The cry of a needy cat. A waiting carriage with its driver folded down in sleep. Condensation against a lit window. A child's ankle, fleeing.

Sam stops before a red building so long its edges disappear into fog. A strange building, windowless and featureless save for one high door. Sam turns to Lucy. Not narrow-eyed, but beseeching.

"Remember, you asked," Sam says, and the door opens.

Later, Lucy will try to remember this first sight. How rich the red house seems, how endless. The dark-stained wood, the drapes and carpets, the candles set low so that their light doesn't reach the ceiling. The building inside disappears into shadow as the building outside disappears into fog. There's a rustling in the room, though there are no windows.

Instead, there are girls.

Seven girls line up against the far wall. Each stands against a square of paint. They look like drawings of princesses in storybooks, gilt-framed. And their dresses—

Lucy steps closer. She's never seen dresses like these, not even in the magazines Anna got from back East. These dresses aren't made for walking or running or riding or even sitting or staying warm. Only for beauty. The nearest girl could have stepped from Lucy's history book. A solemn drawing with this caption: **Last of the Indian princesses**. This girl is just as solemn, as doe-eyed, as fierce of cheek and black of hair. She wears feathers, and deerskin so buttery Lucy's fingers itch to touch.

There is a smell in the room, close and bitter and sweet. It deepens as a woman all in black sweeps toward them. She leans **down** to kiss Sam's cheek because she stretches tall, as her full skirt stretches wide. Hard here to find her edges. In this building, around this woman, a perpetual jackal hour.

The woman says, "Samantha." To Lucy's surprise Sam doesn't scowl. The two bend their heads together, private. They walk off, leaving Lucy to examine the rest of the girls alone.

Beside the Indian princess is a girl with the look of the dark vaqueros from the desert to the South. She wears an embroidered white dress that puffs from her tiny waist. Her brown shoulders show above the fabric. The next girl is white-blond, her eyes rabbit-pink. Her dress is thinner than Lucy's shift, thin enough that Lucy blushes. The next girl is darker than the walls, with a blue gleam to her skin. Gold rings stack her throat into a proud column. The next girl has thick wheaten hair in two braids, her cheeks pink apples, her eyes robins' eggs, a milk pail at her feet. None of the girls move. If not for the slight rise of their chests, they might be statues. And the next girl—

"Pretty, aren't they?" the tall woman asks, stepping beside Lucy. "Give the visitor a whirl, girls."

The seven skirts flare, but the faces don't move.

"What do they make you think of?" the woman asks.

Something about her imperious tone makes Lucy answer. Maybe it's just the smell of her. Lucy tells her about the stories in Ma's books, the drawn princesses.

"You're as clever as Samantha promised. My name is Elske. Will you be partaking too?"

"I'd like a bath," Lucy says.

Elske's smile is thin enough to slice. She tells Lucy to choose any girl she likes. The girls spin once more. As long, Elske says, as Lucy can pay.

And then Lucy understands. This place may look rich, but it's no different from the rooms above the saloons in Sweetwater, the creak of those beds that mingled with the train's whistle. The murkiness hides Lucy's blush. She hangs back as Sam confers again with Elske, as Sam leads a girl up the stairs. Sam doesn't look back this time, and Lucy is glad for it.

———

Lucy dozes, waiting. A clatter stirs her. A girl has set down a tray of food: bread, jerky. And a bowl of leaves topped with a strange orange flower that crunches in her teeth.

Sweet, woody. It's a carved carrot.

Years ago, Lucy boiled water to rinse the sickness from Sam's body. Yet when she found the carrot in Sam's pants, Sam looked at her with hate. That carrot was replaced with a rock. What's replaced the rock now? Lucy doesn't know. But in the rooms above, a stranger unknots Sam's bandana to expose Sam's throat. A stranger undoes the shirt and pants with their special stitching. A stranger lays aside Sam's secret—a stranger who knows Sam more fully than Lucy does.

Lucy overheard a part of the bargaining before Sam went up. The room, the length of time, the girl, the price—almost a quarter of Sam's gold. Sam lied. What bath could cost so dear?

Lucy marches to the girls in their pretty frames. When they stand unmoving, she grabs the nearest skirt. The rip carries through the hush, loud as a scream. Beautiful faces turn to her, for the first time losing their practiced stillness. Anger greets Lucy, and affront, fear, amusement, scorn. These girls looked at and through her when she entered. Now she thinks of what Sam said on the trail: the difference between being looked at and **seen**.

She raises the torn fabric. She asks for Elske.

———

Elske's private room is plain. Two chairs, a desk, lamps in place of candles. And more books than Lucy has ever seen, stacked to the ceiling.

"Samantha said you were formidable," Elske says when Lucy refuses the offered seat. "People like us often are."

"I'm not—"

"I mean gold folk. The city is filled with them. These establishments were intended for men with money and desire. They value the finest restaurants. The finest gambling houses. The finest pipe dens to smoke and dream the finest dreams. My first and most generous investors were gold men. They're remarkably open-minded, in that way. They care only for value."

"Tell me what Sam does here."

"Sam tells me you're quite the reader. Can you read this?"

Elske takes a book down from her shelf, and Lucy accepts it without thinking. The cover is blank blue cloth, stained with blooms of white. Wrinkled pages. An ocean's memory seeped through them: salt water.

Lucy opens it.

There are no words on the first page. Just a strange drawing. She flips. More drawings, much smaller, laid out in columns as orderly as words.

They **are** words, she realizes. Each drawing is a word formed from straight lines and curved ones, dots and dashes. She stops at a drawing she recognizes. Ma's tiger.

And then Elske takes the blue book back.

"Where did you get that?" Lucy has forgotten anger.

"From a client, as partial payment. Information can be as valuable as gold. And so, to your question—I'm not in the habit of giving facts away for free, but I might accept a trade."

Lucy hesitates. She nods.

"Say something." Elske leans forward. "From where you and Samantha come from. Anything."

Lucy doesn't say, **We were born here**. The greed on Elske's face won't be satisfied by truth. She knows what value this woman sees in her—the same value Charles saw. Only Lucy's difference. She speaks the first words that come to her. "Nu er."

Elske sighs. "How very beautiful. How very precious and rare." Her head tips back, her throat exposed. Something nearly indecent about it. And then she straightens, saying, "Samantha worked for the gold men for a time. Quite successfully, it was said. I heard of a falling-out, but didn't ask. I still count many gold men among my clients and I don't like to get between their affairs. You see, hundreds come to buy time with my girls. Each young woman is highly paid and educated, whether in painting or poetry or conversation. Do you know what a harp is? I possess the only one in the territory. My girls are lovely and accomplished. They're highly valued, not common, not—"

The smell is stronger in this closed room. The lap and lull of Elske's voice drowsy-making. All of it a spell. The only way to break it is to remember anger.

"Whores," Lucy interrupts. "You want to say they're not common whores. I'm not a customer. Please get to your point."

"Very well. You asked what Samantha does here? The only service Samantha requests is a bath."

Elske's face is sleek and pleased. She knew the trade would be unequal. The truth she gives Lucy is like an emptied-out box—its contents were already in Lucy's possession. Sam doesn't hide. Sam's been Sam all along.

Lucy turns to go, feeling a fool.

"I was once a teacher," Elske says gently, and curiosity keeps Lucy in the room. "Samantha told me you were an excellent student. If you'll permit me a teacherly question—earlier, when you likened my girls to stories. Why did you say that?"

"They're blank," Lucy says, looking at the blue book. Maybe if she answers to Elske's liking, she can trade for another look at it. She thinks of the girls with their still faces, each different and yet precisely the same. "They remind me of pages." Or clear water. A look Lucy has seen sometimes in her own reflection.

She waits there, hoping, and Elske asks one more question.

Sam returns fresh but wary. Jaw stiff. This time Lucy keeps her gaze direct. She smiles, till Sam smiles shyly back.

"Until next time," Elske says, kissing Sam's cheek.

When Elske kisses Lucy too, the smell comes stronger than ever before. As if the woman chews it and swallows it. Bitter and sweet. Mixed with the heat of Elske's body, it grows musky too. At last Lucy recognizes it. So much like the smell of Ma's trunk. Distant places, a very long time ago. Did another of Elske's clients bring the scent as he brought the book?

"Come back with or without Samantha," Elske whispers while Sam looks on with curiosity. "Don't forget."

But wind and salt scour them. By the time they reach the harbor, Lucy's nose knows only ocean.

The ships spread below.

All her life Lucy imagined ships as fantastical things. She was told their sails were wings, that coasts appeared from water as if by magic. And so she failed to question the facts of a ship's making, as she failed to question dragons and tigers and buffalo. She never expected that ships would look this way: grand yet ordinary.

"What makes a ship a ship?" she asks. She shouts the answer, over and over, bouncing on her heels like a child. "Wood and water. Wood and water. **Wood and water**."

Gold

Slick underfoot, the dock sways. Lucy imagines herself thrown into the gray waters, looking up from the harbor's bottom. Sea grass waving. Fish so thick they block the light.

The ship's captain is steady on his feet while Lucy and Sam stumble, disadvantaged already when they request two tickets. The captain counts their coin and looks at them when he's done. Elske told true: this city sees only a person's value.

"Come back when you've got the rest."

Sam's face darkens. "I asked you about the price last month."

"Seas change. Repairs are costly."

Sam empties the wallet. The last of the gold was meant for tonight's lodging, and a place to stay across the ocean. Still the captain shakes his head. He tosses the pouch back, a nugget bouncing to the dock. Sam ducks to retrieve it, the captain already looking past. Lucy follows his gaze to a tall figure at the shore. Likely that person seeks passage too. What can she offer beyond coin?

And she thinks: a story.

She trips. Clutches the captain's arm for balance. She steps clumsily back on the hem of her skirt, fabric pulling tight over her chest.

"I'm sorry," Lucy says, lurching against the captain. "It makes me dizzy to see a real ship. I've wanted to ride one since I was a little girl. Isn't it majestic?"

She looks yearningly at the ship. When she looks back at the captain, some of the yearning remains. She tells about her fear of the ocean. Her hope of a strong, seasoned man to guide them. Her helpfulness. Her cookery. Sam's strength. "We could be of service," she says, and smiles, and pauses, and lets his eyes drag on her silence.

Elske's girls didn't shock her. Not truly. What she saw wasn't new, but an old, old lesson, learned in Sweetwater, learned at the door of a long-ago parlor from her very first teacher. **Beauty is a weapon**.

Down the dock the figure has gone.

When, in the end, Lucy mentions their horses, the captain hands over two tickets. The paper is damp, the penmanship exquisite. Someone has taken care to edge the letters in gold.

———

A ways down the harbor, Sam punches a fist into the packet of food Elske gave them.

"She charged me extra today," Sam says. "Damn her, she always knows how to press. Otherwise we wouldn't have had to bargain like that."

Lucy shrugs. She's thinking of the blue book, and how she'll get more like it when they arrive. She tosses a strip of jerky to Sam and commences to gnaw her own. Sam twists the strip till it breaks.

"Did she teach you that?" Sam says.

Lucy takes her time chewing. "She didn't teach me anything most girls don't already know. She's not all bad. You know . . . she offered me a job."

On Sam's face, a shattered look.

"Not that kind," Lucy says quickly. "Not like the other girls. She wanted me to work telling stories. Talking to men, nothing more." She doesn't say how Elske added, **Unless you'd like to. There's extra payment for that.**

She expects Sam to rage. Instead, Sam sags.

"She made me an offer like that the first time," Sam says, voice so small that Lucy knows Sam thinks again of the mountain man.

"Bao bei," Lucy begins, then stops. Not the time for tenderness, now. Not the time to pick at old wounds. She rips into the hard bread. Shards of crust dig under her nails as she tears a hunk free.

"None of what came before matters, alright? Once we have water behind us, it'll be like—like—" A long-ago promise fills her mouth. Sweet and bitter. "Like a dream. We'll wake up there and all this will have been a dream."

"You mean it?" Sam says, voice still shrunken. "Everything we did before?"

Lucy considers the bread. It's half-stale. They should force it down and swallow it. They should be grateful for the little they have. But. But.

She heaves the bread into the ocean, where it splashes out farther than she thought possible. And though the gulls swoop and dive, it's a fish that rises up to claim it, longer than Lucy is tall. It could block out the sun if seen from below.

At noon their ship will sail. Till then, the night stretches before them. Apart from a few pennies in Sam's pocket, they've got no coin for beds or meals. One last night in the open, the city's hills around them.

That last night they are ghosts. Half of them already on the ship, halfway toward that misty place they will call home. Half disappeared as fog swallows the dock and frees them of mortal weights: the weight of missing gold, five lost years, two silver dollars, Ba's hands, Ma's words. That night they agree: what came before has vanished. Fog obscures.

Through it, only the clink of their pennies as they sit playing gambling games.

For years after, Lucy will hold this night close to her chest. A private history, written only for herself.

Other players gather. Faces blurred by mist so that no one can ask, **Who are you? Where are you from?** Hard men and women, shoulders in a familiar slump, stained with sweat and whiskey and tobacco. The stink of work and despair. And hope. So much hope gleaming on that wet dock.

That night not a word is exchanged. This city has a language of clink and jingle. Their pennies started the game; their luck keeps them in. Lucy sits in the circle, Sam behind her. When Lucy reaches for the facedown cards she feels a heaviness that calls her hand, tugs her heart. Aims her like a dowsing rod to the right card again and again. She plays with eyes closed. Tapping her feet. She's not on the dock but walking the gold of the hills in the early morning, in the early years, the best years, when Ba's hands held only hope and a dowsing rod. They walked out, but the plume of Ma's cook fire kept them anchored to home. Ba taught her to wait for the tug. Because gold was heavy, she needed something heavy inside her to call to it. **Think of the saddest thing you can. Don't tell me. Keep it inside, Lucy girl. Let it grow.** Among the gamblers, that's just what Lucy does. Sam's hands on her shoulders lend the weight of what Sam carries too. Prospector's children, both of them. **Why, you feel**

where it is, Lucy girl. You just feel it. They swallowed sadness and they swallowed gold. Neither left their bodies but grew within them, nourishing their lengthening limbs. And that night it calls to the cards. Every card Lucy draws is the right one. The other gamblers lay down their hands one by one, in a hush. As if paying respects before a grave. They look at the two strangers in the fog and without faces to judge by—they **see**. Call it luck or call it a kind of haunting.

By the end of the night, a small fortune mounds high.

This is what Lucy will remember on the worst of the days to come: that for one night, at least, they made the hills hold gold.

Silver light pries Lucy awake. For a moment she's twelve again, moonlight ringing off a tiger's skull. **What makes a home a home?**

She lifts her head. A card peels from her cheek. The light comes from a stack of silver dollars. Sam snores beside her on the dock. The harbor is empty but for the anchored ships, a few hours left till noon. Lucy grins, watching a bubble of spit form at the corner of Sam's mouth. She leans to pop it.

The burst shakes the world.

A hole has opened in the dock. A ragged mouth of wood, hungry ocean churning beneath. Sam scrambles. A foot, a leg, slip into the breach. Lucy screams, pulls. Drags Sam away, a hairsbreadth from falling.

Fog's burned off. The sky has a different aspect. A hard, clear light. It shows two men at the end of the dock. One is tall and dressed in black. He holds the gun he fired—so burnished by day that the sun off metal pains her. At long last Lucy has seen the gun such men are rumored to carry. Anna claimed otherwise—but there are things Anna's kind are blind to.

Sam doesn't look at the hired man, or the gun. Sam watches the figure who shambles up behind. An older man, slow, enormously fat and bald. He wears white. The only color is in his cheeks, in the gold on his ringed fingers and dripping from his vest.

"We can sort this out," Lucy says to the hired man.

Not a soul pays her mind. The fat man draws a heavy gold pocket watch from his vest. He taps its face. Looks past Lucy. Straight to Sam. "Imagine my pleasure last night when my man informed me of your return. Now let's settle up."

The coins they won last night are filthy with gunpowder, diminished by day. Inconsequential beside the debt the gold man names.

Lucy starts to laugh.

At last the gold man looks at her. The slow look of a man with all the time in the world. At her shorn hair, at her dirty shift, and finally at her throat. His look disassembles her. He doesn't smile or frown, explain or menace. She understands why Sam fled from saloons where a bald head shone. This gold man is a rock. Impermeable to pleading.

And so when Lucy speaks again, she uses the language of coin. She offers last night's winnings to buy time alone with Sam.

When the two men have retreated a ways down the harbor, Lucy grabs Sam's face.

"What did you **do**, Sam?"

"I only took the gold back. What they took from honest prospectors. There was a group of us together; we agreed."

The amount the gold man named could buy ships. Half a dozen coal mines. Far beyond what Lucy had imagined.

"What did you spend it on?" Surely they can use it to bargain. Whatever goods Sam bought must have more worth than the spread of Sam's brains on this dock.

"I didn't spend it."

"You hid it?" A trickle of hope. Sam can lead the gold man to the stash. That and Lucy's best apologies might do the trick after all. They'll miss today's ship, but there's always next month's. Next year's. They'll find work in the city. Lucy will accept Elske's offer to tell stories. They'll make do.

"It was pure gold. Too heavy to take along." Sam's

chin lifts. Sap begins to rise in Sam's voice. "I split some with the others. Kept what you saw. Then I had an idea—we agreed to dump the rest into the ocean. We gave it back to the land to keep, and we all left something." There flashes over Sam's face that old grin. "Each of us carved a piece of gold. Some wrote their mother's names, or the old names of rivers, or the marks of their tribes. I carved our tiger. That gold won't wash up for ages and ages. Maybe next time someone honest will find it— someone like us. Maybe things'll be different by then. Either way, the gold men will be dead. And the gold will be marked. It'll be **ours**."

You belong here too, Lucy girl. Never let them tell you otherwise.

Sam rolls backward on the dock, overcome with a fit of the giggles—silly as the girl Sam never was. "Dead just like the buffalo!"

No amount of bargaining or planning, no amount of smarts will get that gold back. And yet they've got to try. Lucy says, "We'll ask for time. We'll—"

The giggling stops. "They killed two of the others. My friends. And they killed Nellie. Shot her out from under me when I fled." Sam's voice cracks over the mare's name. "This ain't some game. Quit acting a child. They'll kill me, but I figure they'll let you go if you don't raise a fuss."

"If you knew—" Lucy chokes on the question.

"If you knew they were this dangerous, why'd you risk going all the way to Sweetwater? You could've taken a ship weeks ago. Alone."

Stubborn, Sam is. Won't answer. Only looks at Lucy with speaking eyes. The question Sam asked in Sweetwater fills the silence between them. **Don't you ever get lonely?** All along she called Sam selfish. Turns out it was Lucy who couldn't see past herself—who didn't ask the same.

A thing she learned gambling was when to fold her cards down. She lets go the other questions. She could ask why Sam insisted on carrying this burden alone, why Sam didn't tell her when Sam had a chance, why Sam's so damn proud. So stubborn. But. All this is as much a part of Sam as the bandana and the boots, Sam who lives by different, unbent rules—Sam who could take a fortune and dump it in the ocean. Lucy folds down her anger and her fear. What's left is the old, tired-out feeling of arriving at the end of a long trail to a dirty house.

And then it floats up, the last question that matters. "Why baths?"

Sam shrugs. Lucy yanks hard at the bandana. It slips, showing skin two shades lighter. So soft. This, out of everything, brings the threat of tears close. "You used to hate baths. Tell me why, Sam."

"She looks at me. Renata, that's her name. They don't look at the men who buy time in their beds. You know that? They don't kiss them, or really look. But she looks at me when she's bathing me. She **sees** me. The proper way."

Lucy closes her eyes and tries to see.

She sees Sam, shining.

Sam at seven, shining in dress and braids.

Sam at eleven, shining through loss and grime.

Sam at sixteen, this conviction, these grown-up bones.

She sees the gold. Not what Sam dumped, but the other kind. These hills. These streams. Shining too, despite their history, with a value more than metal. So much lost from this place. So much stolen. And yet the land is beautiful to them, because it was their home too. Sam, in Sam's own way, tried to give that land a proper burial.

All that, Lucy can accept. The dead hills, the dead rivers. She'd shoot the last buffalo clear in the heart if it could save Sam.

Not Sam.

Lucy's whole life, Sam was undimmed. That, she can't see: the world without Sam in it.

Lucy opens her eyes. She reties the bandana. Hiding, once more, the tenderest part of Sam.

"Let me try talking to him alone," Lucy says. "I'm the clever one, remember? I can figure something."

Gold

Alone, she bargains with the gold man.

First they pretend to offer what the other won't accept.

She offers the debt paid at sundown, in gold, if he'll let them go off and collect it.

He offers a cloak made from Sam's skin.

She offers double the debt paid tomorrow morning.

He offers Sam's limbs broken into pretty shapes.

She offers a game of cards, right then and there, for triple the debt.

He offers Sam's lying tongue cut out and served to her.

She offers her loyalty. Her smarts. Her clean hands.

He offers Sam's hands chopped and worn as a necklace.

She offers him the services of a prospector's daughter, a knowledge of these hills that she was born to.

He offers her two graves dug so deep in these hills that no one will find them.

They sit in silence, then. A known silence, as if of old friends swapping a story they've each heard before. She examines her hands, her feet, her skin, as if seeing them for the first time. **Always ask why,** she remembers someone telling her. **Always know what part of you they want.**

The gold man accepts her offer immediately. As if he knew the bargain she would strike before she did. Elske might say he saw her value.

And for a small price, a nothing price atop the existing debt, Lucy buys the right to lie.

She meets Sam alone in the shadow of the ship. In a few minutes it'll be noon. In a few minutes the ship will sail.

She tells Sam she's reached an agreement. She'll work for the gold man. A secretary, of sorts, doing sums and writing histories. A year or two, three at most, and she'll pay off the debt. After that she'll take the next ship over.

Sam's chin goes up, the stubbornness in Sam—

There is only one way.

Lucy leans back through the years and hits Sam across the face. Gulls screech and rise in the hard, clear air. The shadows of their wings darken Sam's cheeks. Sam's eyes. When the gulls pass, the mark remains. Lucy learned from the best. How to pivot and how to swing. How to put the whole weight of your body and your good leg and your bad life, yes, your life weighed down by grief as heavy as gold in the silt of your stomach—how to put it all behind a blow. How to then roar and break a person with words, make a person feel small and stupid. **You think you're smarter than me? I'm the one he needs. You're worthless. Go. Git.** How to stroke a face afterward. **Bao bei.**

And she learns that it hurts, deeper than the sting of her palm, to see that person shrink from your touch. Wondering, as Sam boards the ship, if Sam will ever remember her without the shadow of that blow.

Elske observes Lucy's face when she is marched through the red door by the hired man. It's the man Elske listens to, and his explanation of the payment. Elske doesn't ask Lucy this time. Elske only touches.

A hard touch. Elske's hands press through skin to feel the shape of Lucy's bones. She gathers Lucy's hair and tugs, pulls Lucy's lips back from her teeth as if examining a prize horse. Elske mutters, cocks her head, yanks at Lucy's crooked nose. No longer the gentle teacher—that was a story Elske told so well that Lucy believed.

She'll do, Elske says at last to the hired man. **I'll take a cut, of course. And we'll have to wait until she grows out her hair.**

In the three months it takes for Lucy's hair to reach her shoulders, Elske rewrites her. Elske selects a green fabric to tell the story of Lucy's skin as more ivory than yellow, and a high slit to tell of longer legs. Elske consults books—not the blue one, illegible to her, but books written by travelers in her own language. From these and from the remnants of Ma's stories that Elske plucks from Lucy, Elske writes a new tale. Of poured tea and lilting speech, downcast eyes and sweetness, a story as unlike Lucy's own as fool's gold is unlike true gold—but that doesn't matter.

Lucy brings up the original offer, once. Elske doesn't even bother to smile. **That was then, and between us. This trade is on different terms.**

At the end of three months, hair swept into a bun, Lucy steps into her own frame.

As she stands at the wall she thinks of all those silly arguments she had with Sam, stories against the history books. Back when Lucy was young enough to believe in one truth. She says a silent apology.

———

She pays the debt remarkably fast. It's easy. She dug a grave years ago; now she throws into it every Sam and every Lucy that came before. All her soft, rotting parts.

The parts she keeps are her weapons.

The work is easy. The thirst of all men the same thirst. She goes blank when a man points at her. Some want a wife to listen. Some want a daughter to instruct. Some want a mother to hold their head and rock them. Some want a pet, a slave, a statue, a conquest, a hunt. They look, and see only what they want.

It goes easier after she learns how to look back at them. Their faces blur into the same few faces, repeated like suits in a deck of cards. Some men are Charleses, and these she teases and coddles; some are Teacher Leighs, and to these she plays the pupil; some are ship captains to flatter; some are mountain men to accede to; these men, and these men, and these men. Their wants a pattern as predictable as campfire tale, till she can sense the next word, the next need, the next motion of a mouth or hand before it happens.

It goes easier after her nose is broken. She reads one man wrong, and then blood runs hot over her lips. She doesn't wail as Elske does. She's already thinking of how she should have nudged him, how she should have stepped forward instead of back, the words she should have spoken. She'll be smarter next time; no one can say she's not learning.

Her nose breaks in the same place it did many years back. It heals straight, erasing the last mark of her old self. Elske marvels, and after that adds **Lucky** to the story she tells about Lucy. Gold leaf is spun through Lucy's hair. The men choose her more often.

Her debt shrinks.

It goes easier after a man comes that she mistakes for another. Narrow eyes. High cheeks. She lets her eyes fill with herself, for a moment. Then she sees: his hesitant walk, his weak chin. Wrong. Still she undresses him slowly, observing; still she tips her head close to hear him speak. New sounds. Not a Charles, not a teacher, not a sailor, not a gold man, not a mountain man, not a miner, not a cowboy. Something else. A possibility. When he mumbles in his sleep, she lets herself tremble as she puts an ear to his lips. The words she doesn't understand are a comfort.

That man came on a ship along with hundreds more like him. Men with faces like Lucy's, who choose her often. **Lucky**, Elske says again. Because the gold man has revived a long-abandoned project, joining the Western territory to the others with the last leg of a great railroad. He brings shiploads of cheap workers, men only, from across the ocean.

For a time, Lucy is gentler with them. Their

speech a blank to her as her life is a blank to them; and on it, she writes the stories she wishes. **My day is very well**, she says in response to their babbling. **How did you know red is my favorite color too?** One day, there is a man who pays for a bath. Just a bath. **Oh**, she says as she fills the tub, **I should've guessed that you were a prince in your country.** She soaps his back, his broad shoulders, and then— something makes her kiss the part of his hair. He looks up. Her heart beats as his mouth opens. She is certain the next words will be ones she understands despite their two languages.

But he only puts his tongue in her mouth. He upsets the water, overturns the stool, leaving suds on the rug and bruises on Lucy, till Elske comes up with a hired man to remind him, firmly, of the coin it costs for extra services. As he spits and cusses, dragged out soaking and transformed, she realizes: his hair and eyes may be familiar, but he is no different. Another Charles, another mountain man.

She sits a long time watching the water drain. Herself emptying too. Coming to understand that even among faces like hers, she can still be alone.

It goes easier after that.

The ships come, the tracks grow, the hills are razed to hold them. In the Western territory the dry grass blows, torn up at its roots. There are tales of dust storms, though Lucy, in the red building, doesn't see or smell or taste or swallow their grit. All in service of a great railroad to span the continent.

She hears the cheer that goes through the city the day the last railroad tie is hammered. A golden spike holds track to earth. A picture is drawn for the history books, a picture that shows none of the people who look like her, who built it.

The mountain man said that no man in this country could complete the railroad. He was right, after all.

On that day, Lucy claims sickness. She lies in bed. Her eyes closed. Trying to summon up old images. Gold hills. Green grass. Buffalo. Tigers. Rivers. Trying to remember any story but the ones she spends her days selling. The images flicker like mirage, gone the moment she gets close. She stares as long as she is able, mourning what she can before it slips away.

The trains have killed an age.

It goes easier after Elske gives her a gift. Or rather, Lucy earns it. Twelve months' good work for a key to the room of books. For two days Lucy sits reading, searching, her feet tapping as her eyes race across the pages, an old wandering itch in her though she hasn't left the red building. History after history of other territories across other oceans: hills smeared with jungle, plateaus cold as ice, deserts, cities, ports, valleys, swamps, grasslands, peoples. Lands vast and distant—and all of them recorded by men like those she knows. Even one history of this territory. A book thick with dust, clumsily written, the name of a schoolteacher big across the front. She looks for a promised chapter but finds in those pages only a few lines, herself reduced to something crude and unrecognizable.

At the end of the two days her eyes blur, the words blur; she shelves the books, her limbs gone numb. She falls into a deep, dreamless sleep and doesn't return again to the room. Certain, now, of the truth she's suspected. New places there may be, new languages—but there are no new stories. No lands left wild where men haven't touched, and touched.

She doesn't try the blue book. No point, now, in reading it.

At the end of many months, when her debt is paid, the gold man lies winding his watch in her bed and says he'll give her a gift. Any gift, he says, as if generous, as if he hasn't already extracted all value from her.

He asks her what she wants.

She asks, first, for a mirror. Lets herself look at last—no, **see**. The nose is strange to her, as the face is strange, thin and stilled. She will never be pretty, with a girl's shine. She will be beautiful in a way that makes the chests of certain men ache to behold, as if they hold dowsing rods. She cut her hair, but it came back to haunt her. She checks over her shoulder, but no one stands there. The white of her neck is her own. Her unblemished face, her own. No one can hurt her now. Her body is immortal, or rather it's died so many deaths in so many men's stories that she fears no longer. She is a ghost, inhabiting this body. She wonders if she can ever die.

For the second time, the gold man asks what she wants.

The old word is on her tongue. She hasn't spoken it in a year. She tries to remember oceans, ships, star fruit, lanterns, low red walls. Tries to imagine a piece of them for her. But the storybook images have been replaced by the faces of the men she's known, too close, too clear, their lines and pocks and cruelties. She sees herself on those red streets, coming upon the men, upon their wives and their children. Their horror. Her horror. Stretch wide as it may, that land no longer has a place for her. She thinks of Sam grown taller on that land, longer of stride, more shining. Sam taking up all the space Sam wanted, speaking a language not Lucy's. She holds that image for a moment, brilliant in her head. Then she lets it go. She lets it go. Gives Sam up to a people Sam wanted. Those people were never truly hers, and now never can be.

The word on her tongue she lets go. She does not say it.

For the third and last time, the gold man asks what she wants.

She thinks of the other direction. The hills

where she was born, and the sun that bleaches sky and brightens grass. She thinks about when she stood in a dead lake and held what men desired and died for. She thinks that was nothing, really, compared to the way the noonday sun makes the grass blaze. Horizon to horizon a shimmer. Who could truly grasp it, the huge and maddening glint, the ever-shifting mirage, the grass that refused to be owned or pinned but changed with every angle of light: what that land was, and to whom, death or life, good or bad, lucky or unlucky, countless lives birthed and destroyed by its terror and generosity. And wasn't that the real reason for traveling, a reason bigger than poorness and desperation and greed and fury—didn't they know, low in their bones, that as long as they moved and the land unfurled, that as long as they searched, they would forever be searchers and never quite lost?

There is claiming the land, which Ba wanted to do, which Sam refused—and then there is being claimed by it. The quiet way. A kind of gift in never knowing how much of these hills might be gold. Because maybe if you only went far enough, waited long enough, held enough sadness pooled in your veins, soon you might come upon a path you knew, the shapes of rocks would look like familiar faces, the trees would greet you, buds and birdsong lilting up, and because this land had gouged in you an animal's kind of claiming, senseless to words and laws—dry grass drawing blood, a tiger's mark in a ruined leg, ticks and torn blisters, wind-coarsened hair, sun burned in patterns to leave skin striped or spotted—then, if you ran, you might hear on the wind, or welling up in your own parched mouth, something like and unlike an echo, coming from before or behind, the sound of a voice you've always known calling your name—

She opens her mouth. She wants

Acknowledgments

To the hills of Northern California for holding me in splendor. Bangkok and its lesson of solitude. The half-lit seat at Luka in Silom. The counter at Hungry Ghost on Flatbush. The fireplace at High Ground. Green Foxfire at the Hambidge Center. The Jane Austen studio at the Vermont Studio Center.

To the echo and collage of **Divisadero**. The thick love of **Beloved**. The snap of **The Shipping News**. The long, traveling songs of **Gawain and the Green Knight, Little House, Lonesome Dove**.

To Mariya and Mika, odd friends of the heart. Will and Capp St, steadfast. Mai Nardone, cantankerous and true. Jessica Walker and Tiswit. Brandon Taylor, alien twin. Lauren Groff, champion of women. Bill Clegg and Sarah McGrath and Ailah Ahmed, tenacious believers to the end. Aaron Gilbreath at **Longreads** and the team at **The Missouri Review.** All of Riverhead and Little, Brown.

To my mom and Ruellia, for what is hard to say. My dad, once more. My 奶奶 and family across the ocean. Avinash, my home.

And to Spike, prince among cats, who stayed with me long enough to see this boat to water.

Born in Beijing but mostly an artifact of the United States, **C Pam Zhang** has lived in thirteen cities across four countries and is still looking for home. She has been awarded support from Tin House, Bread Loaf, Aspen Words, and elsewhere, and currently lives in San Francisco.